KAMIKAZE RUN!

"Brace for ramming!" Gloval bellowed. The engines shook the great ship, and drove it in a death-dive.

The two huge booms that reared above the ship's bridge were aligned directly at the space mountain that was the nerve center of the Zentraedi fleet. The booms were separate components of the Main Gun, reinforced structures. Around their tips glowed the green-white fields of a limited barrier-defense, making them all but indestructible.

The Zentraedi, prepared for close broadsides, only realized in a last, horrified moment what the SDF-1's intention was. By then, it was too late.

The SDF-1 had become an enormous stake being driven into the heart of the enemy.

Published by Ballantine Books:

THE ROBOTECH™ SERIES

THE SENTINELS™ SERIES

ROBOTECH™ #5:

FORCE OF ARMS

Jack McKinney

A Del Rey Books

BALLANTINE BOOKS • NEW YORK

A Del Rey Book
Published by Ballantine Books

Library of Congress Catalog Card Number: 86-91659

ISBN 0-345-34138-4

Printed in Canada

First Edition: May 1987
Eleventh Printing: June 1993

Cover Art by David Schleinkofer

FOR BONNIE BADER,
AND HER WORK ON THIS PROJECT

PART I:

SHOWDOWN

PART I

SHOWDOWN

PROLOGUE

IN THE 1990s, A GLOBAL CIVIL WAR SWEPT ACROSS THE planet Earth; few wanted this war, but no one seemed to be able to avert it. It absorbed all the smaller disparate wars, rebellions, and terrorist struggles in the same way a huge storm vacuums up all the lesser weather systems around it.

The War was fought with conventional weapons for the most part, but by 1999 it was clear that its escalation pointed directly to an all-out nuclear exchange—planetary obliteration. There seemed to be nothing any sane person could do about it. By then, the War had a life of its own.

As the human race prepared to die—for everyone knew that the final phase of the War would surely exterminate all life on Earth, the fragile lunar and Martian research colonies, and the various orbital constructs—something like a malign miracle happened.

A damaged starship—a super dimensional fortress created by the dying alien mastermind, Zor—appeared in Earth's skies. It crashed on a tiny Pacific island called Macross. Its descent wreaked more havoc than any war:

there was tremendous damage and loss of life and numerous natural disasters. The human race was compelled to pause and take stock of itself.

Zor had served the evil Robotech Masters, but he had resolved to serve them no more and had hidden his ultimate secrets concerning Protoculture—the most powerful force in the universe—in the fortress. The Robotech Masters needed those secrets not only to conquer the universe but to protect themselves from the vengeful attacks of the savage Invid, a race of creatures sworn to destroy them.

Thus, the focus of an intergalactic conflict came to bear on the formerly insignificant Earth.

The super dimensional fortress was Earth's first inkling of the greater events taking place outside the bounds of human knowledge. Earth's leaders saw at once that the wrecked SDF-1 could be rebuilt and become a rallying point that would unite a divided human race.

A ten-year project began, incorporating the brains and energies of the entire planet. But on the day the SDF-1 was to be relaunched to guard humanity from alien attack, disaster struck again. The Zentraedi—the Robotech Masters' giant race of ferocious warrior clones—struck, bringing devastation to the Earth in an effort to recapture the SDF-1.

The desperate crew of the SDF-1 attempted a spacefold jump to get clear of the attack. Yet a miscalculation resulted in the ship's reappearance far from its intended destination: The SDF-1 and most of the civilian population of Macross Island were suddenly transported out to the orbit of the planet Pluto.

And so the long, perilous voyage back to Earth began. The SDF-1 battled for its life, hounded by the Zentraedi armada at every turn. Returning after more than a year, the crew found that it was no longer welcome on the homeworld—in the view of the ruling powers, they constituted too much of a danger to Earth's safety as well as the rulers' own authority.

A renewed Zentraedi offensive resulted in horrendous casualties on Earth and reinforced the Earth leaders' determination to refuse haven to the SDF-1—even though it had waged the only meaningful resistance to alien invasion.

So the great star battleship was forced to ride an orbit to nowhere, its crew and civilian refugees struggling desperately to stay alive. The Zentraedi continued to plot new war plans, determined to have the ship and the secrets of Protoculture.

Alien agents were planted within the ship, reduced from their fifty- and sixty-foot heights to human size. These spies found themselves strangely affected by the experience of human life as their long-dormant emotions were awakened by the sight of humans mingling and showing affection and in particular by the singing of Minmei—the ship's superstar and media idol and the mainstay of its morale.

Upon their return to the invasion fleet, the spies' stories and souvenirs of their experiences among the humans led to the defection of a dozen and more of the Zentraedi and disobedience in the ranks of those who remained behind.

Aboard the SDF-1, human life fell into patterns of conflict and emotion. Lieutenant Rick Hunter, fighter pilot in the Robotech Defense Forces, experienced constant confusion and turmoil over his love for Minmei and simultaneous attraction to Commander Lisa Hayes, the SDF-1's First Officer.

This triangle formed the core of a larger web of loves and hates, the sort of human emotional blaze that the colossal Zentraedi found so baffling and *debilitating*.

Nevertheless, the Zentraedi imperative was battle, and battle it would be. The aliens deployed a million-plus ships in their armada, restrained from all-out attack only by their need to capture the SDF-1's Protoculture secrets intact.

Breetai, commander of the invasion force, moved in his own intrigues against two of his rebellious subordinates: Azonia, the female warlord, and Khyron the Backstabber, psychotic demon of battle.

But the Robotech War proved to be far more complex than any of them—Zentraedi or human—could have ever imagined.

> Dr. Lazlo Zand,
> *On Earth As It Is in Hell:*
> *Recollections of the Robotech War*

CHAPTER
ONE

I guess Max was the most conspicuous example of the growing war weariness and hunger for peace. As the top VT pilot, he was revered by all the aspiring hot-doggers and would-be aces.

When he came back from a mission, his aircraft maintenance people would always stencil the symbols for his latest kills on the side of his ship; that was their right. But like a lot of us who had been in the eye of the storm for too long, he began avoiding the jokes and high-fives and swaggering in the ready rooms, barracks, and officers' club. He was still top man on the roster, but it was plain that his attitude was changing.

The Collected Journals of Admiral Rick Hunter

"**Y**A AIN'T SO BIG NOW, ARE YA, YA FREAKIN' *alien?*" the big bruiser said, shaking a scarred fist the size of a roast in his face.

Well, no, he wasn't. Karita *had* been a Zentraedi soldier some forty feet tall. But now, having been reduced to the size of a human and defecting to their side in the Robotech War, he was only a medium-build, slightly-less-than-average-height fellow facing three hulking brawlers eager to split his head wide open in a Macross alley.

Even as a Zentraedi, Karita hadn't excelled at combat; his main duty had been tending the Protoculture sizing chambers, the very same ones in which he had been micronized. The situation looked hopeless; the three ringed him in, fists cocked, light from the distant streetlamps illuminating the hatred in their faces.

He tried to dodge past them, but they were too fast. The biggest grabbed him and hurled him against the wall.

Karita dropped, half-stunned, the back of his scalp bleeding.

He cursed himself for his carelessness; a slip of the tongue in the restaurant had given him away. Otherwise, no one could have told him apart from any other occupant of the SDF-1.

But he could scarcely be blamed. The wonders of life aboard the super dimensional fortress were enough to make any Zentraedi careless. The humans had rebuilt their city; they mingled, both sexes, all ages. They lived lives in which emotions were given free expression, and there was an astonishing force called "love."

It was enough to make any Zentraedi, born into a Spartan, merciless warrior culture with strict segregation of the sexes, forget himself. And so Karita had made his error; he had gone into the White Dragon in the hopes of getting a glimpse of Minmei. He didn't realize what he was saying when he let slip the fact that he had adored her since he had first seen her image on a Zentraedi battlecruiser. Then he saw the hard looks the trio gave him. He left quickly, but they followed.

During the course of the war, everybody aboard had lost at least one friend or loved one. The Zentraedi, too, had suffered losses—many more than the SDF-1, in fact. That didn't stop Karita and the other defectors from hoping for a new life among their former enemies. Most humans were at least tolerant of the Zentraedi who'd deserted from their invading armada. Some humans even *liked* the aliens; three of them, former spies, had human girlfriends. But he should have known there would be humans who wouldn't see things that way.

The three closed in on him.

One of the men launched a kick Karita was too dazed to avoid. It was not so much a sharp pain he felt as a tremendous, panic-making numbness. He wondered woozily if his ribs were broken. Not that it mattered; it didn't look like his attackers were going to stop short of killing him. They didn't realize that they had picked on one of the most unmilitary of Zentraedi; given a different one, they would have had more of a fight on their hands.

One of them drew back his heavy work boot to kick Karita again; Karita closed his eyes, waiting for the blow. But the sudden sound of shoe leather sliding on pavement and the thud of a falling body made him re-open them.

He looked up to see one of the assailants down and the other two turning to face an interloper.

Max Sterling didn't look like the conventional image of a Veritech ace. The brilliant Robotech Defense Force flier was slender, wore blue-tinted aviator glasses—with *corrective* lenses—and dyed his hair blue in keeping with the current fad for wild colors.

This young RDF legend looked mild, even vulnerable. In a time of crisis, Max Sterling had risen from obscurity to dazzle humanity and the Zentraedi with his matchless combat flying. But that hadn't changed his basic humility and self-effacing good-naturedness.

"No more," Max told the assailants quietly. The bully on the ground shook his head angrily. Max stepped between the other two, went to Karita's side, and knelt, offering his hand.

Minmei's Aunt Lena had watched the ominous trio follow Karita when he left the White Dragon; it took her a few minutes to find Sterling, so Max said, "Sorry I'm a little late."

This bookish-looking young man who held the highest kill score of any combat pilot in the ship offered the Zen-traedi his hand. "D' you think you can stand?"

The attacker Max had floored was back on his feet, eyeing Max's RDF uniform. "You have two seconds to butt out of this, kid."

Max rose and turned, leaving Karita sitting against the wall. He took off his glasses and dropped them into Karita's limp hand.

"I guess there's gonna be a fight here, so let's get one thing straight: In case you missed the news, this man isn't our enemy. Now, are you going to let us by or what?"

Of course not. They had looked at Karita and auto-matically thought, *We can take him!* And that had de-cided the matter. Now here was the pale, unimposing Max, and their assessment was the same: *We can take him, too. No sweat.*

So the one Max had knocked down came at him first, while the others fanned out on either side.

Max didn't wait. He ducked under a powerful, slow haymaker and struck with the heel of his hand, breaking the first one's nose. A second attacker, a thick-bodied man in coveralls, hooked his fist around with all his might, but Max simply wasn't there. Dodging like a ghost, he landed a solid jab to the man's nose, bloodying it, and stepped out of the way as he staggered.

There wasn't much fighting room, and Max's usual style involved plenty of movement. But it didn't matter very much this time; he didn't want to leave Karita unprotected.

The third vigilante, younger, leaner, and faster than the other two, swung doubled fists at him from behind. Max avoided the blow, adding momentum with a quick, hard tug so that the man went toppling to his knees. Then Max spun precisely so that he had his back nearly up against the first attacker and rammed his elbow back.

The man's breath rushed out of him as he clutched his midsection. Max snapped a fist back into his face, then turned to plant a sidelong kick to the gut of the one in the coveralls. The incredible reflexes and speed that served him so well in dogfights were plain; he was difficult to see much less hit or avoid.

Karita had struggled to his feet. "Stop!"

The three attackers were battered up a bit, but the fight had barely started. Max Sterling wasn't even breathing hard.

"No more fighting," Karita labored, clutching his side. "Hasn't there been enough?"

The first man wiped blood from a swelling lip, studying Max. Indicating Karita with a toss of his head, he said, "Him and his kind killed my son. I don't care what you—"

"Look at this," Max said quietly. He displayed the RDF patch on his unform, a diamond with curved sides, like a fighting kite. "You think *I* don't understand? But listen t' me: *He's* out of the war. Just like *I* want to be and *you* want to be.

"But we're never going to have peace unless we put

the damn war behind us! So drop it, all right? Or else, c'mon: Let's finish this thing."

The first man was going to come at him again, but the other two grabbed his shoulders from either side. The young one said, "All right—for now."

Max supported Karita with his shoulder, and the three stepped aside to let them pass. There was a tense moment as the pilot and the injured alien walked between the attackers; one of them shifted his weight, as if reconsidering his decision.

But he thought better of it and held his place, saying, "What about you, flyboy? You're goin' out there again to fight 'em, aren't ya? To kill 'em if ya can?"

Max knew that Karita was staring at him, but he answered. "Yeah. Maybe I'll wind up killing somebody a lot like your son tonight. Or he'll wind up killing me. Who knows?"

Max put Karita into a cab and sent him to the temporary quarters where the defectors were housed. He didn't have time to go along; he was late for duty as it was.

Waiting for another cab, Max gazed around at the rebuilt city of Macross. Overhead, the Enhanced Video Emulation system had created the illusion of a Terran night sky, blocking out the view of a distant alloy ceiling.

It had been a long time since Max or any of the SDF-1's other inhabitants had seen the real thing. He was already defying the odds, having survived so many combats. The EVE illusion was nice, but he hoped he'd get to see the true sky and hills and oceans of Earth again before his number came up.

Elsewhere on the SDF-1, two women rode in an uncomfortable silence on an elevator descending to a hangar deck, watching the level indicators flash.

Commander Lisa Hayes, the ship's First Officer, wasn't at ease with many people. But Lieutenant Claudia Grant, standing now with arms folded and avoiding Lisa's gaze as Lisa avoided hers, had been a close friend —perhaps Lisa's only true friend—for years.

Lisa tried to lighten the gloom. "Well, here I go again. Off for another skirmish with the brass."

That was certainly putting the best face on it. No previous effort had convinced the United Earth Defense Council to either begin peace negotiations with the Zentraedi invaders or allow the SDF-1 and its civilian refugees to return home. Lisa had volunteered to try again, to present shocking new evidence that had just emerged and exert all the pressure she could on her father, Admiral Hayes, to get him to see reason and then persuade the rest of the UEDC.

Claudia looked up. They were an odd pair: Claudia, tall and exotic-looking, several years older than Lisa, with skin the color of dark honey; and Lisa, pallid and slender, rather plain-looking until one looked a little closer.

Claudia tried to smile, running a hand through her tight brown curls. "I don't know whether it'll help or not to say this, but stop looking so grim. Girl, you remind me of the captain of a sinking ship when he finds out they substituted deck chairs for the lifeboats. It's gonna be hard to change people's minds like that. Besides, all they can do is say no again."

There was a lot more to it than that, of course. Admiral Hayes was not likely to let his only child leave Earth —to return to the SDF-1 and the endless Zentraedi attacks—once she was in the vast UEDC headquarters. Neither Claudia nor Lisa had mentioned that they would probably never see each another again.

"Yeah, I guess," Lisa said, as the doors opened and the noise and heat of the hangar deck flooded in.

The two women stepped out into a world of harsh worklights. Combat and other craft were parked everywhere, crammed in tightly with wings and ailerons folded for more efficient storage.

Maintenance crews were swarming over Veritechs damaged in the most recent fighting, while ordnance people readied ships slated for the next round of patrols and surveillance flights. The SDF-1's survival depended in large part on the Veritechs; but they would have been useless if not for the unflagging, often round-the-clock work of the men and women who repaired and serviced and rearmed them and the others who risked their lives as part of the flight deck catapult crews.

Welding sparks flew; ordnance loader servos whined,

lifting missiles and ammunition into place. Claudia had to raise her voice to be heard. "Have you told Rick about the trip, or have you been too busy to see him?"

Busy had nothing to do with it, and they both knew that. Lisa had concluded that her love for Rick Hunter, leader of the Veritech Skull Team, was one-sided. By leaving the SDF-1 on a vital mission, she was also almost certainly giving up any chance of ever changing that.

"I thought I'd call him from the shuttle," she said.

Claudia exercised admirable restraint and did not blurt out, *Lisa, stop being such a coward!* Because Lisa wasn't—she had the combat decorations to prove it, medals and fruit cocktail that any line officer would respect. But where emotions were concerned, the SDF-1's competent and capable First always seemed to prefer hiding under a rock someplace.

The shuttle was near the aircraft elevator-air lock that would lift it to the flight deck. Lisa's gear and the evidence she hoped would sway Admiral Hayes and the others at the UEDC were already aboard. The crew chief was running a final prelaunch check.

"The shuttle is nearly ready for launch, Captain," a female enlisted-rating tech reported. "Launch in ten minutes."

Captain Henry Gloval crossed the bridge to glance at several other displays, stroking his thick mustache. "Any signs of Zentraedi activity in our area?" His voice still carried the burred r's and other giveaways of his Russian mother tongue.

Vanessa answered promptly, "There's been absolutely no contact, no activity at all."

The stupendous Zentraedi armada still shadowed and prowled around the wandering battle fortress. Time and again the aliens had attacked, but in comparatively insignificant numbers. The defectors' information was only now beginning to shed light on the reasons behind that.

"There's been nothing at all?" Gloval asked again, eyes flicking across the readouts and displays. "Mm. I hope this doesn't mean they're planning an attack." He turned and paced back toward the command chair, a tall, erect figure in the high-rolled collar of his uniform jacket, hat pulled low over his eyes. He clenched his cold, empty briar in his teeth. "I don't like it, not a bit ..."

Lisa was his highly valued First Officer; but she was also much like a daughter to him. It had taken every bit of his reason and sense of duty to convince himself she was the logical one for this mission.

The first enlisted tech turned to Kim Young, who was manning a position nearby. She knew Kim and the two other enlisted regulars on the bridge watch, Sammie and Vanessa, were known as the Terrible Trio, part of what amounted to a family with Gloval, Lisa Hayes, and Claudia Grant.

"Kim, does the skipper always get this ... concerned?"

Elfin-faced Kim, a young woman who wore her black hair in a short cut, showed a secret grin. She whispered, "Most of the time he's a rock. But he's worried about Lisa, and, well, there's Sammie."

Sammie Porter, youngest of the Terrible Trio, was a high-energy twenty-year-old with a thick mane of dark blond hair. She usually didn't know the meaning of fear ... but she usually didn't know the meaning of tact, either. She was conscientous and bright but sometimes excitable.

Lisa's departure had meant a reshuffling of jobs on her watch, and Sammie had ended up with a lot of the coordinating duties Claudia and Lisa would have ordinarily handled.

"Yellow squad, please go to preassigned coordinates before requesting computer readout," she ordered a unit of attack mecha over the comcircuit. The mammoth Robotech war machines were part of the ship's defensive force. Excaliburs and Spartans and Raidar Xs, they were like some hybrid of armored knight and walking battleship. They were among the units that guarded the ship itself, while the Veritechs sortied out into space.

Gloval bent close to check on what she was doing. "Everything all right? No trouble, I hope."

Sammie whirled and snapped, "Captain, please! I have to concentrate on these transmissions before they pile up!" Then she went back to ordering the lumbering mecha around, making sure that the gun turrets and missile batteries were alert and that all intel data and situation reports were up to date.

Gloval straightened, clamping his pipe in his teeth again. "Sorry. I didn't mean to interrupt." Kim and Vanessa gave him subtle looks, barely perceptible nods, to let him know that Sammie was on top of things.

Gloval had come to accept Sammie's occasional lack of diplomacy as a component of her fierce dedication to duty. Sometimes she reminded him of a small, not-to-be-trifled-with sheep dog.

Gloval considered the Terrible Trio for a moment. Through some joke of the gods, it had been these three whom the original Zentraedi spies—Bron, Konda, and Rico—had met and, not to put too fine a point on it, begun dating and formed attachments to.

The normally clear lines between personal life and matters of concern to the service were becoming quite muddied. The Zentraedi seemed decent enough, but there were already reports of ugly incidents between the defectors and some of the SDF-1's inhabitants. Gloval worried about the Terrible Trio, worried about the Zentraedi—was apprehensive that, after all, the two races could never coexist.

On top of that, he couldn't shake the feeling that he ought to be setting curfews, or providing chaperones, or doing *something* paternal. These things troubled him in the brief moments when he wasn't doing his best to see that his entire command wasn't obliterated.

"Shuttle escort flight, prepare for launch, five minutes," Sammie said, bent over her console. She turned to Gloval.

"Shuttle's ready, sir. Lisa will be leaving in four minutes, fifty seconds."

■ ■

CHAPTER
TWO

Of course, idle hands are not the devil's workshop; that is a base canard.

Rather, it is the sort of hand that is always driven to be busy, turning itself to new machinations, keeping the brew boiling, that causes the most trouble. Those who wish to dispute this might do well to consider what happened whenever Khyron grew restive.

Rawlins, *Zentraedi Triumvirate: Dolza, Breetai, Khyron*

MAX STERLING, FLIGHT HELMET CRADLED IN HIS left arm, strode through the frenetic activity of the hangar deck and heard Sammie's voice echo over the PA. "Sammie's substituting for the commander," he said.

At his side was a Skull Team replacement, Corporal Elkins, who had been transferred in from Wolf Team to help fill the gaps in Skull's ranks after the last pitched battle with the Zentraedi. Elkins remarked, "I hope she stays calm. Last time she had me flying figure eights around a radar mast."

Max chuckled, then forgot the joke, distracted. "Hey."

Elkins saw what Max meant. The techs had rolled out a prototype ship, something everybody in the Veritech squadrons had heard about. It was like the conventional VT, a sleek ultra-fighter, but two augmentation pods were mounted above its wing pivots.

The conventional VTs were a kind of miracle in themselves, the most advanced use of the Robotechnology that humans had learned from the wreckage of the SDF-1 when the alien-built battle fortress had originally crashed on Earth twelve years before. The SDF-1 had murderous teeth in the form of its mecha, its primary and secondary batteries, and its astoundingly powerful main gun, but the VTs were the ship's claws. And this new, retrofitted model was the first of a more powerful generation, a major advance in firepower and performance.

"Wouldn't that be something to fly?" Max murmured. He hoped it checked out all right in test flights; the humans needed every edge they could get.

"Whenever they're ready to give me one, I'll take it," Elkins said. "Anyway, watch yourself up there, Max."

At the top of the shuttle boarding steps, Lisa said, "I've made notes on everything that might be a problem."

"Don't worry about a thing," Claudia told her. Then she put her hands on Lisa's shoulders. "I'll see you back here in a few days, okay?"

Lisa tried to smile. What do you say to someone dearer than a sister? "I hope so. You look after things." One of the ground crew whistled, and Lisa stepped back into the shuttle's entry hatch.

The mobile steps moved away from the tubby shuttle. Claudia threw Lisa a salute for the first time in so long that neither of them could remember the last. Lisa returned it smartly. The round hatch swung to, emblazoned with the Robotech Defense Force insignia.

There were no other passengers, of course; contact with Earth had been all but nonexistent since the UEDC rulers decided that the dimensional fortress was to be a decoy, luring the enemy away from the planet. Other than a few canisters of classified dispatches and so forth, she had the passenger compartment to herself.

Lisa found a seat at the front of the compartment, near a com console, and asked a passing crewman, "Is this a secure line?"

"Aye aye, ma'am. It's best to make any calls now; never can tell what glitches we'll run into outside."

"I will."

He was wandering a quiet side street of Macross when the paging voice said, "Repeating: Lieutenant Rick Hunter, you have a call."

For a moment he wasn't even sure where he was, shuffling along in civvies that felt rather strange—the first time he'd worn anything but a uniform or a flightsuit in weeks. He'd been brooding a lot longer, trying to sort things out, to understand his own feelings and face up to certain truths.

He went to one of the ubiquitous yellow com phones and identified himself. The incoming call carried a secure-line encryption signal, keying the public phone with it. While the machines went through their coding, Rick looked around to make sure no one was close enough to eavesdrop.

People were just passing by, not even sparing a glance for the compact black-haired young man at the phone. He didn't mind that; he needed a few hours respite from being the Skull Team's leader—some time away from the burden of command.

He had been a cocky civilian when he first came aboard the dimensional fortress two years before. He had been drawn into military service only grudgingly by Roy Fokker, his unofficial Big Brother—Claudia Grant's lover. Rick Hunter had survived more dogfights than he could remember, had written so many condolence letters to the families of dead VT pilots that he forced himself not to think of them, had stood by at the funeral of Roy Fokker and others beyond counting. He only wanted to shut them out of his mind.

He was not yet twenty-one years old.

The comcircuit was established. "Rick? It's Lisa."

He felt as though he had been under observation as he walked the streets aimlessly. Lisa and Minmei; Minmei and Lisa. His brain failed him in that emotional cyclone where his feelings for the two women swirled and defied all analysis, all decision.

"What can I do for you?" Ouch. Wrong. He knew that as soon as he said it, but it was too late.

"I wanted to let you know, Rick. I'm leaving the SDF-1. I'm on my way to Earth to try to get them to stop the fighting."

He looked around again quickly to make sure no civilians had any chance of hearing. There was enough unrest in the dimensional fortress without spreading new rumors and raising expectations that would in all probability be dashed. At the same time, he felt an emptiness. *She's leaving!*

"Why wasn't I told ab—"

"It's all top secret. Rick, I might not be allowed to come back." Lisa cupped the handset to her, staring at it sadly, as the shuttle was moved onto the aircraft elevator for the trip to the flight deck. Max Sterling's VT was next to it.

"So . . . I want to tell you something," she struggled. *Oh, say it!* Claudia's voice seemed to holler at her. But she couldn't.

"I appreciate all you've done, and it's been an honor serving with you," Lisa said instead. "Your observations about our captivity in the alien headquarters will be an important part of my report when—"

"What are you talking about, Lisa?" Something that had been murky to him moments ago was crystal clear now. "I don't care about reports or anything else if you can't come back here!"

Tell him! Say it! But she ignored the voice, couldn't face the rejection. He loved the luminous superstar, Minmei, and Minmei cared for him. Who could compete with that?

She found herself saying, "Please watch over the Zentraedi defectors, Rick. A lot of our people haven't had time to reason things out yet, and the aliens are in danger."

The stubby shuttle was on the flight deck, boxed up for launch by the cat crew, the hookup people clear, the blast deflector raised up from the deck behind the spacecraft. Off to one side, Max's VT swept its wings out and raised its vertical stabilizers.

Lisa held the handset tenderly. "We're launching. Good-bye. And thanks again."

"What? Wait!" But the circuit was dead.

He got up to an observation deck just in time to watch a tiny cluster of distant lights, the drives of the formed-up flight, dwindle into the darkness.

* * *

"Shuttle craft and escorts proceeding according to flight plan," Vanessa told Gloval quietly. Nobody had actually *said* that Lisa's flight was to be monitored so closely; but no one had objected to the idea, either, and the Terrible Trio were keeping close tabs.

Back at her duty station, Claudia was alert to every nuance of voice, like everyone else there. When Vanessa said, "Captain!" in a clipped, alarmed tone, Claudia's heart skipped a beat.

"Elements of the Zentraedi fleet are redeploying. They're on intercept course, closing in on the shuttle."

Gloval looked over his situation displays, threat boards, computer projections. Claudia kept one eye on the board, one on Gloval.

He sounded very calm. Now that battle had come, he was a well of tranquillity. "Order them to take evasive action as necessary or return to the SDF-1 if possible."

Claudia almost blurted out a plea to send reinforcements, but she could read the displays as well as anyone. More Zentraedi forces were moving into place, apparently to cut the shuttle off from the dimensional fortress. Pummeled and undermanned, the SDF-1 could ill afford to risk an entire VT team to save one shuttle and its escorts.

No matter who might die.

Alarms and emergency flashers brought Lisa out of a dim gray despair. The shuttle pilot was announcing, "Enemy craft approaching. All hands, general quarters. Secure for general quarters."

There was a heavy grinding sound as sections of padded armor shielding slid up into place around Lisa's seat. She calmly pulled her briefcase into the questionable safety of the metal cocoon with her, securing her acceleration harness, and the ship's drive pressed her back into the seat's cushioning.

Max Sterling accepted the news almost amicably. The heritage that was the fighter pilot's proud tradition remained strong. Dying was sometimes unavoidable, but losing one's cool was inexcusable.

"Enemy approaching on our six," he said, with less emotion than most people used talking about the weather. "Form up in gamma deployment and stick with your wingmen."

The other VTs rogered and moved to comply. Max was going to give Lisa an encouraging wave, but the armored cocoon had already swallowed her up.

He peeled off to take up his own position. The aerodynamic maneuvers of the VTs looked strange in the airlessness and zero g of space, but the pilots came from a naval aviation tradition. They thought a certain way about flying, and thinking was half the key to Robotechnology. The aerodynamic maneuvers wasted power, but Robotechnology had plenty of that.

Max hoped this was another feint. Like Gloval and many others, he had noticed that there seemed to be two distinct factions—almost a schizophrenia—among the enemy. One side was playing a waiting game, determined to capture the SDF-1 intact for reasons that the humans still couldn't guess and that the low-ranking defectors, not privy to strategic information, couldn't clarify.

The other element—rash, unpredictable, almost irrational—mounted sudden, vicious attacks on the dimensional fortress, apparently intent on destroying it with no thought to the consequences. It was becoming clear that the enemy commander responsible for this had a name known to, and even feared by, all Zentraedi.

Khryon the Backstabber.

"Commander, the target has changed course," a Zentraedi pod pilot said, the facebowl of his combat armor lit by his instruments. "And the Micronian fighters are redeploying for intercept."

The alien mecha, two dozen and more, were in attack formation—huge ovoid bodies quilled with cannon muzzles, mounted on long reverse-articulated legs so that they resembled headless ostriches. Most would have been considered "armless," but the Officers' Pods mounted heavy guns that suggested gargantuan derringers.

In the lead pod was Khyron the Backstabber.

He didn't fit most stereotypes of the brutal warlord. Quite contrary to the Zentraedi conventionalities—their Spartan simplicity, their distaste for mannerisms— Khyron would have been called a fop if such a word or concept had existed among his race.

Youthful-looking and sinisterly handsome, he gazed into the screens of his pod's cockpit, contemplating the kill. He had been forbidden to attack the SDF-1 again on pain of immediate execution, but no one had issued any orders with regard to a juicy little convoy.

Four times now, the Micronian vermin had humiliated him. With each defeat, his hatred had grown geometrically. It went incandescent when he saw the sorts of perversions the humans practiced: males mingling with females, the sexes somehow coming into contact and expressing weak-willed affection for each other. They behaved seductively, something unknown to the Zentraedi. The Micronians paired off, sometimes forming lifelong bonds, driven by impulses and stimuli Khyron was only beginning to perceive.

It repelled and fascinated him; it obsessed and possessed him. So he knew he had no other choice but to destroy the Micronians utterly or go completely insane.

"Nothing can save them," he gloated. "All units: Attack immediately!"

The pods closed in, riding the bright flames of their drives, guns angling, answering their targetting servos. The VTs swept out to meet them.

"Captain, the shuttle has reached coordinates Lambda thirty-four," Sammie called out. "Should we send reinforcements?"

The bridge crew watched Gloval, hoping he would say yes as much as he himself wanted to. But that would have left the SDF-1 underprotected; the Zentraedi had already tried similar diversionary maneuvers to set up a major attack.

With the number of spaceworthy VTs critically low until the Robotech fabrication machinery could produce replacements, he simply couldn't risk sending out another team of fighters or risk the pilots who were so crucial to the ship's survival.

"Not unless we absolutely have to," he said stonily. The women turned back to their jobs in silence. Gloval did not elaborate on the question of reinforcements, but he had already decided: He couldn't risk a flight of VTs, but there *was* one desperate gamble he could take if the shuttle's situation got worse.

In the volume of empty space designated Lambda thirty-four, Max Sterling's Veritech went through a lightning change. It was what Dr. Lang, the eerie Robotech genius, termed "mechamorphosis," the alteration of the fighter's very structure.

Max had pulled the lever that sent the ship into Battloid mode, thinking the mecha through its change. The VT shifted to Battloid, looking like a futuristic gladiator in bulky, ultratech armor, bristling with weapons. Two pods drove in at him, cannon blazing.

CHAPTER
THREE

That undisciplined showoff? That wet-nosed civilian joystick pilot? What a waste of time and effort!

Remark attributed to Lisa Hayes upon being informed that trainee Rick Hunter had qualified as a VT pilot 2009 A.D.

THE PODS FIRED AWAY WITH THE PRIMARY AND SECondary guns that protruded from their armored plastrons, but the blue bolts converged on utter vacuum. Max's Battloid wasn't where it had been a split second before.

The Battloid had its autocannon in its metal fists, riding its backpack thrusters with the agility of a gymnast, darting like a dragonfly. It whirled on one pod, opening up.

The chain-gun was loaded with depleted transuranic rounds, big as candlepins and much heavier—high-powered, extremely dense projectiles that delivered terrific amounts of kinetic energy. The pod's armor flew like shredded paper; it exploded in an outlashing of energy and debris.

Max was still dodging with blinding speed, turning his sights on the second pod. He riddled it before the enemy pilot could draw a bead on him, putting a tight shot group of holes in the center of the egglike alien mecha. The pod became a brief fireball.

No system of manual *or* computer controls could

have come up with such astounding maneuverability, such instantaneous responses and deadly shooting. Only the "thinking cap," the interface of mind and mecha, could work the seeming magic of the RDF.

Other VTs had already paired off against the foe. The mecha swirled and pounced; their missiles corkscrewed and sizzled while energy bolts and powered gatling rounds lit the darkness. But the pods had the advantage of numbers by more than two to one, enough to occupy every Veritech and leave more pods to go after the shuttle.

The shuttle pilot was taking evasive action and running for safety at full emergency power. But there was no safety; the shuttle was no match for the pods' speed, and the Zentraedi closed in, firing. The shuttle's light armaments and lack of maneuvering ability made it easy prey, but the shuttle skipper did his best, trying to evade. He was hoping he could eventually make a dash for the tantalizingly nearby Earth, knowing that the UEDC would never allow any of its forces to intervene or otherwise risk turning the Zentraedi wrath on Earth itself. He could hope for no help from that quarter.

A Zentraedi cannon burst stitched holes in the shuttle's port wing in a line of three, ringed by molten metal. Lisa felt the ship rock in her armored cocoon, and gripped the padded armrests, waiting to see what the outcome of the battle would be.

The attacking pod was a modified standard type, carrying augmentative particle-beam cannon for added firepower. It turned to come back for the kill, but just then Max arrived, his Battloid diving headlong into the fight. The Battloid knocked the pod aside like a football player, driving a huge, armored shoulder into it.

Then the Battloid that was Max Sterling flipped neatly on foot thrusters and fired. The rain of armor-piercing slugs punched a dozen holes in the enemy, and it was driven back like some wounded living thing. There was no secondary explosion—very unusual, since the enemy mecha's power systems usually turned them into firecrackers once their armor had been pierced.

Two more pods came in at him, one with extra missile

racks and another with the strange rabbit ears of a Zentraedi signal-warfare ship. Max went at them, juking and evading to stay out of their cross hairs, his Battloid firing short bursts from the autocannon.

One of the escort VTs had been lost, another damaged by the first onslaught. Several more were still engaged in combat, but the rest, like Max, had come through their first duel and were taking on new opponents. Some help arrived, and Max began to feel confident that he could keep the pods away from the damaged shuttle.

But just then, Elkins yelled over the tac net, "More pods! We've got more pods coming at us—half a dozen!"

Max's mouth became a thin line as he drove in to deal with his current opponents as quickly as he could. He thought back with a certain pilot's superstition on what he had said to the men in the alley. Perhaps the taboos were right and it was lethal bad luck to talk about not coming back.

"The escorts are outnumbered," Kim called over her shoulder without taking her eyes from her instruments.

"More pods closing in on them!" Vanessa added. "Cutting off the shuttle's escape."

Gloval sat slumped in his command chair with his cap visor pulled down low over his eyes. A Veritech flight couldn't possibly get there in time, and he didn't have them to spare. But . . .

"How long would it take the armored Veritech prototype to make it there?"

Sammie already had the figures. "Approximately four minutes from launch at max boost."

Claudia bit her lower lip, watching Gloval. The captain's head came up. "Prepare it for launch!"

Claudia relayed the order, sending up a silent prayer, while Sammie asked, "Who'll be flying it, sir?"

"Get Lieutenant Hunter to the hangar deck at once. Tell him we don't know how much longer Sterling can hold out."

* * *

The ship's PA and a few seconds on a comcircuit had Rick on his way, anxious and very intense, in a commandeered jeep he flagged down in the middle of a Macross boulevard. The enlisted driver was a capable man who liked having an excuse to break all traffic laws.

Rick suited up virtually on the run, and minutes later the aircraft elevator was lifting the humpbacked-looking armored VT to the flight deck.

"Lieutenant, your destination is Lambda thirty-four," Sammie told him over the command net.

"Lambda thirty-four? What're you talking about?"

On the bridge, Claudia turned to Sammie. "Didn't you see to it that all pilots had the new map-reference codes?"

Sammie looked devastated. "I was so swamped—I didn't think he'd need one until he went on duty later."

Aircraft status was relayed; the armored VT was boxed and ready for launch. Sammie gritted her teeth, ignoring the silent stares of the rest of the bridge watch, especially the ominous quiet from Gloval. She couldn't let her mistake spell Lisa's death!

Sammie opened the mike again, concentrating, eyes shut, matching coordinates and codes by memory. "Coordinates in superseded code are at Weasel twenty-one!"

Rick launched without taking time to acknowledge. The armored VT poured on speed like nothing any other human-produced mecha had ever demonstrated. A single man in an untested ship, flying out against terrible odds —and if he lost, the woman who was humanity's best hope for peace would die too.

From the first, Max had known that the chances of help arriving from the SDF-1 were slim. Now he was resigned to the fact that there would be no help, though he didn't let on to the dwindling survivors of the escort flight.

The other VT pilots had flown well and bravely; their kill ratio was high, but still they went down to oblivion, one by one, in the silent globular explosions of a space rat race—a mass dogfight. Max Sterling flew like no

pilot before him, a grim reaper, a deadly wraith, an un-
defeatable mecha demon in the form of a Battloid.

The Battloid changed vectors and zoomed out of a
pod's salvo, jamming some of its missiles with ECM
equipment and dodging the rest, a masterful performance. Max turned the gatling on it and hosed it with a
tracer-bright stream of heavyweight rounds, blowing it
away.

But still the enemy came, and more were arriving. It
looked like a day for dying.

He turned to get back with Elkins, to stick together
and protect the shuttle to the last. But Elkins's ship vanished in an ugly blossom of fire and shrapnel. The escort
had been whittled down to five. Four times that number
came in at them now.

Hanging back from the action in his Officer's Pod,
Khyron watched gleefully. He suspected that the enemy
leader, the amazingly fast and deadly blue-trimmed Veritech, was the same one who had sent so many Zentraedi
to defeat and death—had even humbled the vaunted
Miriya, female ace of aces of the Quadronos.

Khyron was in no hurry to lead the attack and tangle
with the Micronian devil in person; it would be enough
to dispose of the rest of his command by attrition and
pull the Veritech wizard to bits by sheer weight of
numbers. Then, Khyron would have a boast to fling in
Miriya's face and the faces of all the others who secretly
laughed at him!

More pods converged. But at that moment a new-
comer arrived.

"Only one," a pod pilot reported, and Khyron dismissed the matter coldly. One more Veritech wouldn't
matter now.

His opinion changed a moment later. The fighter accelerated to unprecedented speeds, maneuvering more
nimbly than any Micronian mecha ever had. Its humpbacked profile didn't match any computer ID.

Then the strange new machine let forth a storm of
fire: murderously fast and accurate missiles of some new
type; autocannon rounds with even greater velocity, de-
livering far more kinetic energy on impact; phased-array

laser blasts as powerful, at close range, as any plasma bolt.

The new arrival, faster than the escort leader, was in and out among the pods, striking and vanishing, blowing two Zentraedi mecha to smithereens and going on to take out another while the first two explosions were still ballooning.

Suddenly, the pods were like so many fat pigeons before the attack of a rocket-driven hawk.

Rick's initial success was so overwhelming, so pronounced and irresistible, that he got careless.

After seeing a dozen and more of the ambushers go up in flames, he began the switch to Guardian mode. But he'd forgotten what a hot ride he had, and the ship's sudden retro thrust almost put his head through the instrument panel and split his thinking cap down the middle.

He barely recovered, shaking his head, the breath knocked from him by the strain of the safety harness across his torso. Trembling, he got control of himself and his ship and pressed the fight again.

And once more the Zentraedi pods were fat targets at his mercy. He went swooping in at them, the VT laying out a staggering volume of fire, skeeting pods as if they were clay targets.

Khyron had seen enough; he had no desire to go up against this bewilderingly fast, fearsomely armed intruder. He made sure his own withdrawal was well under way before he ordered his troops back.

It didn't mean his thirst for revenge was slaked, of course; if anything, it was worse. It was a constant torment now; it would be until he destroyed the enemy insects once and for all.

Max's report came over the bridge speakers. "The enemy has broken contact and withdrawn. The shuttle has sustained minimal damage and is continuing on.

"With your permission, I am returning to the SDF-1 with the remaining escort ships, due to damage suffered during the attack. Lieutenant Hunter will escort the shuttle to Earth."

Gloval granted permission. To Claudia's doubtful look, he responded, "That armored Veritech has so much speed and firepower, it's the equal of ten regular fighters."

And a thousand more like it wouldn't put us on an equal footing with our foe, he thought to himself. *Still, we must have as many as we can, as fast as we can!*

Sammie stretched and yawned. "I'm exhausted! I wish Commander Hayes was back."

Claudia glared at her. "We almost lost her permanently with that code snafu of yours!"

Sammie looked dismayed, young and tearful; she was even more upset by the danger to Lisa than by Claudia's temper, which could lead to *very* serious problems for anyone who angered the bridge officer.

But Claudia softened after a moment. After all, Sammie *had* pulled things out of the fire.

"That's okay, kiddo," Claudia said, turning back to her console. "Everybody learns from mistakes."

Gloval thought about that, silently gazing through the forward viewport. Did that apply to the Zentraedi, too? And the UEDC rulers?

Could they all be convinced the war was a catastrophic mistake?

The protective shielding swung back to show Lisa a passenger compartment that seemed unaffected by the battle. She was still a little winded and bruised from the tossing around she had taken in the padded, armored cocoon.

The shuttle pilot had kept her abreast of the battle and she felt a bit limp with relief. It was so vital that she get to Earth, that she speak for peace—long ago she had resigned herself to the likelihood that she would die in war, but to have died at that moment was a tragedy too vast to contemplate.

"Commander Hayes," the pilot's voice came over the intercom. "We have a commo call for you from Lieutenant Hunter, who's now flying escort for us. I've patched it through."

So Rick was the one who had ridden to the rescue in the armored VT; she had hoped it was and yet had feared for his life all through the fight. She picked up the handset.

Armored panels were sliding back from all the viewports. She was looking out at the humpbacked new-generation Veritech. "Lisa, are you all right?" she heard him say.

"Yes. Because you came to help." She saw him through the VT's canopy, looking at her worriedly.

I was never cut out for emotional drama, she thought. *I should have known I couldn't get away with a rehearsed exit speech.*

"No problem," he was saying. "Now, what's all this about you not coming back?"

"There are reasons, Rick."

"Even though your father's on the UEDC?"

"*Especially* because of that. Besides, they aren't going to like what I'm going to tell them."

There was a choppy sensation as the shuttle entered the Earth's atmosphere. He fumbled for something appropriate to say, knowing he had to turn back in seconds. "I hope you'll be safe" was all he could come up with.

"Thanks. I'm sure I'll be fine."

"Um." He knew the call was patched through the shuttle's com system, accessible to the pilots—presuming they weren't busy with their atmospheric entry maneuver. "There's something else—sorta private. Here; look."

He had fallen back, out of the pilots' line of vision, up close to the shuttle. She could see him clearly, watching her. She was confused. "What is it?"

"Prosigns." He began flashing his VT's running lights in prosigns—brief dot-dash combinations that represented whole words, for quick manual Morse code communications. Lisa was a little rusty but found that she could read it.

LIKE YOU MUCH. COMPLAIN SOMETIMES BUT BELIEVE IN YOU. MISS YOU MUCH IF YOU DON'T RETURN. PLEASE RETURN SOONEST.

He could read her lips, so close were VT and shuttle. *I'll try. So long, Rick.*

He threw her a salute—a joke between them, given his lack of military discipline when they had first met and clashed.

The armored VT peeled off and vectored for the SDF-1, the blue vortices of its thrusters shrinking to match flames, then disappearing. The shuttle jostled more as it hit the denser atmosphere.

CHAPTER

FOUR

> *I have familiarized myself with the enemy's culture, to better carry out my espionage mission. What a repulsive, contemptible thing it is!*
>
> *All seems to revolve around their gruesome, sadistic method of reproduction, and it obsesses them constantly. The humans—Micronians—even make up false legends about it! They immerse themselves in stories where males and females poison one another or stab themselves or simply expire from some unexplained thing called "pining away." Or else the imaginary couples go off together and spend all their time in revolting, pointless intimacies.*
>
> *Our enemies languish in these falsehoods the way we might enjoy a hot soak at the end of a long campaign.*
>
> *What perversion! Truly, this is a species that must be exterminated!*
>
> Miriya Parino, from her interim notes for an intel report to the Zentraedi High Command

SHE WAS STRIKING ENOUGH TO DRAW STARES EVEN in the crowded Macross plaza, where people were usually in a hurry and some of the more attractive women in the dimensional fortress were to be seen.

Boots clicking on the swirling mosaics of the plaza, the green-dyed hair flowing with the speed of her walk and the light air currents of the ship's circulation blowers, she looked neither right nor left. People made way for her; she was barely aware of their existence, even that of the men who looked at her so admiringly.

Miriya, greatest combat pilot of her race, exulted a bit *I've finally discovered one of the reasons these Micronians have developed such amazing skill in handling their mecha!* It wasn't the reason she had come to the SDF-1 as a spy, but it was a step in understanding her quarry, and that was elating. The intelligence data would also be of interest to the Zentraedi High Command, another coup to her credit.

Not that Miriya needed one. As a demigoddess of battle, she was without equal, her kills and victories far outnumbering her nearest rival's. She had lost only once in her life, and had submitted to micronization and come to the SDF-1 to make amends for that.

Miriya left the street and its EVE noonday, entering the dark and blinking world she had only recently discovered. All through the media-game arcade, people stood or sat hunched toward the glowing screens, playing against the machines.

The screen-lit faces of the players were so intent, their movements so deft and quick—what could account for it other than military indoctrination and the hunger for combat? What other motive could there be for the Micronians' relentless practice? They were so highly motivated that they even subsidized their own training, feeding money into the machines.

The young ones were the best and most diligent, of course. *By the time they reach maturity, they will be superb warriors!* she thought. This, even though the very concept of human reproduction, the parents-child-adult cycle, made her feel queasy and dizzy. The discovery of that vileness, as she thought of it, had rendered her inert and dazed when she first stumbled on the truth of it. But in time, bravely, she had shaken off the horror of human reproduction and resumed her search.

Miriya came to the most significant machine, though they were all cunning and instructive. She vaulted into the little cockpit, inserting a coin in the slot. One hand went to the stick, the other to the throttle, as she watched the screen. Her feet settled on the foot pedals.

Her finger hovered near the weapons trigger as she waited for the game to begin. Miriya looked around quickly to see if her nemesis was there.

She couldn't spy anyone who might be that greatest of Micronian pilots and therefore assumed he wasn't present. Surely a pilot who was good enough to have defeated Miriya Parino, the indisputable champion of the Zentraedi, would draw great attention and recognition.

She would know him when he came or when someone mentioned him. She would find him eventually.

And then she would kill him.

The face in the family portrait was pale, thin—but open and kind, the mother's features very much like the daughter's. Admiral Hayes glanced down at the framed photo, not realizing that many minutes had gone by while he sat, thinking and remembering.

He was looking at himself, years ago, only a lieutenant commander then. Next to him in the photo was his wife, and in front of them a shy-looking little girl wearing a sun hat and sun dress with a Band-Aid on one knee.

Whenever I look at this picture, I wish Andrea were still here to see how her little girl turned out—to see what an extraordinary soldier Lisa's made of herself.

A comtone from his desk terminal broke his contemplation. "Pardon me for interrupting, sir," an aide said. "But you left word that you be informed when the shuttle made final approach."

Hayes shook himself; there had been that last, terrible fear when the shuttle was attacked and not even he could countermand UEDC orders and send help. More to the point, there was no help that Earth could send that would be of any use; the SDF-1 and its Veritechs were the only effective weapons against Zentraedi pods. Hayes could only wait and hope.

When the shuttle survived its gauntlet, he had nearly collapsed into his chair, staring at the photograph of the past. There was so much to heal between himself and his daughter, so much to put behind them.

Now, he looked to the aide's image on his display screen. "Thank you."

"The craft should be landing very shortly. Shall I meet you at the elevators, sir?"

Hayes pressed against his big, solid oak desk with both hands, pushing himself to his feet. "Yes, that would be fine."

The headquarters of the United Earth Defense Council was a vast base beneath the Alaskan wilderness. Very little of it was aboveground—surveillance and communications equipment, aircraft control tower—but the surface was guarded by the few remaining Battloids on Earth.

Years before, when the SDF-1 made its miscalculated spacefold jump out to the rim of the solar system, it took with it most of its Robotech secrets and all the fabricating equipment humanity had discovered in the huge vessel when it originally crash-landed on Earth. Earth had turned back to largely conventional weapons for its defense with the exception of one gargantuan project that was already under way: the Grand Cannon.

The Grand Cannon took up most of the sprawling, miles-deep base, a doomsday weapon that let the UEDC live the fantasy that it could defend itself against an all-out Zentraedi onslaught. Admiral Hayes had been largely responsible for the Grand Cannon's construction; Gloval's simple disdain for such a massive, immobile weapon system was one of the major stresses that had ended their friendship.

Waiting by the landing strip, the brutally cold arctic wind whipping at his greatcoat, Hayes recalled those days, recalled the bitter words. His once-warm bond with Gloval, solidified during their service together in the Global Civil War, had shattered as Hayes accused the Russian of timid thinking and Gloval sneered at the "hidebound, Maginot-Line mindset" of the Cannon's proponents.

Hayes's thoughts were interrupted by the aide. "Admiral, we've just received word that the shuttle's ETA has been moved back by twenty minutes. Nothing serious; they're just coming around for a better approach window. If you like, I'll drive you back to the control tower; it's warmer there."

The admiral said distractedly, "No, I'll wait here. It's not that cold, anyway." Then he turned back to watch the sky, barely aware of the biting wind.

The aide sat back down in the open jeep, shivering and buttoning up his collar all the way, burrowing his chin down and tucking gloved hands under armpits. He always thought of his commander as rather a comfort-loving man; certainly, Hayes's living quarters and offices gave that impression.

But here was the Old Man, indifferent to an arctic

blast that would send an unprotected man into hypothermia in seconds. None of the base personnel knew much about this daughter; her last visit to the base had been rushed and very hush-hush. Hayes rarely mentioned her, but he had been remote most of the time since he had received word she was coming. The aide shrugged to himself, swearing at the shuttle, wishing it would hurry up.

In an officers' mess onboard the SDF-1, Max sat toying with his coffee cup, glancing over at the table a few yards away where Rick Hunter sat immersed in thought, an almost palpable cloud of gloom surrounding him.

He's been sitting there by himself for half an hour twiddling his spoon, and it's like his food isn't even there, Max reflected. He made a quick decision, rose, and went to approach his team leader.

"Lieutenant, it's too early to be depressed about this," Max jumped right in. "I'm sure Commander Hayes will get back here somehow."

Rick turned away from him, chin still resting on his hand. "First of all, I'm *not* thinking about her, and secondly, what makes you think I'm depressed?"

Rick decided it was all far too complicated to explain to Max Sterling, the bright-eyed boy wonder of the VTs, the cheerful, unassuming ace of aces. A man who never seemed unhappy, at a loss, or in doubt of what he was doing. *Eager beaver!* Rick thought huffily.

"Maybe you need a little excitement—some distraction," Max persisted. "How about a game? I know just the place! Let's go!"

Before Rick could object or even consider pulling rank, Max had him by the arm and yanked him to his feet, tugging him toward the door. It seemed easier to give in than to start a tug-of-war in the middle of the officers' mess; Rick went along compliantly.

It didn't take long to get there; Max even paid for the cab. The Close Encounters game arcade was alive with noise and lights, like some Robotech fun house.

Max's eyes were shining. "Great place, huh? You're gonna love it!"

More war games? Rick groaned to himself. "I don't know. Maybe I'll just head home—"

But Max had him by the elbow again. "A coupla games'll make you feel like a new man, boss."

"Max, I don't think—"

"Look, I've been here before; I know what I'm talking about!" He dragged Rick through the entrance.

As they moved deeper into the arcade, Rick recognized a face. Jason, Lynn-Minmei's little cousin, had stopped to watch a young woman playing a game. Rick went past without saying anything to attract the child's attention; talking to Jason would only remind him of his feelings for Minmei and compound his doubts and gloom.

In passing, he did notice the young woman: a very intense player with green-dyed hair and an expression like some beautiful lioness ready for the kill.

The shuttle had barely rolled to a stop when Hayes reached it, running. His aide watched him in astonishment.

By the time the ground crew got the mobile stairs in position, Lisa was waiting in the open hatch. The wind tugged at her long, heavy locks of brown-blond hair and her too-light trench coat. She was wearing fur-trimmed boots she had borrowed, but the cold sent ice picks through her and numbed her skin instantly.

She halted, shocked to see her father waiting for her. Their previous meeting and parting had been anything but cordial, with the admiral doggedly taking the UEDC line against Gloval's common sense and compassion. Coldly formal to her in the meetings, her father had later sought to get her reassigned to headquarters base, to get her out of the danger of her SDF-1 assignment. Lisa had torn up the conciliatory note he had sent her and returned to the dimensional fortress with Gloval. She was unaware of how that tormented her father.

Now, looking up at her, he said, "Lisa! Thank goodness you're here at last!" She came down the stairs carefully, holding the railing with one hand as the wind buffetted her, clutching a dispatch case.

"You're finally off that cursed alien Flying Dutchman." He was smiling, tears forming. "We've got a lot of talking to do!"

But when she reached the bottom of the stairs, she came to attention and snapped him an exacting salute. "Admiral, Commander Lisa Hayes reporting, sir. I'm carrying a special dispatch from the captain of the SDF-1 to the United Earth Defense Council."

He was taken aback, the smile wiped from his face. It was her turn to be formal and distant now, her right, as it had been his the last time.

If she was giving him back his own, he was willing to accept it. Nothing was as important to him as the fact that his daughter, his only family, was with him again. He returned her salute crisply, straight-faced.

"Welcome home."

Dante's Inferno was one of the more popular games there, but Rick just didn't feel like following old Virgil down through the nine circles to the demanding Ultimate Player level. Dragonbane, with its swirling nightmare reptile attackers and Nordic swordsman, seemed a little too much like his own duel with inner demons.

Nor was he inclined toward Psycho Highway Chainsaw Bloodbath. Eventually, though, Max convinced him to take on a pair of side-by-side Aesop's Gauntlet machines, mostly because the easy chairs before them were thickly upholstered and comfortable.

Down below, on the main level, Miriya sharpened her skills at the Veritechs! game. She found grim amusement in being a simulated Micronian pilot, blowing Zentraedi Battlepods to whirling fragments. She was disappointed that there were no Quadrono powered-armor opponents in the game; her own unit was by far the elite of the alien armada.

She also approved of the training machine—as she thought of it—for not introducing trainees to the realities of warfare at this early phase of their instruction. It was clear that the gamesters would need a little hardening and proper military discipline before they could deal with the horror and bloodshed of real warfare. This clean, neat gaming gave them appropriate affection for combat without any confusing exposure to certain unpleasant aspects of a real warrior's life. Clever.

She sent another pod to computer-modeled oblivion, pretending it was that of Khyron, whom she had come to despise. The score credit flashed, and little Jason, still watching, piped up, "Wow! Look at that!"

She tried to ignore him as tokens stamped with a big M poured into the payoff tray. The little Micronians were intriguing to her, but disquieting. And the small ones were always so boisterous or emotional—certainly impulsive and rather simpleminded. At first she thought that they were a slave underclass, but that didn't square with the indulgent treatment they got from the bigger Micronians. She forcefully shut from her mind the truth about human childbearing; compared to it, the war and slaughter were simple, comprehensible, painless things.

And such thoughts were not in keeping with her true mission aboard the SDF-1. She looked around, wondering when she would find her quarry. The memory still burned in her: of how the Micronian ace had outflown her and then, in the very streets of Macross itself, she in her Quadrono superarmor and he in his Battloid, faced her down, made her flee.

Her face burned again at the thought of it. She had difficulty eating or resting and would until she regained her honor.

The dimensional fortress was big, but not big enough that her enemy could hide forever.

CHAPTER

FIVE

Considering the staggering expense involved in any Robotech operation, the match that took place in the arcade that day certainly ranks as the most cost-effective VT mission of the war—and perhaps the most fateful.

Zachary Fox Jr., *VT: the Men and the Mecha*

EVERY ANIMAL IN AESOP'S BESTIARY SEEMED TO have it in for Rick, while Max progressed through the ascending levels with ease.

"The points're piling up, Lieutenant," Max said, referring to his score. Rick, teeth gritted, was trying to wax the fox that was leaping for the grapes. Damn thing moved faster than a Zentraedi tri-thruster.

After a lot of bleeping, ringing, and flashing from Max's machine, a flood of tokens, glittering like gold, slid into the payoff tray. The tokens could be used for more games, of course, or redeemed for prizes, vouchers of various kinds, or—if one really pressed the issue—cash.

"That's great! I always make more than I can cart off."

"Well, you left *me* behind," Rick admitted. *Wasn't this supposed to make me feel better?*

Actually, it did. "Max, look at that!" More and more tokens slid down into the tray until they were spilling all over the place.

* * *

Close Encounters's assistant manager, Frankie Zotz, a nervous young man in white pancake makeup and black, owllike hairdo, rushed into the manager's booth. "Hey, boss! We're gettin' wiped out at some of our most difficult machines!"

Blinko Imperiale, the manager—he of the goggle shades and two-tone Mohawk and vaguely intimidating lab coat—sat with chin on fist.

"Dincha hear me?" Frankie Zotz yelped. "That pilot's upstairs again, and the green-haired dame's inside turnin' a VT game every which way but profitable!"

Blinko didn't even move, sadly staring off at nothing. "Oh, boy. I knew I never shoulda opened this place near where those RDF maniacs hang out!"

The split-screen comparisons were obvious even to nontechnical personnel. The DNA strands and analysis workups spoke for themselves.

The presentation flashed along as Admiral Hayes muttered, "Interesting...hmmm..."

It was much more than that; it was astounding. It shook the very foundations of human knowledge.

It had long been thought that wherever the basic chemical building blocks of life coexisted in the universe, they would preferentially link to form the same subunits that defined the essential biogenetic structures found on Earth. In other words, the ordering of the DNA code wasn't a quirk of nature. Tentative evidence dated back to long before the SDF-1's crash landing on Earth, both from meteoric remains and from spark-discharge experiments.

The new data pointed up a universal chemistry—that the formation and linking of amino acids and nucleotides was all but inevitable. The messenger RNA codon-anticodon linkages that blueprinted the production of amino acids seemed to operate on *a coding intrinsic to the molecules themselves*. This meant that life throughout the universe would be very similar and that *some force dictated that it be so*.

Admiral Hayes skimmed over all that; it had little to

do with the war. He skimmed some of Dr. Lang's hypotheses and preliminary findings, too: that somehow the very energies that drove Robotechnology were identical to the shadowy forces governing molecular behavior. There was also mention of this irritatingly mystical Protoculture, something none of the alien defectors had had sufficiently high clearance to have learned much about.

Lang, it appeared, was monumentally frustrated that the hints and suspicions couldn't be verified. But he was vocal about his suspicion that this Protoculture the Zentraedi were so obsessed with was the key to it all—molecular behavior, the war, the origins of life, ultimate power.

The point of the presentation was obvious even to an aging flag-rank officer whose Academy biochemistry classes were far behind him. "Let me see if I'm completely clear about what you're telling me.

"You believe our genetic backgrounds, the Zentraedi's and that of the human race, are similar. And because of the possibility that we might all be part of the same species, you hope to promote peace talks."

Lisa was nodding, wide-eyed as the little girl he remembered. "But will all this convince the UEDC to open negotiations, sir?"

He sighed, the heavy brows lowering, staring down at the briefing file before him on the coffee table. Lisa held her breath.

"I'm not sure," her father said at last. He looked up at her again. "But I'll present it to them and make sure they listen, then we'll see what they say."

For the first time since she left the SDF-1, Lisa smiled.

Miriya bent over the VT machine, refining her game. Next to her, on the floor, were two plastic pans filled with playing tokens. Frankie Zotz had had to refill the game's reservoir twice to pay off all her winnings. She ignored his sweaty invitations to go play some other game—or, better yet, take a rain check and just *go*—with a slit-eyed amusement and a dangerous air that kept him from pressing her too hard about it.

Max came downstairs with Rick, holding his own tray of tokens. Suddenly, he stopped yammering his over-cheerful encouragements about how Rick would eventually get the hang of the computer games. That was fine with Rick; he had had just about enough light banter.

Max paused on the stairs. "Oh! *That girl!* Sitting at that game!"

Rick looked at the green hair. She wore a tight brown body suit that showed off a lithe figure, and a flamboyant yellow scarf knotted at her throat. "So? What about her?"

"Isn't she incredible?" Max said, more excitely than Rick had ever heard Max talk about anything. "I've been seeing her everywhere."

"Well, she *is* sort of attractive," Rick had to admit, his mind too full of Lisa Hayes and Minmei for him to go on at any greater length.

Max, the renowned VT wizard, wasn't much when it came to the pursuit of females; his few fumbling attempts with one or another of the Terrible Trio had failed, and he retreated completely when Sammie, Vanessa, and Kim became involved with the three Zentraedi ex-spies, Konda, Bron, and Rico.

Max's modest, self-effacing shipside persona made him a sort of uninteresting doormat for women. Perhaps he wasn't suave or seductively menacing enough. So when he wasn't out in a Veritech, he kept to himself for the most part.

But this was different; the Close Encounters arcade was his turf. "Maybe I can get her in a game with me!" Max said, as he went racing down the stairs.

There was quite a crowd around Miriya; she had rolled up one of the largest scores ever on the Veritechs game. She felt a little irritated, even a bit strange, with all these Micronians gathered around. Yet she endured their gaze, proud and pleased to show off her prowess.

She briefly considered the idea that her strange sensations had something to do with the damned Micronian food. It was nothing like the cold, processed, sanitized rations of the Zentraedi; human food had strange textures and flavors, odd biological constituents. It was all animal tissue and plant substances, and she suspected it was affecting her system.

She shook off the feeling and kept playing, rolling her score higher and higher, until she went over the top, beating the game, and more tokens poured into her tray. Getting enough money to survive in Macross had been no problem for Miriya since she had discovered the arcades.

Now someone pressed through the crowd: an unremarkable-looking VT pilot with a tray of token winnings in his hands. She was inclined to dismiss him; dozens of men had made overtures to her since she first came to the SDF-1.

But there was something different about this one, she thought.

Max worked up the nerve to say, "'Scuse me; would you be interested in playing a game with me? From what I've seen, I think we'd be equally matched. Don't you?"

He looked so young and eager that she almost laughed in his face and ignored him. Then she considered the tray of tokens in his hands. Miriya knew enough about the arcades to appreciate how good he must have been to have accumulated so many of the glittering pieces.

Of course it was beyond the realm of possibility that this slim youngster could be the premier enemy killer, but if he provided some competition, it might make for useful practice.

She looked at him languidly beneath long black lashes. Max felt his heart pounding. "Are you willing to bet all that?" Miriya asked.

He gasped happily. "Yes, I am!" He set his tray down next to hers, then scooted around into the seat opposite her. He babbled, "This is absolutely terrific! I know we're gonna have a great game!"

Watching from the sidelines, Rick wondered if there wasn't something *else* Max could do to screw up his chances of impressing her. Trip over her, maybe, or throw up.

But once in his seat, Max took on the air of confidence and aplomb that was his in matters regarding the VTs. "How about starting with level B? All right with you?"

She shrugged, somehow making it seem alluring and yet indifferent. "Fine."

"All right. Here we go."

He deposited the tokens, and the screen lit. Miriya had picked red for the color of her VT; Max selected blue, for the trim on his own ship. He didn't notice that Miriya's eyes suddenly narrowed at that choice.

Little animated Minmei figures walked out from either side of the screen to strike a gong in the center, and the action began. They guided their VTs through the twisting, changing computer-modeled landscape, using control sticks and foot pedals, maneuvering at each other and firing.

It didn't take long for Miriya to lose her nonchalance. Try as she might, she couldn't gain the advantage on him, couldn't shake him once he'd gained on her. A frown crossed her face, then a sudden flare of rage, when his fighter destroyed hers. She hid the expression in an instant, looking at him more closely.

The video warriors gathered around them were aghast. It had been a master-level fight. Max grinned at her. "Whoops! Looks like I won, huh? Wanna go on to level A?" He winked at her.

Rick groaned to himself. Somewhere along the line, Max had learned *exactly* how to antagonize beautiful young women.

She regarded him coldly. "Yes. Let's go on to level A. That should prove quite interesting." This time she would give the fight serious attention.

Max fed in more tokens; this time a blue hemisphere sprang from the game, a holoprojection. The muttering of the growing crowd became louder, until the real purists silenced everybody.

The miniature Veritechs flew over the flat surface of the gaming table now, going to Battloid mode and taking their autocannon in hand at high port. There was a moment in which Miriya gazed through Max's blue-trimmed, ghostly mecha, through his blue aviator glasses, into his eyes.

Somehow, she knew in that moment; all the rest of the game would only be proof of what her instincts were telling her.

The little Battloid computer images looped and fired, maneuvering on each other, going to Guardian or Veritech as their players decreed. There were outbursts and yells from the onlookers as the game moved. It was the fastest, most canny maneuvering anyone had ever seen; even though side bets were strictly illegal, everybody was making them.

Frankie Zotz projected it onto the arcade's main screen. Veteran players looked on in awe at the amazing dogfight. Tiny missiles and tracers spat; the computers could barely keep up with the instructions coming from the control sticks. The minuscule mecha circled and attacked.

Miriya used the same tactics she had used that day in her Quadrono armor; his responses were the same. For a moment, it seemed to her that her simulacrum Battloid had *become* a miniature Quadrono. Any doubts she had were swept away.

Max was thinking, *Boy, is she beautiful!* as he played his best at the machine. Another VT pilot, a lady's man, might have lost to Miriya on purpose. But then, another VT pilot probably couldn't have won.

People were whooping and cheering on the sidelines. In her mind's eye, Miriya saw the apocalyptic combat in the streets of Macross, as her own powered armor smashed through buildings and wreaked havoc, backpack thrusters blaring. She also saw that one-on-one final confrontation, when she had bolted rather than die in a point-blank shootout.

And just as his autocannon rounds had defeated her that day, Max's VT image destroyed hers. The red VT fragmented and flew into modeled, spinning bits, then de-rezzed to nothingness.

The blue hemisphere faded away, leaving her open-mouthed and blinking. *I lost! This cannot be! I will not be humiliated again!*

The victorious Battloid image's head turret swung back, and a little figure that looked suspiciously like Rick Hunter appeared, crying the word "STRONG!!" as a tiny Minmei raced up to throw her arms around his neck, kissing him and kicking her feet. The real Rick Hunter, still standing on the staircase, edged back in order to be more inconspicuous and thought dark thoughts about the sense of humor of video game designers.

An onlooker was saying to Max, "I dunno how you pulled that off, buddy."

"Aw, there were a couple of tight spots in the middle and near the end, but all in all, it wasn't too tough."

"*Oh!*" Miriya breathed. The insult of it. So she'd presented him with little challenge, eh? She rose, turning on one booted heel.

Max forgot his warm victory feelings and plunged after her. He caught her wrist, not knowing how close he was to getting a fist in the throat. "Wait, I've been wanting to speak to you for a long time. I think you're wonderful, and I want to get to know you better. This is my only chance to get your name and phone number."

His grip was very strong but not painful, his palm very warm. For a moment Miriya felt as though her wrist were burning.

"My name is Miriya," she said coldly. "And I don't currently have a phone number." She turned to go, tugging at his grip. The feel of his skin against hers made her feel a typical Zentraedi loathing of contact between the sexes but stirred something else, something she couldn't put a name to.

Now that she had met her archenemy, Miriya was confused. Killing him on the spot was out of the question; she suddenly didn't know *how* to cope with her mission. What he said about her brought back the strange, blurry feelings that the Micronian food gave her.

Max kept hold of her wrist. "Then, would you meet me in the park this evening? By the Peace Fountain, at nine o'clock?"

Fool! You've sealed your fate! she thought. Somehow the thought of slaying him made her angry rather than exultant. "Oh, whatever you want! Just let me go!"

His fingers loosened, and she snatched her wrist away, saying an icy, "Thank you." Then she whirled and ran, fleet as a deer, driven by a storm of conflicting emotions.

Max watched admiringly, breathing, "Isn't she something? Whew!"

Looking down from the staircase, Rick silently wished Max better luck than *he* was having.

CHAPTER
SIX

When you're caught up in a war and thinking mostly about the enemy, it's easy to forget that there are other fronts on which you should at least attempt to strike a truce.

Lisa Hayes, *Recollections*

IN A CORRIDOR DEEP IN UEDC HEADQUARTERS, LISA Hayes sat fretfully, shifting and fidgeting. She heard footsteps approaching and looked up to see her father. "Well, I talked to them," he said.

Tension twisted her middle. "Did they make any decisions?"

"You can never be certain about these things, but I think they're ready to accept the idea of peace talks."

She drew an excited breath, then smiled at him fondly. "I'm so proud of you for having the courage to take on this fight!" She stood on tiptoe to kiss his cheek.

Later, as they sat on an upholstered bench in a lift car, she asked him, "Is anything wrong, Father?" He had been staring at her strangely for minutes.

"I've been thinking of how you remind me of your mother. And how proud she'd be."

She blushed, very pleased. "Thank you, Father."

He shocked her by saying, "So, tell me how your love life's going these days. Are you going out with anyone special? Anybody I should know about?"

It took her so off guard that she found herself admitting, "Well, there *is* a young man . . ."

"He's military, of course?" her father said.

"Yes, he is. In fact, he's the one who rescued me from the alien ship."

Admiral Hayes nodded slowly. "Ah yes. Sounds like a good man."

They walked and chatted as they hadn't done in more than three years. The admiral led Lisa through the enormous base, coming at last to a vertical shaft nearly a mile across. It was lined with operations ports, energy systems, and power routing. High above, at ground level, a faceted dome like a cyclopean lens covered the shaft.

"Was there something in particular you wanted to show me out here?" After the relative confinement of the base passageways, it *did* feel like being outside.

Her father led her out to the end of a gantry overlooking the cavernous shaft. They could see down for miles, see up almost as far.

He waved a hand at it. "I wanted you to see the Grand Cannon, Lisa. Before we enter into any peace negotiations with the aliens, we're going to fire it at them."

She couldn't believe her ears. "What?" The cry seemed lost in the abyss that was the cannon's barrel.

Admiral Hayes wore a grim look, his strong jaw set. "Even though the satellite reflector system isn't in place yet, we expect to wipe out a large segment of the enemy fleet by pulling off a surprise attack spearheaded by a volley from the Grand Cannon. Once they've seen its power, we think they'll enter the negotiations in good faith."

The original plan had been to put huge orbiting mirrors in place to direct the cannon's bolts as needed; otherwise, its field of fire was very narrow indeed. But with the alien warships so numerous and so close to Earth, it was really only a matter of time before part of their fleet drifted into range.

Lisa spat, "This Grand Cannon probably couldn't wipe out a small division of Battlepods, much less one of their nine-mile-long mother ships! Don't you understand? We *have* to approach them without trying to escalate the war!

"Some of them have defected to us already! I'm sure

the Zentraedi will listen to our peace proposals *without* the use of weapons."

The admiral looked out at the barrel of the gun. "Lisa, how can you be so naive?" He turned to her. "The only thing a warlike power understands is a demonstration of *greater* power! We can't let the Zentraedi mistake our peace overtures for a sign of weakness. We must deal from strength!"

He paced to the observation platform at the very end of the gantry, hands clasped behind him. "How can you expect peaceful intentions from a race bred and trained for nothing but war? Even if their genetic structure is identical to ours, we have no real knowledge of what factors in their background motivate them, or how strongly."

"But Father," she began hopelessly.

He forged on. "No, Lisa! If history tells us anything, it's that caution and strength are needed when dealing with an unpredictable foe. We've already set a date for the firing of the cannon; we'll see about the peace talks after that."

She stood mutely, hair stirred by air currents in the yawning shaft. "I'm sorry, dear," he told her. "But there's nothing more to discuss."

"Yes. So I see."

Even with strange rumblings of unseen events on the war front, the public demanded that its hunger for other news be fed. The interest in celebrities and media idols was never satisfied for long.

A press conference had been called in the lobby of Macross General Hospital. It was crowded with print and broadcast journalists, shoving and elbowing, aiming lights and lenses and microphones. In the middle of it all was Lynn-Minmei, the reigning queen of Macross and the SDF-1.

Not even nineteen yet, she was used to the lights and attention, a gamine, black-haired lovely. Her tremendous charm and vivacity had bolstered the ship's morale through its darkest moments and won the heart of almost everyone on board.

Next to her sat her costar and third cousin, Lynn-

Kyle, a saturnine, sullen young man with flowing black hair that reached down past his shoulder blades. Kyle, the pacifist who was nonetheless an unbeatable martial-arts expert, wore a bandage around his head. He was completing his convalescence after having saved Minmei from a falling spotlight during a Zentraedi attack on the battle fortress.

Lynn-Kyle glared at the reporters and the camera and sound people. He always held the public in some contempt, scorning them for their willingness to let the military prosecute the war.

"Minmei," one man was saying, waving a mike at her, "is it true you've been helping Kyle recover, remaining *right beside his bed for the whole week*?"

Minmei frowned at him, and Kyle glowered, but they were used to that kind of innuendo by now. "I don't think I'd put it quite that way," she replied.

A woman persisted. "Rumor has it both of you are about to get married. Got anything to say about that?"

"Absolutely untrue!" she fired back.

That didn't keep another guy from asking, "Can you tell us how your ex-boyfriend reacted when you told him about these marriage plans?"

She felt like blowing her stack, then saw that this might be a chance to divert the focus of the interview. "Oh, you must mean Rick Hunter." She gave a silvery laugh. "He was just a friend."

Sitting up on his bunk, knees clasped to himself, watching the live coverage, Rick made a sour face, shaking his head. "Yeah. I guess that's all I was."

He felt like an idiot, a complete sucker. Time and again he had convinced himself that Minmei cared for him.

There was something about her, something flirtatious and impulsive. It was something that didn't want to release anyone who had fallen under her spell because, he supposed, that would be too much like rejection. So every time he had come close to getting over her, she had shown up to raise his hopes all over again.

Well, it looked like that wouldn't be a problem anymore. A little trip down the aisle for the two darlings of

stage and screen would at least cut Rick free once and
for all.

But the reporters weren't having any of Minmei's
evasion. "Oh, come on, now! That's not what *we* heard!"
"You used to be pretty close to him, right?" "You mean
to tell us you and Hunter never discussed marriage at
all?"

Minmei looked vexed but didn't answer. Rick thought
back once again to those long days they had spent together, stranded and lost in a remote part of the SDF-1,
when they first met. When it looked like they weren't
going to make it, she had admitted to Rick her lifelong
desire to be a bride.

They held a mock ceremony, marked by a very real
kiss, only to be interrupted by rescuers before they could
say their vows. Rick wondered if any of that was passing
through Minmei's beautiful head or if she had dismissed
it from her mind as she seemed to dismiss anything that
didn't fit with her desires and attitudes of the moment.

He told himself that he would probably never get a
clearer sign. It was finally time to put her out of his
thoughts and try to get back to living his life.

In other quarters, the micronized Zentraedi defectors
were gathered around a screen, utterly enthralled as they
gazed at Minmei.

They were dressed in ordinary work clothes and came
in the assortment of sizes and shapes that any random
group of human males might include. Except for a few
skin tones that seemed a little odd—mauve, albino-
white, a pale, pale green—there was nothing to mark
them as alien. Since the incident with Karita and the
muggers, they all took great pains to avoid trouble. The
military's decision to keep them all confined to their
quarters chafed but was accepted.

The SDF-1 authorities had provided them with
quarters and rations and so forth and were spending long
hours debriefing them, though as low-ranking warriors
there was little of strategic value the defectors could tell.
No one had yet begun a systematic orientation program
to familiarize them with human life; since the military
believed there was always the chance they might return

to the Zentraedi fold, the less they knew, for now at least, the better.

But they could watch Minmei and listen to her voice —the voice that had enticed them away from war making.

Now, one of them said, "Rico, what do they mean by 'marriage'? Why do they keep talking about it?"

There was some grumbling, as others were troubled by the enigma, too. Rico considered his answer. He understood only a little more about human existence than the others, but they looked to him for answers, and he didn't want to seem at a loss.

"Um, because marriage is something important. When two people get married, they go off someplace private and spend their time pressing their lips together."

This business of pressing lips had been mentioned before among the Zentraedi, had been one of the prime matters of fascination that had led to the defections. But still, the thought of such unbridled contact between the sexes sent the erstwhile warriors into a tizzy.

"Maybe they won't make us do it?" "My lips aren't ready for that sort of thing!" "I dunno; something tells me it might feel good." "Lemme at 'er!"

Some babbled and exclaimed to one another; others started shaking visibly or gnawing their fingernails. A few tried rubbing their top and bottom lips together and concluded that they were doing it wrong somehow. At least one swooned.

At the interview, Kyle found another microphone shoved into his face. "Tell the truth: *have* you proposed marriage to Minmei?"

He was calm, unflappable, on the outside. "No, I haven't."

He and Minmei were not close by blood, although their families had kept close bonds due to friendships and shared business investments in the White Dragon and Golden Dragon restaurants. He had grown up with Minmei very much like an adoring little sister to him.

But that had changed over time, as much as he'd fought it. It was the tremendous battle inside him compared to which mere physical fights were children's antics. Everyone thought the self-discipline he brought to the martial arts was a reflection of his inner calm; in fact, it was a reflection of the iron will that barely kept him from yielding to temptation. He'd spent all his young adulthood locked in fierce battle against his own impulses.

And most difficult of all were the movies they made together, the shared work and intensity of their scenes, especially the love scenes. It was so easy for acting to slide over into the real thing. The impulses were very patient and unrelenting. He drove them off each day, only to have them return fresher and stronger than ever the next.

But no more. Being with Minmei aboard the SDF-1, seeing the others who coveted her, had decided Kyle. No one else could have her.

"Sounds like a pretty weak denial." The interviewer grinned at him. "Maybe you just haven't had the chance, right?"

Kyle said in his calm, measured tones, "No, I've been thinking about, um . . ."

The newsman was watching him like a ferret. "Yes?"

"Thinking about how I'd actually say it to her. Because I don't mind telling you, it's something I've considered."

He heard Minmei's gasp next to him, and the mass intake of breath by the reporters. Flashbulbs began popping, and everyone began talking at once.

"Minmei, what d' you have to say?" "Have you set the date?" "Tell our viewers: Would you accept if he proposes?" "Give us a shot of you two holding hands!" "Kiss 'er, Kyle!" "Where d' you two plan to honeymoon?"

But they paid the reporters no attention. "Kyle, are you serious?" Her eyes looked enormous. They sat there, gazing at each other, while the furor boiled around them.

His screen switched off, Rick lay with head pillowed on elbows, feeling utterly wretched. *I can't believe it. All this time she's been waiting for Kyle to propose to her.*

There was a knock at the door, and Max showed up,

dressed in civvies: sports jacket, slacks, sweater, and tie. He wore a cheerful, eager look that made him seem sixteen or so.

"Sorry to bother you, boss. But I'm thinking of wearing this tie to meet Miriya. And I wondered if it made me look too sophisticated, you know? Or maybe I should go the other way, wear a gold chain . . ."

After Rick got rid of Max, he decided to get some fresh air. He wandered up to a parklike area on one of the observation decks and stared out a viewport as high as a billboard and longer than two.

Earth swung by above him, a crescent of swirling blue and white in the darkness. He sat and tried to spot Alaska.

After a while a familiar voice, holding a trace of mischief, said, "Well, if it isn't Lieutenant Hunter, as I live and breathe!"

He looked up to see Claudia standing nearby. "Oh. Hi, how're you?"

They hadn't seen each other a great deal lately, partly because they had been so busy and partly because they both still ached with the grief of Roy Fokker's death, and seeing each other brought it up all over again.

But now she came over to sit next to him. "Not bad. But what're you doing up here at this hour?"

"Couldn't stand my quarters anymore."

"Ah. You saw the press conference."

"Mm-hm."

She sat down, crossing her knees, resting her chin on her hand, helping him watch Earth. "You *could* get along without her. She isn't that terrific."

"She is to me!" Rick wouldn't have taken that from anyone else now that Roy was gone. But Claudia had an honesty that was hard not to respect and give its due. And she was quite capable of getting mad right back at you if she felt it was warranted. Claudia was not someone you wanted to be mad at you if you could avoid it.

"You're bright; you should be with somebody else," she said after a bit.

"I don't know that I want to be. I'm stuck on her."

"Why, Rick?"

"I don't *know* why! Maybe she's just my type."

Claudia put one finger to her chin, eyeing him side-long. "I don't know. I sorta picture you being with some-body more mature. You know: someone more experienced? Who's been through a big romance and a broken heart?"

Oh, great, just what I need! Rick thought. *Some other walking wounded to hang around with!* But he couldn't help listening very closely.

"It'd be good for you to be with someone who can appreciate a relationship. Those people're around, y' know. Sometimes they turn out to be your next door neighbor. Or even . . . your superior officer."

"Huh?"

She rose. "Gotta go."

"Claudia, you mean Lisa, don't you?"

She glanced back over her shoulder at him. "Did you hear me mention anybody by name? I only said people like that are around. Sometimes they've been known to pass by so close, you can't even see them."

She started off once more, throwing back over her shoulder, "Now, don't stay up too late. Things will look a lot better in the morning."

He watched her go and said very softly to himself, "Wow."

Rick sat, watching Earth again. The way he had it figured, the SDF-1's orbit would bring Alaska into view in a little while. He went over the message he had flashed to Lisa by prosign dots and dashes.

He wished he had said more.

CHAPTER
SEVEN

The myths of selfless humility and humble allegiance to ideals aside, there is no warrior culture, not that of Japanese samurai, medieval knight, or any other, that does not, upon close scrutiny, have a ruthless, entirely practical side to it. Also universal are egotism and a hypocritical willingness to dispense with all the high-flown language and poetic vows when the grim business of life and death is at hand.

How much more so, then, among the cloned, bred-for-battle Zentraedi? In the case of Miriya Parino, female warlord of the Quadronos and arguably the greatest fighter of her race, the matter is certain: Her soaring pride and utter self-confidence had been her hallmark until she was bested both in the air and on the ground by Max Sterling. Her emotional ferment was such that the law of her kind, the vendetta, was the only road open to her—vengeance, by any means possible.

Is it any wonder, then, that what happened next has provided fuel for songs, arguments, dissertations, and grand opera for generations since?

Altaira Heimel, *Butterflies in Winter: Human Relations and the Robotech War*

THE SUPER DIMENSIONAL FORTRESS PROWLED CAUtiously through the void, vigilant against attack and yet resigned to battle as only a seasoned veteran can be.

The Zentraedi had come pressing battle upon the ship many times before, would come again. Life in between clashes was, therefore, to be lived that much more fully. Death was all around—the war had gone on for years; nobody aboard thought, any longer, that it couldn't as easily be *their* number that would come up the next time around.

In the center of Macross was a park, lovingly and

carefully put together by the inhabitants almost blade of grass by blade of grass. Overhead was an Earthly summertime evening, courtesy of the EVE system. There was even the sound of crickets—descendants of good-luck pets who had somehow survived the war.

Max Sterling paced fitfully under a streetlamp near the Peace Fountain that trickled and gurgled a few yards away. He checked his watch for the seventh time in two minutes.

"Jeez; it's almost nine. I hope she's all right."

He was worried that Miriya wouldn't show up—worried even more, really, that she would. Just an average-looking young man straightening his necktie and hoping his only sports jacket didn't look too shabby, and recalling with a sudden sinking feeling that he had forgotten to pick up the flowers he had ordered.

He didn't know that death hunted afoot and that the pounce was near; he wouldn't know for several seconds yet that cruel eyes were watching him from the shadows.

"I can't believe I asked her to meet me in the park—a girl, at night!" he muttered. "She could get mugged or something."

In fact, street crime in Macross was all but nonexistent. And punishments were such that recidivism was just about nil; but that sort of reasoning meant nothing to a young man waiting for a woman who had him mesmerized, entranced, enraptured. A woman he had met only a few hours before.

A woman who stood in the dark poised, to kill him.

Then he heard running footsteps behind him, and her voice. "Maximillian, prepare for your doom!" It was a literal translation of a Quadrono war cry.

Miriya had gotten to the spot well in advance, seen him arrive, watched him. She had been set to kill him precisely at their appointed meeting time, a quarter hour before. But she had only watched him, hating him all the more but feeling strange—feeling drawn to him in some mysterious way she couldn't fathom.

She told herself she was merely studying her enemy's movements and possible vulnerabilities and fought down the *liking* she had for seeing him in motion. She told herself that she was merely waiting for the most opportune moment; yet though that part of the park was absolutely deserted, she let the minutes slide by.

Miriya observed his eyes, his lips, the way he moved. She felt a trembling in herself that no military mind/body discipline known to her could quiet. But at last, by a tremendous application of will, she hurled herself into battle.

Max was unaware of all of that, of course. At first he thought it was some kind of joke.

He saw her charging at him with the quick grace of a panther, a gleaming knife held high. Miriya's heavy waves of green-dyed hair snapped and flew behind her like a flag. She still wore the brown body suit, the knee-high boots of blue-dyed leather, and the yellow scarf at her throat.

Her eyes started madly. She was Quadrono, a Zentraedi warrior, and yet this miserable human had somehow made her vacillate—made her feel weakness where once there had been only strength! But that would end; Sterling would die, to expiate his sin of defeating her, and she would once more be Miriya the unconquerable.

Max was fumbling through a little greeting he had been rehearsing, his habitual whimsical half smile appearing on his face. "Miriya, it's nice to see you . . . glad you could . . . uh . . ."

This, while she bore down on him, the blade gleaming. The knife was a kind of hybrid cross between a Japanese-style *tanto* and one of the midlength Randall hunting models, with a circular guard. She saw that she had a lot of ground yet to cover and, afraid that he might elude her, hurled it at him, clawing in the meantime for her second blade.

The knives weren't quite like the Zentraedi weapons she was used to, but the balance and heft weren't too different. Although a firearm would have been faster, her incandescent need for revenge had made Miriya choose a more traditional weapon. It had to be reflexes, muscle, eye-to-eye confrontation, and cold steel that settled her score with the hated human.

And in that moment Max Sterling proved that all those dogfight kills weren't some kind of fluke. His psychomotor responses were the fastest the SDF-1 meds had ever measured—his coordination and reflexes were unprecedented.

Max was still trying to figure out what she was talking about when his body saw the flash of steel, understood, and ducked; he was doing his best to recall the awkward, rather romantic little speech he had meant to make to her when those supreme and somehow *strangely given* combat reflexes cut in.

His evasion was barely a flicker of movement; the knife flashed past him to land solidly in a tree trunk.

This was the first time she had ever missed. But she kept coming at him.

Stunned, Max watched her charge headlong toward him. She threw the sheath of the first knife far from her; it made no sound, landing in the grass.

"Hey, are you *crazy*?" Everything had suddenly slid into place within him; he already loved her so, but the physical Sterling, the part that made him unbeatable, was broadcasting warnings and threat updates, putting his body in motion.

She drew a second, sheathed blade from the open front seam of her body suit. "I am Quadrono Leader Miriya Parino: Zentraedi warrior!"

Max gulped. "There goes our first date."

But something in him had already changed; his balance was forward, on the balls of his feet—he felt nearly weightless—and his hands were curled into the fastest fists on the SDF-1.

However, he was still infatuated with her; he held himself in check when all his impulses were to counterattack. A little thing like attempted murder couldn't alter the fact that he was hopelessly in love with her.

She had seen him pacing, heard his concern for her. The weakling human fears—for the safety of an imagined loved one, of all things!—were so contemptible and misplaced, and yet . . .

Somewhere deep inside of her she knew, with a clear and pure knowledge, that Max's worry was a reflection of his regard for her. Who else, in the course of her matchless military career, had ever shown such simple, loving concern for Miriya Parino's well-being?

No one. Not ever. The very thought galvanized her, launched her forward to murder.

The sheath hissed briefly with a metallic rasp as the blade glimmered wickedly under the soft park street-lights. "You're such a fool! Fight for your life!"

There was something nauseatingly vulnerable and adoring in his eyes; the expression with which he regarded her was unworthy of any true warrior—but it sapped her determination so.

Yet inside her, a furnace as hot and powerful as any Protoculture engine burned. *Kill him! Kill him now, at once! Before ... before he can ...*

"My life? But why attack me?" Max asked bewildered; but his body was already set—they were both so locked into the physical language of hand-to-hand that a fight was inevitable.

She brought the glitter of the blade up into their line of sight like a fencer so that they could both consider its cold blaze. *"I will have my revenge!"*

His hand went to the hilt of the knife embedded in the tree trunk, and she made new calculations based on his being armed. Sterling's having a knife was so much the better as far as Miriya was concerned; she wanted to kill him in a fight on equal terms, wanted to humble him as he had humbled her—before ... before he could ...

His hand came away from the haft of the knife—very reluctantly, very slowly, very deliberately. He turned back to her. "I'm afraid I don't know what this is all about."

He left the weapon aside when he might have taken it. His life was in danger, but in another way his life was there, staring at him, a knife in her hand—the person, he was sure, he couldn't live without.

I wonder what the court-martial punishment is for falling in love with the enemy?

"What d' you mean, revenge? If you're a Zentraedi, I understand why we have to—to fight." He barely got the word out. "But why d' you want *revenge*?"

She held the short, *tanto*-style knife high, a miniature samurai blade, burnished and keen, that threw the light back like a mirror. "I ... have ... *reasons!*"

With that she sprang at him, fast as any jungle cat.

But Max Sterling's emotions and misgivings were subject to a sudden override; body and reflexes took over.

An edge so fine that it would have cut a hair floating in the air sliced through the spot where he had been standing, with a curt, sinister sibilance. Max was already aloft.

She spat a Zentraedi oath in frustration, watching him dive and flip to momentary safety. He whirled on her when he might as easily—and more sanely—have run for it. "Miriya, what'd I ever do to you?"

She wasn't blind to his decision to stand when it would be more advisable to run. Like a Valkyrie, she lifted the knife blade again, so that it threw back shards of light.

"You defeated me. And you don't even know who I am, do you?"

She swirled the blade around, *en garde*, so that there was a contoured trail of light between them. "I am the Zentraedi's greatest pilot! And I will not be humiliated by a human *insect*!"

She plunged at him, the razor-sharp edge slitting the air. In less than a second she executed two masterful infighting moves that would have disembowled a lesser opponent.

But Max Sterling simply wasn't there. He made no countermoves, but he avoided the cuts and thrusts like a shadow. Miriya was even more enraged to see that he wasn't terrified, but rather mystified. That he still felt weakling human emotions for her.

She fought down the chaotic impulses that flared up within her. She slashed again, but the knife hissed through empty space once more.

And she began to know a certain fear. *By the Protoculture! He's so fast!* Her fear had nothing to do with dying; she was Zentraedi. In this strangest battle of her life, she wasn't quite sure *what* that ultimate and most dire of terrors was, the dread that was somehow bound up in Max Sterling. She had had many mental images, wondering about what this utter demon of war would be like; none of them were anything like the truth.

"The first time you were lucky! The second time was your final victory!"

She cut at him, barely missing, Max dodging with that same uncanny speed. "Nothing can save you now!" Miriya hissed. *I will defeat you!*

She hurled herself at him, the blood thirsty edge coming around in an eviscerating arc.

CHAPTER
EIGHT

> *There are old soreheads and young soreheads in our*
> *ranks who still denounce the events that occurred near the*
> *Peace Fountain that night. Chances are, they won't get the*
> *point of this book, either.*
>
> *To paraphrase Robert Heilbroner, "These people bring*
> *lots of rigor to our cause, but alas, also mortis."*
>
> Betty Greer, *Post-Feminism and the Robotech War*

MIRIYA WAS QUICK, TOO, NEARLY AS QUICK AS
Max, and a clever knife fighter. She maneuvered the
next sequence of cuts so that his route of evasion would
be past the tree's great roots, and sure enough, he stumbled and went down.

She dove at him gleefully, the white throat open for
her death cut. By all rights the duel was hers; it needed
only the flick of a wrist to end Sterling's life and expunge
her shame. Nothing could explain her slight hesitation,
she who had never hesitated before and had lost to no
other foe. Nothing could explain it except the sudden,
vivid image of what he would look like when she killed
him.

Flat on his back, Max looked up at her. *This* was the
powered-armor pilot he had fought to a standstill days
before, first in a furious dogfight over the SDF-1, then in
a toe-to-toe confrontation in the streets of Macross itself.

He should have been afraid for his life. But all he
could think of was the fact that, squaring off with Miriya's mecha, he'd kept hearing Tex Ritter's old song from
High Noon, "Do Not Forsake Me, O My Darlin'," echo-

ing through his head. And now he just couldn't help hearing that haunting line—

on this, our weddin' day-ayy...

Miriya sprang at him; the blade cleaved the air, aimed at his heart. His body responded before he had time for coherent thought; he held up a flat disk of rock, and the knife point skidded from it, striking sparks, nearly taking two of his fingers off but missing but a hair's breadth.

The miss put her off balance; he worked a leg trip. As she rolled to get free and try for his life again, he catapulted toward the first knife, which was still buried in the tree.

She was after him at once. To kill him before... before he could...

"It's no use!" she cried triumphantly, slashing at him. They maneuvered and feinted, the other knife's haft only inches beyond Max's reach. "You're no match for me! Oh, you may be a great man, but what's a man compared to a Zentraedi?"

He faked her away from the tree, turned, and had the knife in his hand like magic, her belated cut only chipping bark.

"Now, we'll see." He held the knife in a fencing grip, almost hesitantly. She went at him.

Impossibly, they set aside any sane knife-fighting style to fence as if they held sabers. The knives struck scintillas of light from each other. Max had learned to fence in school and had sharpened his combat skills in the Robotech Defense Force; Miriya was a Zentraedi— she lived and breathed warfare.

Amazingly, Max engaged her blade in a bind, whirling it around and around, whisking it from her grip. It flew high, landing yards away. The point buried itself in the ground, tantalizingly close and yet so far, too far.

Max held the point of his knife close to her throat. She raised her chin proudly. "I guess I win again," he said, yet there was something in his tone that made him sound unsure.

It was the moment Miriya Parino, warlord of the Quadrono, had never thought she would face. And yet there was such a thing as dignity in defeat, such a thing as her warrior code. "I've lost to you."

This is a shame I cannot endure. She sank to her knees, pulling the scarf down and baring her throat. She waited for the cold kiss of the blade, hoping it would come soon to end her suffering. She couldn't help it, but tears welled up in her eyes—not from fear or even anger but from impulses to which she could put no name.

He was hesitating for some reason; she thought that perhaps he was going to show the cruelty a Zentraedi might in his position. She didn't blame him and was bravely determined to endure whatever he might mete out, but she thought that perhaps he simply needed a word from her to acknowledge her defeat.

"End my life." She lowered her head; the long green tresses hung about her face. "Please. Do it now."

But what she felt wasn't the final cold fire of the knife's edge. His fingers were under her chin, lifting her face. "But I couldn't! You're so beautiful..."

Suddenly everything was so unreal, so difficult for her to understand, that it came as only a minor shock to see that he had let the knife fall.

Miriya looked up blissfully into a face that held confusion, wonder, and a certain something else she was only beginning to comprehend.

She never felt herself come to her feet; perhaps she didn't, and the zero-g, flying feeling was real. One final spasm of Zentraedi warrior training made itself felt, telling her to stop him, to stop him before...before he could...

But he already had, and they were kissing, embracing, Miriya in Max's arms. For a while, in the little meadow in Macross's darkened park, there was a place apart from all other worlds. No word was said for a long time, until Max got up his nerve.

"Miriya, this is gonna sound crazy, but—will you marry me?"

"Yes, if you wish. Maximillian, what's 'marry'?"

The three former Zentraedi spies, Rico, Bron, and Konda, were sitting in the RDF crew lounge not far from the bridge, doing their best to show the Terrible Trio a good time.

Sammie, Vanessa, and Kim were feeling downhearted. It seemed that the SDF-1's voyage would never end, that there was no refuge for the starship anywhere.

No one wanted to guess how much longer the dimensional fortress could last against the Zentraedi armada that hounded them, but the unspoken consensus was that it had pushed its luck to the limit and that they were all living on borrowed time.

"D'you think the Canadians will offer sanctuary to the SDF-1, Konda?" asked the burly Bron.

If the Canadians could be persuaded to defy the United Earth Defense Council and let the ship land, offer her crew and refugees asylum, there might be hope. It would be the most strenuous test yet of the UEDC's authority as opposed to the autonomous rights of its member states, could perhaps lead to a new civil war, but it was the SDF-1's only hope.

Bron's friend and fellow warrior chewed a bit of food. "I'll tell you one thing: If our request is denied, it means we'll be stranded out here in space *forever*."

The three young women exchanged agonized looks. Little Sammie shook her head, intense and frightened. "Konda, please don't say anything like that!"

Kim, her coffee cup forgotten in her hands, suddenly looked lost and vulnerable. "Surely . . . *someone* will help us!"

Konda didn't contradict her, but neither did he agree. The six usually had fun when they were together, but now they just stared gloomily into their coffee.

"We must have faith," Rico said—an odd thing coming from one whose only belief had, until some months ago, been the Zentraedi warrior code.

None of them noticed Max Sterling pass by, looking every which way for his commanding officer. "Ah! Just the man I want to see," he muttered, spying Rick Hunter.

Rick sat alone at a table on an upper level of the place, lost in thought, staring out the deck-to-overhead viewports that had space on three sides of him. He was exhausted from the constant flight duty and the added burdens of being a team leader. He was worried about the ship, about his men, and about what he could possibly do to set his love life straight.

Rick looked surprised when Max broke in on his reverie, but he invited him to sit. "It's about last night," Max began. "I think I'm gonna get married."

Rick spat out his coffee and choked a bit until Max patted his back. "That's the most ridiculous thing I ever heard!" he sputtered at last. "You only went on one date! Man, you know she won't be leaving town, so why don't you take some time?"

Max looked stubborn, struggling a bit before he said, "We're in love."

Rick plunged into a lecture that he never would have imagined giving before he became Skull leader. But before he could get too far into why no one should rush into matrimony and how that went triple for VT fighter pilots, Max cut him off.

"Lieutenant, that's not the part that's bothering me." He mopped his brow with his handkerchief. "Y' see, it's ah, I'm not sure how to say this. She's the enemy. Miriya confessed to me that she's a Zentraedi."

Rick stared at him blankly for a long moment. If it had been practically anyone else, he would have doubted his sanity; but he was Max's friend, and besides, he had seen his latest psych evaluation. "How could you let this happen?"

"I love her," Max said, a bit more forcefully than he usually said anything.

"You're talking nonsense! What could you possibly have in common with her?" This, even though the three former spies and the bridge bunnies were keeping company on the other side of the lounge. Rick had been trying to unsnarl his *own* stormy emotional life and couldn't see why other people would want to complicate theirs.

"I'm telling you, I love her," Max insisted. He suddenly hit the table with his fist, making cup and saucer dance. "And there's no problem love won't solve!"

Oh yeah? Rick thought ironically; he wished that for just a moment he could do something about his hopeless yearning for Minmei, could understand his complex feelings toward Lisa Hayes. *Max, you've got a lot to learn!*

"There's one problem it won't solve, pal, and that's your silly idealism. Love isn't gonna make you happy, take it from me."

Max was furious. "It doesn't matter what you say, Rick. I'm going to marry this woman with or without your approval."

"Okay, look, so you're attracted to her. How many times does *that* happen to a guy?"

"She's special!"

"Take it easy; I'm sorry. I can tell you like her very much."

Max calmed a bit. "I want you to meet her."

"This should be interesting," Rick said, realizing someone had come up to the table.

Miriya Parino of the elite Quadrono battalion of the Zentraedi hordes looked like the cover of a fashion magazine. Rick didn't know what he had expected; he had never met a female Zentraedi and had seen few males who didn't look ugly enough to stop a clock.

What he *hadn't* expected was a gorgeous young woman in a simple, graceful pink summer frock set off by a blue sash about her slim waist. She wore her dark green hair in a single lush tail drawn forward over one white shoulder.

"We were just talking about you," Max told her with a sublime, starry-eyed smile.

Rick blinked, flabbergasted, then got out haltingly, "You were right, Max. She *is* beautiful. I—I think I understand now."

Miriya smiled serenely. "I'm so pleased to meet you. You look just the way Maximillian described you."

She was terribly happy that she and Max were to marry, though this odd, strangely thrilling human custom was more a mystery than anything else. She suddenly looked and felt nothing at all like a Zentraedi commander and warrior, but she didn't mind. Everything was so clear and bright and wonderful...

Max's decision to buy her new clothes had plainly been a good one; the looks she'd drawn from people, and from Rick in particular, were not the kind one directed at an enemy.

It was difficult to believe that only hours before, she had been trying to kill Max. He had spent much of the intervening time trying to clarify what "love" meant. She decided she wanted more clarification—a lifetime's worth.

"You're a lucky man, Max," Rick told him, without taking his eyes off Miriya. Then he grinned. "And forget all that nonsense I told you."

Max was all smiles again. Rick added, "And to guarantee you two have a great wedding day, I plan to be there to kiss the bride!"

Max shrugged and nodded cheerfully, a little irony creeping into his tone. "I knew I could count on you, boss. Only—"

He reached out to take Miriya's hand. "You'd better hold off on that until I explain it all to the future Mrs. Sterling. The RDF forces are shorthanded as it is, and I'd hate to see Skull Leader wind up in intensive care."

The preparations for the wedding began that same day. Gloval was strangely silent, except to give his permission and authorize the sort of major bash the ship's media moguls hungered and cried out for. Rick knew Gloval well enough to know that the captain had good reasons for a move like this, and he wondered what those might be.

News of the coming nuptials had the entire dimensional fortress abuzz. It galvanized crewpeople and refugees alike, a reason at last to celebrate and forget the war for a while. Mayor Tommy Luan and the director of the in-ship broadcasting system and a hundred others threw themselves into the arrangements.

Somewhat to their surprise, they found that Gloval had ordered that no effort be spared in making the occasion a major event. Miriya could have had ten thousand bridesmaids if she wanted; the RDF people and the Veritech pilots in particular kicked out the chocks to mount a pageant worthy of a royal wedding.

The preparations went quickly; the marriage became the center of existence for quite a few people. They were sewing, cooking, decorating; the RDF personnel rehearsed their drills, and the engineers rigged the most special of special effects.

All the activity didn't go unnoticed. In the alien armada, cold and merciless eyes watched the peculiar goings-on. Fateful, dire decisions were near.

CHAPTER
NINE

> *These letters pile up, Vince dear, perhaps to be read by
> you someday or perhaps not, but today especially I have to
> set down how full my heart is—more so than at any time
> since Roy was killed.*
>
> *I heard Gloval murmuring something astounding while
> he was sitting in his command chair: "Capulets and Monta-
> gues." I thought he was going soft; heaven knows the rest of
> us have. But when I looked at the clipboard he had been
> studying, it was an intel rundown on books Miriya had
> screened from the Central Data Bank while she was here—
> when she was hunting Max. Shakespeare was there, of
> course.*
>
> *I don't know what to think, except—damn it! We've got
> to change the ending this time!*

> Lt. Claudia Grant, in a letter to her brother Vincent

THE SPECTACULAR FIREWORKS LIT UP THE SPACE ALL
around the SDF-1. It was only the beginning, but *what* a
beginning. The whole area was illuminated in bright
colors; civilians and RDF people alike crowded every
available viewport, oohing and ahing.

Then the fighting mecha appeared, to execute their
part in things. From the flight decks of the fortress and
the two immense supercarriers that had been joined to it
like stupendous metal forearms, Veritechs swarmed out
to take up their places.

A broad, flat roadway of light, radiant in all the colors
of the spectrum, sprang from the bow of the flattop *Daedalus*, like a shining runway. The Veritechs zoomed out,
retros flaring.

Excitement hit fever pitch all through the ship. It was
more than just the occasion of a wedding—even the first

wedding that anyone could think of that had taken place in outer space. There was something about the joining of a human and a Zentraedi that spoke directly to the humans' longing for peace and a return home. It was a ray of hope that the terrible Robotech War might yet be ended short of catastrophe.

For Max and Miriya, it was simply the happiest day of their lives. They came swooping out of the void in Max's VT fighter right on schedule, Max wearing his tux and sitting in the forward seat, piloting. Miriya sat in the rear, making constant corrections to the fall of her wedding veil, the arrangement of her bridal bouquet. She had won so many decorations for bravery and courage under fire, yet she found herself unable to stop trembling.

The VTs had gone into Battloid mode, looking like giant ultratech knights. They positioned themselves in pairs, facing one another across the rainbow runway of light. They lifted weapons, the long gray autocannon that had been used on other occasions to wage savage war on the Zentraedi.

Now, though, the weapons had been fitted to throw forth brilliant beams of light into reflective aerosols that had been misted around SDF-1 for just that purpose. They shone like scores of crossed swords over the gleaming approach path. Max flew his ship under the military salute at low speed as Miriya looked around at it open-mouthed, delighted beyond words.

The fighter set down on *Daedalus*'s deck, and there were more mecha—the attack machines of the tactical corps ground units. Monstrous Destroid cannon, Excaliburs, Raidar Xs, and the rest sent harmless beams to form a canopy overhead as Max taxied for the elevator that would lower his ship to the hangar deck.

Cameras were already tracking the VT, and close, total coverage was planned for every portion of the ceremonies. Max and Miriya didn't mind; they wanted everybody to share in their total joy.

But not everyone did.

Breetai, the mountainous commander of the Zentraedi armada, gazed into the projecbeam image from intercepted SDF-1 signals. "This is the oddest Micronian custom we've observed yet, is it not, Exedore? Can you explain to me what Miriya Parino is doing?"

What she was doing was evident: She was walking slowly next to a blue-haired human, dressed in a rather elaborate and inconvenient-looking outfit, clutching what appeared to be a handful of plants.

She was also clinging to the Micronian's arm, causing Exedore to speculate that perhaps she had been wounded in the leg or fallen ill. Although she didn't *look* ill; she looked—Exedore didn't know *what* that expression on her face could mean.

Breetai gazed at the image. He was a creature who would have had no trouble passing for a Micronian himself, except that he was some sixty feet tall. Terrible wounds received in battle against the Invid species, implacable enemies of the Zentraedi, had left him with a glittering metal half cowl covering the right side of his skull, the eye replaced by a shining crystal.

Next to him was Exedore, a hunched and fragile-looking Zentraedi, far smaller than Exedore—almost a dwarf by the standards of his race. But within Exedore's big, misshapen skull was most of the accumulated lore and knowledge of his kind and a mind that Breetai relied upon heavily.

Exedore's bulging, lidless, pinpoint-pupilled eyes were fixed on the projecbeam image of the wedding, too. "Your Excellency, if I am not mistaken, she is getting 'married.'"

They were standing in Breetai's command station, overlooking the vast bridge of his colossal flagship. The flagship, nine solid miles of weapons, shields, and armor, was in a state of disrepair after its furious engagements with the SDF-1 and the RDF mecha. The transparent bubble surrounding the command station had been shattered; only jagged pieces of it remained around the frame.

Zentraedi were warriors, not slaves or drudges; they had little taste for anything that smacked of common toil, and even less talent for it. Those predjudices were approved of and reinforced by their Robotech Masters; without the Masters, the Zentraedi would sooner or later find themselves without functioning tools of war.

Exedore explained, "According to my research, it is a condition in which male and female Micronians live together."

Breetai was stunned. His harsh, guttural bass voice filled the command station. "Live together? Miriya Parino and this puny Micronian male?"

"Correct, m'lord."

But for what reason? The towering Zentraedi warlord, master of a cloned race that didn't know love, family, or sex, tried to imagine what the purpose could be, why male and female might conceivably desire such *intimacy*. But when he tried, he was assailed by waves of distaste and confusion, by nameless half-seen visions that made him physically ill. He shunted the images aside.

Breetai lowered himself into his enormous command chair, still considering the import of the wedding. "It seems she's taking this spying mission of hers very seriously. Perhaps more seriously than she should."

His first conclusion was that Miriya the dedicated fighter was simply undergoing the tremendous torment of such behavior to infiltrate the enemy and learn the perverse secrets of their obscene social practices. But Breetai saw something in Miriya's face, something that made the towering commander doubt this analysis.

It was like the three spies, Konda, Rico, and Bron, all over again. Breetai felt a certain dread. "Unless my senses deceive me, it would seem she's enjoying herself in some peculiar fashion. Could it be that she too has found the Micronian way of life too enjoyable to resist?"

Exedore answered, "It would appear, sir, that she cannot resist the charm of that Micronian pilot."

Breetai had seen kissing demonstrated when he captured Rick Hunter and Lisa Hayes. He shuddered, recalling the disgusting display, and wondered how any intelligent creature could bring itself to indulge in such baseness.

But the lure of the humans was undeniable; scores of Zentraedi soldiers had secretly conspired to undergo micronization and had gone to live among their former foes. It was the first such mutiny ever to have taken place in the history of the warrior race. Part of the madness had to do with the young human female Minmei and the oddly hypnotic power called "singing" that she exercised.

"Our forces may be in more jeopardy than we believed," Exedore said. "What if the traitors who went over to the human side were not merely mental defectives, as we thought, but rather the first wave in a sea of such deserters?"

Breetai rubbed his huge jaw, the one giant black eyebrow lowering. "It appears this 'love' business is a very powerful thing."

Exedore replied, "I'm afraid I agree with you, sir. It's an emotional factor against which we Zentraedi have no defense. This 'love' could be used as a powerful weapon against us."

Breetai scowled at the image of laughing, joyous humans, of the radiantly happy Miriya and proud, smiling Max. "Weapon, eh?"

"Yes. We must beware."

The intercepted coverage of the wedding showed them flashbulbs popping and people applauding as Max and Miriya cut their cake. The wedding cake was a ten-foot-high model of the SDF-1 in its knightlike Attack mode.

Breetai, growling in his rumbling bass, watched the proceedings angrily. What was there about the blissful looks of Miriya and the Micronian that exerted such a fascination, such a deep pull, on him? He told himself that it was only a commander's need to study a dangerous enemy, refusing to believe that he could feel such a thing as envy for the puny foe.

At the reception, the master of ceremonies was calling for quiet.

"Ladies and gentlemen, today is a very special day. It's more than just a wedding celebration; it's the bonding of two souls dedicated to the protection of our Robotech colony. I'd like to introduce the man who's done so much to make this a unique occasion, the commander of the SDF-1, Captain Henry Gloval!"

There was plenty of applause even though people were still passing around cake and freshening up their champagne after the several toasts that had been drunk.

Gloval stood up, decked out in his dress uniform, laden with medals, braid, and campaign ribbons galore. Rick, who knew the captain a little better than most people there, got the impression that they were going to find out why he had spared nothing to turn the wedding into a major occasion.

Gloval spoke. "Well, to begin with, I extend heartfelt congratulations to Max and Miriya. This wedding carries with it a great historical significance.

"As you all know, Miriya was a Zentraedi warrior who destroyed many of our ships. She comes from a culture that we have grown to fear and hate."

Oh, no! Rick thought. What could Gloval be thinking of? Miriya sat rigid as a statue, staring down at her plate. Max was white. The gathered guests were listening in stunned silence.

"It is the Zentraedi who have caused our present situation," Gloval pressed on. "They alone prevent our return to Earth—our homes and our beloved families." One hand was balled into a fist now. "It is they who have caused injury, destruction, and endless suffering!"

"Captain, *please!*" Max burst out, just at the same moment that Rick yelled, "Captain!"

Gloval forged ahead. "Now, I know what you're thinking: 'Why is he choosing this time to remind us of these terrible things?' I remind you of them, ladies and gentlemen, because we *must learn to forgive our enemies.*"

His image and his voice went out over screens throughout the fortress—in the barracks, the lounges, the giant monitors in the public squares of Macross City. "Not blindly, not out of ignorance, but because we are a strong and willing nation. We cannot blame the Zentraedi for their inexplicable lust for war. They have never known another way of life, and it has been their only means of survival."

All through the battle fortress, people gazed up at the screens in amazement—some with burgeoning hope, others with growing antagonism.

"Nor can we condemn individuals of that society for the mass insanity of their leaders. Instead, we must look to their good nature. As you may know, dozens of Zentraedi defectors are now aboard the SDF-1, having been reduced to human size. They have made a request to stop the fighting, and I believe it is a genuine request."

He turned to indicate the newlyweds. "The blood of these young people was tested before the ceremony. Zentraedi blood was found to be the same as human blood."

That started murmurs and whispers in the reception hall; in the ship and the city at large, it ignited a thousand arguments and marked a turning point in human thinking.

In the White Dragon, the Chinese restaurant belonging to Minmei's uncle Max and aunt Lena, Mayor Tommy Luan and some others had come over to watch the ceremonies on television. They heard Gloval say, "There is no reason why we cannot coexist in peace. Let this occasion represent a future where all people live in harmony."

Cheers and applause were rising, evidence of the general hunger for an end to war. Gloval held his hands up to silence it. "Please, let me speak a moment longer."

Voices in the background were heard, saluting Gloval for his leadership, courage, and convictions. In the restaurant, Mayor Tommy Luan nodded his head and wiped at a tear. "Captain Gloval is truly a man of peace. A great man."

There were others in the ship who didn't feel the same way, others who smashed bottles in the street or shook a fist at Gloval's image. There had been so many losses, so many deaths, and so much suffering since the aliens' first attack that the hunger for revenge would not die easily.

Gloval had anticipated that, of course. "All of us have lost loved ones, and it will be difficult not to harbor ill feelings toward the Zentraedi. But somehow we must overcome these feelings! We must stop this senseless destruction."

Far beneath the surface of the bleak Alaskan tundra, in the lowest levels of the United Earth Defense Council's headquarters base, Admiral Hayes pointed a remote unit at the TV, and it went dark.

He turned to his daughter and spat, "He's crazy! I

don't understand Gloval talking about peace at a time like this!"

Lisa was quick to spring to Gloval's defense, both because he was her former commanding officer and because he was inarguably right. "Father, it's the only way to avoid our own destruction! If we don't start talking peace, it will mean the end of this planet, and not even you would want that!"

He suddenly looked pained. "Lisa!"

"I'm sorry," she told him, "but you *must* stop the Grand Cannon operation immediately!"

Admiral Hayes stubbed out a cigarette and avoided his daughter's gaze. "Plans for use of the Grand Cannon are already set. There's nothing to be done about that now."

CHAPTER
TEN

I heard someone next to me saying something about a marriage literally made in the heavens. I held my tongue and was glad no one took the obvious bait, to mention a honeymoon in hell. I silently said my chants for the newlyweds and for us all.

Jan Morris, *Solar Seeds, Galactic Guardians*

GLOVAL STILL HELD HIS AUDIENCE TRANSFIXED.

"Each and every citizen must develop a responsible attitude toward the efforts for peace. We must learn greater tolerance and meet this challenge. I'm not proposing we lay down our arms but rather that we *extend* the hand of friendship.

"There is a chance for a peaceful solution, and we must make it come to pass. As Max and Miriya, here, have done.

"The Zentraedi are a strong and intelligent people. Let this ceremony stand as a symbol of our desire for peace. We must emulate Max and Miriya: They are the heroes of today and our hope for tomorrow."

It took a moment to realize he was finished, as Gloval turned to let the newlyweds retake the spotlight. Then all at once the cheers and applause were deafening. Streamers and confetti showered around the SDF-1 cake, and everybody was hailing Max and Miriya and blessing their union.

The crowd hailed Gloval as well, and friendship between human and Zentraedi. The Terrible Trio threw themselves into the arms of the three onetime Zentraedi spies—Vanessa to the husky Bron, little Sammie with Rico, and Kim embraced by purple-haired Konda. The joyous crowd called out toasts and salutes to peace.

Gloval hoped that it had been enough—hoped that the commitment and the determination would still be there when the cheering had stopped.

The headquarters of the Zentraedi supreme commander, Dolza, hung like some titanic hive in the blackness of space. It was the size of a planetoid, an armored moonlet so immense that Breetai's flagship and hundreds of thousands more like it could fit within. Around it, the Zentraedi Grand Fleet was assembling, a force so incredibly vast as to dwarf even Breetai's armada.

Dolza, the Old One, largest of his race, paced within his headquarters. Standing at attention before him were his assembled subordinates. Dolza stopped pacing and looked down at them.

"We can no longer permit this condition to exist. It's becoming a significant threat to Zentraedi power. It seems that we have underestimated the powers of these Micronian vermin."

In the end, it seemed Breetai's trusted adviser Exedore was right: The ancient Zentraedi warnings against any contact with Micronians had been handed down for good reasons, though the reasons had been unknown until now.

A race that could subvert the Zentraedi, make them violate their warrior code—a race that could weaken them so with talk of love and peace! Dolza had seen that it was a threat infinitely more dangerous than the ravaging Invid, that it was something that could end Zentraedi greatness forever, at a single stroke, unless something was done immediately.

"The battle fortress has become too dangerous to continue to exist. Even though it means destroying so many of Zor's secrets and losing valuable knowledge, you are ordered to totally annihilate the SDF-1. The Grand Fleet will soon be mustered and prepared to set forth."

The subordinates smote their chests with their right fists, roaring in unison. *"Ho!"*

Then, Dolza thought grimly, *we shall incinerate the planet Earth and end this threat once and for all.*

At the reception, there was the roll of a snare drum, and the master of ceremonies brought out Lynn-Minmei. Rick Hunter sat with his arms folded across his chest and didn't know what to feel.

She was even more beautiful than the first time he had met her—a black-haired, blue-eyed stunner with a naturally winning stage presence. She wore a gold lamé gown cut high on her left hip.

She took the microphone; the crowd was eating out of her hand before she even opened her mouth. Minmei paid lavish compliments to the newlyweds, then broke into one of her biggest hits, "To Be in Love."

Rick recalled the first time he had heard it, marooned with Minmei in a deserted portion of the SDF-1, lost and seemingly doomed. He had fallen in love with her there and had thought she felt the same.

Her wonderful voice took the notes with a sure, sheer beauty, caressing the words, taking the crowd under her spell.

Rick saw Miriya take Max's hand shyly. The three alien ex-spies were hugging the bridge bunnies. Konda and Bron and Rico had initially been won over to the human side by that same voice, that same face.

Claudia was trying not to cry; she had done a good job controlling it since Roy was killed, but Minmei's voice had something mystical about it. Rick saw moisture on Claudia's cheek.

Rick looked out the viewport to the emptiness of space. Roy, his best friend, was gone—and Ben Dixon and how many hundreds, how many thousands upon thousands of others? The losses had been terrible.

Deep under the frozen Alaskan ground, Lisa had turned the ceremonies back on. She watched Minmei work her magic and despaired of ever being able to compete, of ever being able to win Rick's love. *How can I? She's so beautiful; her singing—it's like a kind of miracle.*

* * *

The broadcast was also intercepted by the armada as it swam like a school of a million bloodthirsty deep-sea creatures in the depths of space. The great warships, bristling with weapons, spiny with their detection and communication gear, prowled hungrily.

In his command station, Breetai looked up at the image and heard the music. "This woman has a voice that...can make a man feel sorrow," he said slowly, heavily. Exedore looked at him worriedly.

Just as Minmei was about to start another song, a priority signal replaced Minmei's image. One of Dolza's staff officers looked down at him.

"Commander Breetai, forgive this interruption, but I bring you top-secret orders from Commander in Chief Dolza."

Breetai shot to his feet, hand outflung. "Hail, Dolza!" He shook off the effects of Minmei's siren song.

"You are ordered to begin a full-scale assault on the SDF-1," the officer informed him. "There are to be no survivors whatsoever, no matter what the cost. That is all."

He disappeared, and Minmei was singing once more. "Well, Your Excellency?" Exedore asked softly.

Breetai stared up sadly at Minmei's image. "It grieves me that the time has finally come. I do not look forward to this task at all, Exedore. That may sound strange, but it's true."

And the haunting beauty of Minmei's voice put that same heavy sorrow in him once more, until he willed himself to reach out and shut it off.

Loyal, insightful Exedore looked at his lord with concern. Half a dozen times he almost spoke of the fear and apprehension that those words, coming from Breetai, put into him. But in the end the small, slight giant held his peace.

But Breetai did not have the only receiving equipment in the fleet. Everywhere in the teeming warships it was the same: Clusters of huge, hulking warriors had gathered around to watch and listen to Minmei—and had heard Gloval as well. The first sounding of the alert signals, the call to arms and to glorious Zentraedi warfare, had touched off more dissent than they had ever experienced before.

"I don't *want* to fight," growled a much-decorated pod commander. He was staring at something tiny that lay in the palm of his hand as though examining his own heart line. Another PC, standing near, tried to get a look at whatever it was; but the first closed his fist.

He did it carefully; he didn't want to damage the tiny Minmei doll that lay there. Bron had given it to him before he and the others defected, seeking shelter and an uncertain future among the humans. The PC had listened to the doll sing until the batteries were all but exhausted. He couldn't explain its appeal . . . or the power of Minmei's music over him . . . or why he was unwilling to go out and destroy the SDF-1 when his former comrades in arms were aboard.

The harsh Zentraedi language had few or no words for these concepts, but that didn't change the PC's feelings.

All around them, colossal warriors raced to don combat armor, seize weapons from the racks, grab gear, and get ready for the great assault. The decks thrummed under their massive iron-shod feet.

The second PC opened his palm to the first for an instant. They had been thinking the same thing, for he held another of the tiny souvenir Minmei dolls. He closed his fist again. Opposing the war felt much different, sparked a higher flame of hope, when each realized that the man facing him felt the same.

"It's as though I'm going to be fighting against my own people," the second PC said, struggling to put his thoughts into the limited Zentraedi battle tongue.

NCOs and officers were yelling at various scurrying units to move it, move it, move it. Go! Go! The deckplates thundered.

But one body-armored NCO, having caught a bit of the exchange, skidded to a halt, his disrupter rifle gripped in one hand.

"D' you realize what the penalty is for disobeying orders in combat?"

Others had been listening to the two pod commanders, half swayed by what they were saying, recalling Gloval's words and Minmei's song. But all of them knew the dreadful punishment the NCO was talking about. Death would be preferable.

One of the bystanders declared, "He's right! We will *have* to fight!"

"Let's move!" someone else cried, and with that they were in motion, scrambling to prepare and race to their battle stations. Everyone, that is, but the first PC. He watched the others go as he reclined back on his bunk, hands behind his head, brooding. At last he brought his hand forth and spent a long time looking at the tiny Minmei doll.

The vast armada began shifting formation, spreading and realigning for the attack.

At the wedding reception, alert sirens began sounding at just about the same time Gloval took the call on a mobile com handset and got the crowd's attention. With the banshee song of the sirens behind him, he announced, "Ladies and gentlemen! It grieves me to say this, but we are now on red alert."

He had to raise his voice to speak over the confusion and outcries of the crowd. "All military personnel report to battle stations at once. Civilians proceed to emergency duties or to designated shelters. The SDF-1 is about to come under full-scale attack."

He swallowed once, with effort. It was the first time the enemy had thrown its massed strength at the fortress, and there was little question as to what the final outcome would be.

"God be with you all. Now, move quickly!"

Only a few actually lost their heads and bolted; everyone aboard had been through the fire of battle, and most moved swiftly but with a deliberate calm.

The Terrible Trio finished what they were eating and swapped hugs with the Zentraedi spies before dashing off to the bridge. Striding for the door, Rick Hunter exchanged a brief glance with Minmei but had no time to stop and talk to her, though he wanted to do that more than anything in the world.

A VT duty officer halted amid the flow of people and looked back to the wedding party's table as Max came to his feet, unable to believe what was happening.

"Max, you're excused from duty. Captain's orders! You sit this one out!" Then he was on his way.

Max slowly tugged his bow tie, opening his collar. He sighed deeply, feeling Miriya's eyes on him, and turned to her. "I can't let them down when they need me the most, love."

She drew off her wedding veil. "Of course not, Max. I'll go with you."

He stared at her. *"Huh?"*

Miriya came to her feet. "I've seen your Veritechs, even flew yours for a bit, remember? I can handle one was well as any of your pilots."

"No—"

"I promised in our vows that I would stay by your side, and I will. From now on, we fight together."

And a brief fight it might be, he knew. The RDF needed every hand it could get, and Miriya's battle skill might be a critical plus. He took her hand, and they managed an even more loving look than they had exchanged during their vows.

"Then I guess I have no choice," he said. "Even though we may die together."

"Oh, but Maximillian! I would accept no other death!"

"Me, either." He kissed her quickly, then they raced off hand in hand. "There goes the honeymoon," he said as they ran.

"I don't think you understand true Zentraedi determination." She smiled.

Alone in the ballroom, the master of ceremonies had no more strength to seek shelter or follow the war over the screens. The wedding had been the best thing that had happened to him in two years aboard the SDF-1, the thing he was suited to, that he did best.

Now he sank to his knees, head lowered to the forearm he rested on the shambles of the wedding party's abandoned table. The fortress model, symbol of Max and Miriya's wedding, looked down at him. He sobbed what everyone in the ship was thinking, as the Zentraedi dreadnoughts moved in in their hundreds of thousands.

"Please, save us all."

CHAPTER
ELEVEN

Dolza, my old friend, old watchdog; the naive straight-forwardness of the Zentraedi could be your downfall some day.

All things are so simple to you: The eye sees the target, the hands aim the weapon, a finger pulls the trigger, an energy bolt slays the enemy. You therefore conclude that if the eye sees clearly, the hand is steady, and the weapon functions properly, all will be well.

You never see the subtlety of the myraid little events in that train of action. What of the brain that directs the eye and the aim? What of the nerves that steady the hand? Of the very decision to shoot? What of the motives that make the Zentraedi obey their military Imperative?

Ah, you call all of this sophistry! But I tell you: There are vulnerabilities to which you are blind.

Remark made by Zor to Dolza shortly before Zor's death—known only to Dolza, Exedore, and Breetai

AGAIN THE BAYS OPENED, THE ELEVATORS LIFTED the fighters to the flight decks. The SDF-1 and the *Daedalus* and *Prometheus* catapult crews labored frantically to launch the all-important fighters as fast as possible. On the flatdecks, waist and bow cats were in constant operation, and the crews' lives were in constant danger; it was very easy for something as small and frail as a human being to meet death during launch ops, especially in the airlessness of space.

The Veritechs rose to the flight decks, deploying ailerons and wings that had been folded or swept back to save space on the hangar decks. Their engines screamed like demons, and they hurtled into space in a meticulously timed ballet, avoiding collisions with one another and forming up for combat with the sureness of long experience.

Gloval watched from a tall viewport as Rick Hunter went out, leading Skull Team. And the rest, scores of them, fell in behind to do battle against the aliens' total attack.

"May every one of you make it home safely," Gloval murmured, the old briar pipe gripped in his teeth. But he knew it was too much to hope for.

Rick was running the fighter wing now; even though there were those who outranked him, there was no one with more expertise.

"Remain in Fighter mode until I give the word," he told them. "We are now approaching intercept zone."

Flying at his wing was Max, with Miriya in the seat behind wearing an RDF flight suit and "thinking cap."

The pods were coming in droves to soften up the target and eliminate and suppress as much counterfire as they could before the Zentraedi heavyweights came in for the kill.

Rick's autocannon sounded like a buzz saw multiplied a thousand times; high-density slugs went out in a stream lit by tracers to pierce an oval armored body through and through. The enemy disappeared in an expanding sphere of red-hot gas and flying shrapnel an instant later.

The Veritechs peeled off, wingmen trying their best to stick together, and threw themselves into swirling, pouncing dogfights against the enemy. The pods advanced in an unstoppable cloud, as the desperate VTs twisted and swooped.

Gloval agonized over the fact that ongoing repairs and retrofitting made it impossible to fire the ship's main gun. But the ship's primary and secondary batteries opened up, turrets swinging, barrels traversing, hammering away.

A pod was hit dead center by an armor-piercing discarding-sabot round and blew to incandescent bits. Another was riddled by kinetic-energy rounds from an electromagnetic rail-gun, projectiles accelerated to hundreds of thousands of g's, hitting at such high speed that explosives would have been redundant. A VT in Guardian mode spun and tumbled, chopped to fragments by the energy blasts of a pod's plastron cannon.

But more and more pods came at the humans in vast waves, pushing them back. The SDF-1 was surrounded by the globular explosions of space battle, hundreds of them every second.

Max had a pod square in his gunsight reticle, thumb on his stick's trigger, when Miriya cried, "No! Wait! Don't shoot!"

"Huh? But they were right in my sights."

She took over, maneuvering until the computer-aided sights were centered on a structure behind the articulation apparatus that joined the pod's legs. Whatever it was, it wasn't on the VT pilots' menu of sure-kill shots.

But Miriya told her husband, *"Now!"* Max zoomed in on a close pass, letting a short burst fly. The target structure disappeared in a burst of flame.

The Zentraedi wobbled and careened out of control, its main thrusters sputtering and coughing every which way, guns going silent after a moment. Trailing fire, it drifted away, limping toward safety with feeble gusts from its attitude thrusters.

VT pilots were taught to go for the sure-kill shots at areas of the enemy mecha most likely to expose themselves to fire. He felt like he had just been taught a secret *Shao-lin* pressure point.

"But we could've lost him while we were trying for that shot," he pointed out, craning around to look over his seat at his bride of less than an hour.

"I don't want anybody else to be hurt in this war," she told him.

"But Miriya, we don't want to jeopardize our own lives, right? Or the ships?"

She looked him in the eye. "Remember what the captain said? Max, it's time to do more than just talk. We must act. And now I've given you the key."

"Oh, boy. You're right. We'll just have to give this a try."

"Thank you, Maximillian."

Max took out two more to make sure it really worked.

"What in heaven's name is going on in that plane?" Rick yelled over the tac net.

He saw Max's face on one of his display screens. "Boss, I'm sorry those last few weren't kills."

"Don't bull *me*, Max." Rick could see what was going on. "I think I understand."

He dove at a pod, his forward lasers vaporizing the vulnerable component that Miriya had revealed. "We'll stop this war *without* bloodshed!"

Captain Gloval was right. "The time has come for peace," Rick muttered.

The secret of popping the enemy pods without killing anyone within was made easier to share because the small, vulnerable component was located behind and slightly below the leg juncture. This made it easy and even fun for the VT fighter jocks to tell each other where to shoot and to vie with each other at making perfect shots.

The structures were also located in a spot difficult for the pods to defend. The VTs had never concentrated on that place before because most of that area was heavily armored and the target in question was so small.

But once they knew what they were after, the VT pilots began enthusiastic, almost crazed disabling runs. Pods got their fundaments blown out from under them by VTs on long passes, predatory banks, high deflection shots. One guy on Ghost Team got three in one pass.

But the pods had closed in tightly around the SDF-1 as the alien battlewagons came up behind. The dimensional fortress shook to a ferocious blast of concentrated fire.

"Captain, our number two thruster's been damaged," Vanessa said.

Gloval gritted his teeth, saying nothing; he knew it was going to get worse.

The Zentraedi officer dashed angrily into the readyroom hatchway, furious when he saw that the crew there had not even so much as donned their armor.

"Lord Breetai commands that you prepare to attack!" he roared.

One crewmember was standing by a viewport, looking out at the starlit darkness, holding a tiny Minmei doll in his palm, small as a pea in his giant hand.

"So beautiful yet so small," he whispered to himself in his rumbling voice as the others looked over his shoulder. He thought of her songs again, and the memory filled him with longings no Zentraedi career could ever answer. He closed his enormous fingers gently around the doll.

The officer bawled, "You're all in direct violation of Lord Dolza's orders! Report to battle stations at once, or I'll have you all court-martialed!"

They were Zentraedi beguiled by the songs and peace talk of humans; but they were still Zentraedi, with the pent-up fury of their race. One whirled on the officer, bringing up an assault rifle, clacking off its safety.

"*What* did you say?"

Others turned, weapons clacking, and the officer found himself staring into a half dozen rifle muzzles and then a dozen. "Don't be insane!" he screamed. "Think of what you're doing!"

"It doesn't matter what you say," one of them told him icily. "We aren't fighting anymore. We have friends on that ship. We have vows we've sworn with those friends, sacred warrior oaths. We won't attack them; that's where we draw the line. Now, *leave!*"

He threw the rifle to his shoulder, bracketing the officer in his sights, finger tightening on the trigger. The officer gave a yowl and disappeared from the compartment hatchway, boots echoing on the deck.

The warriors stood listening, lowering their weapons. "Look at him run, like a trog with his tail between his ears," one said, laughing.

Breetai spun on Exedore. "What? It's mutiny!"

"Your Excellency, a large number of our best pilots will not leave the mother craft. *They refuse to acknowledge that the order was given!* Mutiny in time of battle is a thing that has never happened before in Zentraedi history."

Although, he added to himself, *those warnings from*

the ancients must have had a basis. If they're right, we face disaster!

"But—with all respect—they have some justification," Exedore went on.

Breetai glowered down at him. "There is no rationale for mutiny!"

"But you know there are Zentraedi on the battle fortress. And now they know, too. To attack their own is a direct violation of the laws that bind us together as comrades in arms—"

"Enough!"

"And then there is this baffling new tactic of the enemy, disabling our pods rather than destroying them, sparing our warriors when they could more easily have killed them. Some pod commanders in the attack force are preparing to turn on their fellows if the attack isn't broken off—"

Breetai turned and strode away. "Exedore—"

Exedore hurried his shorter strides to catch up. "And the transmissions from the wedding—"

Breetai stopped and pivoted instantly. *"I said enough!"* His boulderlike fist hung near Exedore's face, clenched so tight that the huge knuckles and tendons creaked loudly, trembling with Breetai's anger. Exedore fell silent.

After several long seconds, Breetai retracted the fist almost unwillingly but regained control of himself. He started walking again, the overhead lights gleaming off his polished skullplate and crystal eye; Exedore followed meekly.

"Stop your blathering," Breetai rumbled. "I'm aware of the situation. Issue the order to withdraw immediately! Recall all Zentraedi mecha."

Exedore halted, mouth agape. "Yes, sir, but that is in direct disobedience of the Zentraedi High Command—of Dolza's own orders!"

Breetai stormed on his way, neither looking back nor answering.

On the SDF-1's bridge, no one quite knew how to take it.

"It's a miracle," was all Sammie could say.

"Yes, we're very lucky," Gloval said softly, sitting in his command chair. *Could it have to do with the wedding? Did it work?*

Claudia began calling the Veritechs home.

The newlyweds had received generous offers of living quarters in crowded Macross City, even from some who could ill afford the space. But there was no question of staying so far from the fighter bays while the current emergency remained.

Ship's engineers had hurriedly taken out the partition between two adjoining compartments to give the Sterlings a small connubial bower: a living room—kitchenette and a tiny bedroom. There hadn't, however, been time to soundproof it; that would have to wait until the next work shift.

So Rick Hunter lay in his bunk, head pillowed on hands, listening to the muffled turmoil in the kitchenette on the other side of the bulkhead.

"Max, why is it on fire?" came Miriya's voice. "Is this another weird human recipe?"

"Uh, honey, get out of the way; I'll put it out," Max yelped, and there was the gush of a small fire extinguisher. Rick didn't hear the ship's main fire-fighting systems cut in and concluded that Max had gotten it.

"Strange, strange day," Rick sighed.

He caught snatches of their conversation without meaning to. What had she done? Just used a dash of that liquid, the cooking oil. Nothing on the bottle *said* it shouldn't be used in the coffeepot.

Max would be perfectly willing to do all the cooking for a while; Miriya insisted that she wanted to do her share. That was what comrades in arms and lifelong mates *did*, she insisted.

After a bit longer, they were both giggling and the hatch to the bedroom closed. Rick slugged his pillow like he was in a title fight, then threw his head against the mattress and pulled the pillow over it.

I hope they'll be happy, he forced himself to think. Then he found himself thinking about Minmei, and of Lisa, and then of Claudia, grieving for Roy Fokker—so brave; stronger than Rick would be in her place.

Roy had tried to tell him something once, something the original Skull Leader had discovered during the course of his tempestuous love affair with Claudia Grant.

Before you can love someone, you have to like them.

The thought came into Rick's mind unbidden, along with the image of long, light brown hair and a slender form—a quick, disciplined mind and a commitment to a set of beliefs that Rick found more worthy every day. And—there was the remembrance of a kiss before alien captors, a kiss that had been so much more than he had expected and had haunted him since.

I like Lisa; maybe I even—

He tossed on his bunk, head on top of his pillow now, staring out at space through his cabin's viewport. Next door there was still silence.

In a few moments he was blinking tiredly before he could sort out just what it was he felt.

I'm so beat. I feel like just—

He fell asleep with Lisa's face before him.

CHAPTER
TWELVE

> *Khyron was always different from the rest of us, and the ways of the Micronians held some dark fascination for him, however much he fought it.*
>
> *But the Micronians are mad! Is it any wonder this drove him over the brink, so that as he perceived it his only relief was to liquidate them all?*
>
> Grel

"ALIEN VESSEL, BATTLESHIP CLASS, SIR," Vanessa said tightly from her monitoring station on the bridge.

This time Gloval was ready. "Prepare to fire main cannon! Lock all tracking systems to target!"

In the respite that had followed the last attack, engineers had completed retrofitting and new installation. At long last, the SDF-1 had been brought into Attack mode without major damage to Macross City and accompanying loss of life.

The ship could use its fearsome main gun in this configuration, standing like a monumental armored gladiator in space with the two tremendous supercarriers held out like menacing forearms.

"All systems go; booms now moving into position," Claudia said in clipped tones. The booms had stood like horns above the fortress; now, brute servomotors swung them down so that they pointed out straight from both of the ship's huge, bulky shoulder structures.

"Main gun standing by to fire on your command, Captain," the message was patched in from engineering. Claudia couldn't help but wish Lisa were back on the bridge. The Terrible Trio and the other techs were good and were doing the best they could, but nobody except perhaps Dr. Lang knew as much about the ship as Lisa.

Sammie watched the preparations, wide-eyed. "I bet this is a trick or something," she declared in her young, breathless voice. "A Trojan horse!"

Kim spared a moment from her own problems to gaze at Sammie dubiously. "Trojan horse? They know we'd never fall for that! Where on Earth would you get an idea like that from?"

"The Trojan War! Besides, that's the way it always happens in the movies."

For two years now, they've been trying to wipe us out, and she still thinks about movies! Kim groaned to herself and went back to her job, resolving to slug Sammie later.

Sammie said with high acrimony, "Okay, if you've got a better theory, let's hear it!"

Vanessa cut through the squabble.

"Captain," Vanessa said, "I have a message coming in in cleartext from the alien ship."

Gloval came halfway out of the command chair. *"What?"* He tried not to let himself hope too much.

"They're asking permission to approach the SDF-1. Shall I put it up on the monitor, Captain?"

Gloval grunted approval, and Vanessa complied. Suddenly, Sammie's flight of fantasy didn't sound so zany.

"I say again: We are sending an unarmed ship to dock with your battle fortress. We request a cessation of hostilities. Please hold your fire."

The enemy flagship drew near at dead-slow speed, straight into the line of fire of the main gun. The battleship might be nine solid miles of supertech mayhem, but surely by now the Zentraedi knew that it would be as defenseless as a helium blimp before the holocaust blast those massive booms could generate.

"Let them come," Gloval told Claudia. "But stand ready to fire."

Claudia flipped up the red safety cover with her thumb, exposing the trigger of the main gun. Sweating, she watched the battlewagon close in, ready to fire the instant Gloval gave the order but forcing herself to be calm. She was unaware that everyone else there, captain and enlisted ratings alike, was glad that Claudia—whom they saw as a tower of strength—was trigger man that day.

Gloval let the flagship come at him, come at him. Sammie's Trojan horse remark was much in his mind. He wondered about this Breetai, whom Lisa and Rick had described to him. The three Zentraedi spies and the deserters who had come after them had contributed more, as had Miriya. Gloval wondered and hoped the vagaries of war would let him meet Breetai face to face; he suspected that the alien commander felt the same.

The flagship slowed to a stop, a sitting duck of a target, reassuring him. But abruptly there were dozens of streamers of light swirling from behind it, bearing in on the fortress at high speed. Gloval didn't have to look at the computer displays; he had seen these performance profiles before.

Vanessa yelled, "Picking up large strike force of tri-thruster pursuit ships, closing rapidly!"

The tri-thrusters were right in the line of fire; Claudia's forefinger hovered by the trigger.

What are they up to now? Gloval thought with dismay. Peace had seemed so suddenly, tantalizingly close. But what could this be except betrayal?

The tri's were out in front of the flagship, closing in on the SDF-1, their drives leaving bright swirling ribbons of light behind them. The command to fire was on Gloval's lips.

But all at once a hundred batteries in the enemy flagship's forward section opened up, and the tri-thrusters were blown into fragments, dozens disappearing per second in ballooning clouds of total annihilation. The blue-white lines of energy from the enemy dreadnought, thread-fine against its enormous bulk, redirected immediately upon destruction of a target, to the next. In moments, the massive sortie fell apart and space was full of briefly flaming junk.

Gloval swallowed. "Secure the trigger but stand by," he said.

Claudia closed her eyes for a moment, breathing a prayer, thumbing the safety cover over the trigger. But as he had ordered, her thumb rested on it still.

* * *

Breetai stood at his command station, hands clasped at the small of his back. As he expected, Khyron the Backstabber didn't take long to appear by projecbeam image.

"Breetai, have you gone mad?"

Breetai studied him coldly. "Your ships were interfering with a diplomatic mission, as you well know. And so I disposed of them. Henceforth you will address me by my proper rank."

Khyron fought a fierce internal battle, then managed, *"Commander,* what happens now? I refuse to spare the Micronians! We all know Dolza's orders!"

"You know nothing, Khyron! And I will hear no further word from you on the subject. Just consider yourself lucky you didn't choose to lead your troops this day!"

"Ridiculous!"

Breetai swung his command chair away from the screen, cutting the communications circuit, muttering, "Hardly."

Like some immense killer whale, the flagship came to a stop directly in front of the SDF-1's most powerful weapon.

"They're just sitting out there, Captain; I guess they're waiting for us to make a move." Claudia's thumbnail stood under the edge of the trigger's cover.

If they don't want peace, why would they destroy their own fighters? Why would they not overwhelm us, as they so easily could?

"They wish to send an emissary. Very well," he decided. "So be it."

The Veritechs flew forth accompanied by other mecha, like the cat's-eye intel ships, detector-loaded and studying everything about the emissary pod.

The pod was standard except that it mounted only auxiliary commo gear: no weapons. The cat's-eyes and other emissions-intelligence detectors said that it wasn't the Trojan horse of Sammie's nightmares.

Rick Hunter quieted his Skull Team, telling them he

knew it was weird and getting weirder all the time but reminding them the team hadn't suffered any casualties in a while.

That strangest of all convoys came to rest in an SDF-1 bay, the VTs now in Battloid mode with their chain-guns leveled at the pod.

Things moved quickly to the hangar deck, while PA voices went on about the normal checklist procedures and the extraordinary precautions surrounding the emissary's arrival. No one wanted to take any chances on a double-cross or, perhaps worse, on a vengeful human's violent act robbing the SDF-1 of this chance for peace. Security was—in some ways literally—airtight.

The enemy mecha knelt, its prow touching the deck as the rear-articulated legs folded back. A rear hatch swung open; a Brobdingnagian enemy trooper stomped forth to glare around.

"Aren't you forgetting something?" called a reedy, highly miffed voice from within the pod.

The mountainous trooper was immediately contrite, almost afraid. "Oh, please forgive me, your Eminence! My humblest apologies!"

The trooper reached carefully into the pod and came out with a small figure, which he set down with exaggerated, painstaking care. It had been explained exactly what would happen to him if he allowed his micronized passenger to come to any harm.

Exedore, dressed in the blue sackcloth robe that was all the Zentraedi had to give their micronized warriors, stepped off the warrior's armored palm.

His toes clenched, and his arches arched a bit higher against the cold deck. "*Hmph!* How *do* these Micronians survive with such frail little bodies?"

He turned to regard the huge flight deck, but it made little impression because its size would have been imposing for human *or* Zentraedi.

Exedore's pilot was another matter, staring eye to eye with a chain-gun-wielding Battloid. "Rather an imposing sight, aren't we, hah?" he said, rubbing his jaw.

Still, he was one among the Zentraedi to know that size didn't count for everything—counted for nothing, in some cases.

"Ten-HUT!" the PA said as a line of military vehicles came screeching up. The Battloids snapped to present-arms, and to Exedore's great pride, the Zentraedi pilot stood at perfect attention. Exedore abruptly noticed that there were Micronian personnel, ground crew and what-not, scattered around the compartment as they, too, came to attention.

Men leapt from the cars to form ranks smartly, and a man in a uniform not so different from the Zentraedi's own came toward Exedore, hand extended.

"Colonel Maistroff, Robotech Defense Forces, sir. I bring you greetings from the super dimensional fortress commander, Captain Gloval."

Exedore sighed a bit to see that Maistroff was taller than he, to see that all of them were. Perhaps there was something in the micronization process that dictated that, or perhaps it was just something about destiny.

Anyway, Maistroff's open hand was out to him. Exedore blinked at it in bewilderment. "This is how we greet friends," the human said.

Ah, yes! The barbarian custom of showing that there was no weapon! Exedore put his dark mauve hand into the other's pale pink one, trading the grip of friendship.

"I am Exedore, Minister of Affairs."

Maistroff, a former martinet and xenophobe who had been salted and wisened up a bit in the course of the Robotech War, looked him over. "That sounds rather important, sir."

Exedore shrugged blithely. "Not really." He smiled, and Maistroff found himself smiling back.

The colonel indicated his staff car. "If you're ready, we'll get you some more comfortable clothes and then take you to the captain. Have you eaten?"

Exedore sorted that out, recalling the wedding transmissions and dreading a lot of ceremonies stalling the beginning of the peace talks. "Ah, yes; yes."

As they walked, ground-shaking impacts began on the deck behind them, jostling them as they moved. They turned to see that the Zentraedi pilot had naturally fallen in to follow his lord. The Battloids hadn't *quite* brought their chain-gun muzzles back up.

Exedore was quick to see the problem and also to understand some of the humans' apprehension.

Maistroff kept his composure. "Excuse me, Minister Exedore, but—could you ask him to wait here on the hangar deck?"

"Oh!" It didn't take a genius of Exedore's caliber to see that those little hatches wouldn't allow for much full-size Zentraedi wandering. Clever!

He turned to look up at his pilot. "Stay here and guard the pod." It did irritate him how much higher and less forceful the transformation had made his voice.

The pilot pulled a brace, biting out, "Yes, sir!"

Maistroff turned and jerked a thumb at two aides. "You men find him something to eat."

They saluted as one, "Yes, sir!" under the eyes of the Zentraedi warrior, just as precise as he. Then they watched as Maistroff cordially aided Exedore in boarding the staff car, just about as unlikely a sight as anything yet in the war. Motorcycle outriders led the way, and the motorcade moved off.

The two staff officers relaxed, looked up at the Zentraedi, then looked back at each other. "Something to eat?" the first one exclaimed. "He's got to be kidding!"

"Maistroff *never* kids," his companion answered. They both had comrigs in their jeeps, and the second staff officer reached over now to get a handset, telling his friend, "You call ration distribution and break the bad news."

Then he turned to his own mission. "Hello, transportation control? Listen, I'm gonna need a coupla flatbeds..."

The thoroughfares of Macross City were as confusing to Exedore as they had been to the spies. So much undisciplined, disorganized activity! So much aimless milling about! There seemed to be no point to a lot of it—all this gaping through display windows and strolling haphazardly. He wondered if it was some deceptive show that had been mounted for his visit.

And, of course, he averted his eyes from the males and females wandering the city holding hands or with arms around each other's waists. Of the tiny-model Micronians, the noisy, poorly regimented smallscales that the human called "children," Exedore could make neither head nor tail. Just seeing them gave him a shuddery feeling.

But he had to admit the ship was in a good state of repair, especially after two years of running battles with the warrior race. There would have been no hiding the damage in a Zentraedi ship, no fixing it. Intelligence reports had already indicated what Exedore saw evidence of all around him: The Micronians knew how to rebuild —perhaps how to *create*. It was an awesome advantage, a critical part of the war's equation.

Very few Micronians were in uniform; none of them appeared to be under close supervision.

"Why, this is our shopping district," Maistroff explained when Exedore asked.

"Ah, yes! I believe this is where you use something called money to requisition goods."

Maistroff scratched his neck a bit. "Um. That's not too far off, Minister."

They cruised along a broad boulevard, and Exedore suddenly broke out into a cold sweat and began to shudder. Maistroff sat up straight, wondering if something about the ship's life support was incompatible, but that was impossible.

Then he saw that Exedore, teeth clenched, was staring up at a billboard. The billboard advertised the Velvet Suntan Clinics, with a photo of the languorous Miss Velvet, a voluptuous, browned, barely clad, supremely athletic looking young woman whose poster popularity in Macross City was second only to Minmei's.

"Ee, er, oh, th-that picture on the building over there," Exedore got out at last, looking like he was having a malaria attack. "Would you mind explaining it?" He forced his gaze to the floor of the staff car.

Maistroff reached up to the back of his cap and tilted the visor down over his eyes to keep good form with the minister, coughing into his other hand. "Well, actually, it's a little hard to explain."

Exedore crossed his skinny arms on his narrow chest and nodded wisely. "*Aha*! A military secret, no doubt! Very clever! Indeed!"

Maistroff didn't even want to think about what damage he might have done to interspecies relations—didn't want to complicate things.

He tilted his visor farther down. "Right, that's it. Classified."

The motorcade raced for the conference room.

CHAPTER
THIRTEEN

> *RUSSO: What are they doing up there, Alexei? Don't those RDF pantywaists of yours even know how to fight?*
> *ZUKAV: I believe that what we should worry about, Senator, is that they and the aliens are teaching each other how not to.*

> Exchange believed to have taken place between Senator Russo and Marshal Zukav of the UEDC

THE SDF-1 AND THE FLAGSHIP FACED EACH OTHER, unmoving across a narrow gap of space, almost eyeball to eyeball.

Gloval left instructions with Claudia that she open fire with the main gun if there was any hostile action at all. A few minutes later he sat at a judicial bench in the ship's biggest hearing chamber with Colonel Maistroff on his right, an intelligence major to the left, gazing down at Exedore. Except for a few functionaries, the place was empty.

The misshapen little fellow fell far short of Gloval's mental image of a ravaging alien warmonger, the captain had to admit to himself. If anything, he seemed rather ... prissy.

"At last we meet face to face, Captain," the alien said in a not-uncordial voice, glancing at him from the distant witness stand.

"Yes," Gloval allowed.

An attractive young female ensign brought a tray and put a glass of orange juice where Exedore could reach it. Gloval and the others watched Exedore's reaction to the woman closely, but apparently he had gotten his responses under control as he merely nodded his head in gratitude.

Exedore raised the glass and took a cautious sip. The flavor was delightful, but the beverage had a certain savor, something he couldn't define. It was something dizzying, almost electric.

"Mmm. This is very refreshing." He looked up at her. "What is it?"

She checked with Gloval by eye to make sure that it was all right to answer. Gloval gave the barest nod, which Exedore in turn caught. "It's orange juice, sir. From our own hydroponics orchards."

Exedore didn't quite understand for a moment. When he spoke, he tried to keep the tremor from his voice. "You mean, you *grow* it?"

She looked a little confused. "We grow the fruit the juice comes from."

"Ah, yes; just so. That is what I meant." He downed the rest of the orange juice to hide his amazement.

These creatures consumed food that had been alive! Who knew; perhaps they consumed things that still *were* alive! He shuddered and reminded himself that this was only the juice of a plant, but his self-control was tested thoroughly.

Here was something those three imbecile spies hadn't mentioned, or had perhaps omitted from their reports on purpose, or had even failed to realize. Zentraedi food, of course, was synthesized from its chemical constituents; that was as it had always been, by the decree of the Robotech Masters. To eat living or once-living food was to risk the consumption of rudimentary energies somewhat related to Protoculture.

Exedore finished the glass so as to give no hint of what he was thinking—fearing. It crossed his mind that perhaps these men were testing him. If so, he would reveal nothing.

"That was very refreshing," he enthused.

The ensign gave him a bright smile. "Here, have another." She picked up the empty and gave him a full one from her tray.

"If you insist," he said lightly.

Gloval was rubbing his dark mustache. To Maistroff, he said, "I think we're missing some people, aren't we?"

"Some." The colonel nodded. "But they should be arriving any minute now. In fact, this may be them."

He was indicating the door signal. Max and Miriya entered, both in RDF uniform. Max snapped off a sharp salute. "Sir. Reporting as ordered."

Exedore was on his feet, the drink put aside. "Ah! Hello, Quadrono Leader!"

She gasped as she turned to him and saluted by reflex. "I'm sorry, sir; I didn't realize *you* were the emissary."

He shrugged to say it was unimportant. "I found your pairing ritual—marriage?—quite ... provocative."

She didn't know what to say. "You are probably wondering why we did it."

"Yes, just as you're no doubt wondering what *I* am doing here. And this must be the male half of your pair."

Suddenly Miriya looked young and a little forlorn, standing before the great genius of her race, the Eldest, the repository of all Zentraedi lore. "Ah, that's right, sir."

"Gee, y' don't sound too thrilled about it," Max murmured. He almost gave in to his impulse to take her in his arms and kiss her, top brass or no, and remind her emphatically of what their pairing *really* meant.

But just then Rick Hunter reported as ordered, saluting. Then he spied Max, who was in a bit of a snit. "Hey, you don't look so good," Rick confided.

Exedore was still on his feet. Now, he pointed at Rick and Max, yelling, "That's it!" He clucked to himself. "The micronization process must have affected my memory! *You're two of the hostages from Dolza's flagship, aren't you?*"

"Does somebody want to tell me what's going on here?" Rick asked slowly.

"This time the circumstances are a bit different," Exedore rattled on excitedly. "But tell me: How did you and the others manage to escape? Was it some hidden Micronian power?"

What had really happened was that Max had come aboard in a Battloid disguised in a Zentraedi uniform, but Rick wasn't sure he should let that particular cat out of the bag. He didn't see Gloval or the others giving him any help, so he improvised, "Uh, I guess you could say that."

The frail little emissary sat, fingering his jaw. "Hm, another one of your military secrets." It was all so confusing and illogical, even to him. Who knew what eons of eating live food had done to these creatures?

The door signaled again, and Gloval said, "Here are the others now." Rico, Bron, and Konda filed into the hearing chamber. They caught sight of him and cringed as he gave them a death's-head smile.

"It's Minister Exedore!" they all yelped at once, looking like mice facing a hungry lynx.

"I did not expect to see the instigators of our mass defection show up here today," he remarked.

Trembling, Rico drew himself up. "Your Excellency, it *wasn't our fault!*"

"That's right! It was just something that we couldn't help!" Konda put in. And the stout Bron maintained, "We had no control, sir!"

Exedore brushed that aside with a prim flick of his fingers. "You may relax. I have no intention of harming you."

The breath they let out was audible as they wilted with relief. When everyone was seated, Colonel Maistroff said, "Captain Gloval, the ship's computer will record the proceedings."

Gloval squared his cap away. "Very good; let us begin." To Exedore he said, "Minister, we are unclear as to the exact purpose of your mission here. You've told us very little so far. Won't you please enlighten us?"

Exedore's eyes swept across them. "Your curiosity is understandable, but—not everyone is present yet, Captain."

"What?" Maistroff growled under his breath.

"We would like to know more about two of your kind, gentlemen. The first possesses powers and fighting skills that are truly extraordinary, and there is a female who is the core of your psychological assault."

"Incredible," mumbled Gloval, watching Exedore.

Colonel Maistroff had read some of the defector debriefing reports. In an aside to Gloval he said, "I think he means that movie, *Little White Dragon*. They must've seen it too, and think Lynn-Kyle's movie stunts were for real."

Little White Dragon was the first feature film produced on the SDF-1. It featured Lynn-Kyle in some spectacular stunts and fights, downing ferocious giants with his fighting arts and using a death beam that he could shoot from his hand thanks to an enchanted medallion.

"There is clearly a misunderstanding here," Gloval told Maistroff. To Exedore he declared, "I can't think of anyone who would be at the core of a psychological assault. It would be helpful if you could be more specific about this female."

Exedore blinked at him with bulging, pinpoint-pupiled eyes. "She appears to be performing some kind of ritual. A strange little chant."

Bron leaned over to his fellow ex-spies. "Do you think he means—"

"No! He *couldn't*!" Konda whispered.

"Sure he could!" snarled Rico.

"*You* know," Exedore said impatiently. And he rose to stand next to the witness chair, strike a coquettish pose, and sing:

> Stage fright, go 'way,
> This is my big day!

Rick groaned, not wanting to be the first to say anything. If he wasn't seeing what he thought he was seeing, Colonel Maistroff would probably report him to the flight surgeon and get him grounded on a mental.

But the three spies burst out, "He *is* talking about Minmei!"

Exedore went on singing "Stage Fright" with a terrible, cracking falsetto that was seriously off key. He struck poses and postures that looked like he was auditioning for Yum-Yum in an amateur production of *The Mikado*.

Gloval drew his head down into his high, rolled jacket collar like a turtle, making a low sound. "I do not believe this."

"They must think Minmei's singing is a weapon of some kind," Maistroff observed.

"Have the girl brought here," Gloval ordered. "And her cousin as well." Then he tried to figure out what the most direct and yet diplomatic method would be for asking the emissary to please stop singing.

As soon as Minmei appeared in the doorway, Exedore cried, "That's her! Yes!"

She stood looking around like a startled deer. A moment later, Kyle slouched into the room, sulking and hostile, saying, "I'm getting tired of being pushed around by the military."

"Now," Minmei said in a tired voice, "would someone mind explaining why it was so important for us to come here?"

She was as beautiful as ever, delicate and haunting as a princess from a fairy tale; try as he would, Rick couldn't keep the familiar longing from welling up in him.

Kyle stepped before her as if to shield her from harm, glaring all around. "Don't expect any answers from them. They only care about their fascist war schemes; they don't care about people, and they—"

"Enough of this nonsense!" Gloval thundered, and even the truculent Lynn-Kyle was a bit intimidated. Exedore thought how like the great Breetai this Micronian commander was.

"You will answer our questions," Gloval said to the two of them. "These proceedings are strictly classified, and if you mention them to anyone, I will personally see that you rue this day. You will give us your total cooperation. Do you both understand?"

"Yes." Minmei nodded. When Kyle stood unspeaking, unresponsive, she put a hand to his shoulder. "They need our cooperation. Hostility won't do us any good, don't you see?"

Gloval had turned to Exedore; he let his irritation show in his voice. "Now, Mr. Minister, if you would *kindly* tell us what your mission here is all about?" He began stoking up a favorite meerschaum.

"All in its proper sequence," Exedore said earnestly.

"But I assure you: My reason for being here is of crucial importance for you as well as for the Zentraedi."

Gloval puffed out a blue cloud that his officers tried to ignore. *Reading this alien's mind is impossible,* he reflected. The song and dance had convinced him of that. *I'll just have to wait and hear him out.*

In the UEDC's subterranean complex, Lisa Hayes sat at the end of long rows of techs who were manning monitor screens. All attention was focused on the SDF-1; Lisa had gotten the impression, in subtle ways, that the world rulers were chewing their nails, waiting to see what would happen.

She had stopped wishing that she was back onboard to help in what was going on; it hurt too much. The emergency, the shortage of good officers, the dangers of space travel during the current hostilities, the fact that she had had access to classified UEDC information, her value as an intelligence source—her father had a dozen justifications for keeping her right where she was, and there was little she could do about it.

Now, she stared up at her own master console. The more she learned about the Grand Cannon, the more convinced she was that it would serve little purpose except to get the Zentraedi angrier.

She started, realizing that her father had come in to bend down near her. The other technical officers and enlisted ratings kept diligently at their work; it was unwise to be seen letting one's attention stray when Admiral Hayes was around.

She was beginning to understand that her father wasn't a popular officer. She had never found it easy to make friends, and now that she was known as the admiral's daughter, she was effectively frozen out.

She removed her headset in time to hear him say, "How do you like your new job? Everything okay?"

"Fine, fine," she lied, and attempted to smile. "I understand that the SDF-1 and the Zentraedi fleet have reached a cease-fire agreement."

"That's what I hear," her father said noncommittally. She tried to sound as upbeat as she could. "Well, if things keep going this way, maybe we won't have to use the Grand Cannon, after all."

"It's possible, but I doubt it."

She turned away, dropping her eyes in discouragement. They were all so blind down here in their little rabbit warren! Then she felt his hand on her shoulder.

"Listen, Lisa. We can't trust the Zentraedi; we have to *prove* what we can do."

It would do no good to tell him again that the SDF-1's main gun was easily a match for the Grand Cannon, and it hadn't kept the Zentraedi from waging their war. The UEDC planners, engineers, and rulers had too much at stake and only scoffed when she tried to make the point.

He saw she wasn't going to yield the point; she simply gave up arguing it for the time being. He turned to go, saying, "I have work to do. If anything comes up, I'll be in the central core."

"Yes, sir," Lisa said wearily.

CHAPTER
FOURTEEN

I was close enough to Lang in those days to be certain that he had no confidential knowledge of the hidden Protoculture source to which Exedore was referring. Had he but known the secret of those great, sealed reflex furnaces, he might have formulated an immortal update to Einstein's remark: Protoculture doesn't play dice with the universe, but It certainly knows how to palm an ace at the crucial moment!

Dr. Lazlo Zand, *On Earth As It Is in Hell: Recollections of the Robotech War*

"**O**FFICER LYNN-KYLE, WHAT IS YOUR MILItary rank?" Exedore asked in the vaulted hearing chamber.

Kyle gave him a surly look. "I'm a civilian."

Exedore made a brief, mocking chuckle. "With your superpowers? I doubt it."

Kyle bared his teeth at the alien. "I have no idea what you're talking about!"

Exedore looked around, confused. He was satisfied that these Micronians were doing their best to, to "level with" him, as Colonel Maistroff had put it on the way over.

Gloval intervened. "Mr. Minister, he's telling the truth. This man possesses no superpowers. For that matter, none of us in this room possess the powers you're referring to."

Gloval was taking a gamble. The bluff of human superpowers hadn't made the enemy go away and couldn't be sustained for very long. But there was something murky about the whole war, something that made him suspect that a basic breakdown in communication was responsible for the whole thing. It was time for someone to try to get to the bottom of it.

"But—we saw him on our monitors," Exedore protested.

"Oh, that was a *movie*, merely a form of entertainment," Gloval replied, scratching his head to try to think how to explain better. "It's not true, it's . . . simply for enjoyment."

Exedore decided to table that for now; he knew the enjoyment he found in the ancient lore and history of the Zentraedi, but those were *factual*. "Then what about your energy barrier and destruction waves?"

"These are merely defensive and offensive weapons based on technology discovered in this ship when it originally crashed on Earth."

"Ah, but you've forgotten the Protoculture!" Exedore said slyly. "The great genius of the Robotech Masters' race, Zor, hid the secrets of Protoculture and its last great manufacturing source in this vessel before he dispatched it here."

Now, at last, Gloval was seeing some of the aliens' cards, and he was sure the talks were worth it. All the questions of who the Robotech Masters were, who Zor was and why he had picked Earth, had to be set aside, intriguing as they were. The life of the human race might be measurable in hours, even minutes.

Gloval opened a comline. "I think we're ready for Dr. Lang now."

Lang entered, the greatest mind of his time, an intellect worthy to sit with Newton and Einstein and yet a man frustrated by the many mysteries of Robotechnology. He had been monitoring the exchanges in a waiting room and was eager to talk to Exedore.

The Zentraedi, Minmei and Kyle, and the others there who had never seen Lang before got a bit of a shock and understood why he shunned the limelight. Normal-looking in every other way, the man had eyes that seemed to be all dark, liquid iris—no pupil or white.

Gloval remembered that day well, hours after the SDF-1's crash in 1999, when he, Lang, and a few others had first boarded the smoking wreck. They had discovered an astounding technology, fearsome mecha guardians, and bewildering time paradoxes.

They had also discovered a recorded warning that they couldn't fathom. And Lang, yielding to an unquenchable thirst for more knowledge, more interface, had somehow subjected himself to direct contact with whatever it was that animated the ship. That was when his eyes changed, when he himself became *different*, as if he were hearing celestial music. Nevertheless, it was his genius that had allowed the rebuilding of the SDF-1 and the construction of the Robotech Defense Force.

Now, Lang said to Exedore, "We've heard Protoculture mentioned many times, Emissary. Will you tell me now what it is?"

Exedore's brows shot up. "You mean you still insist that you Micronians don't know? Protoculture is the most powerful energy source in the universe."

Lang's deep, dark eyes bored into him. "I have been able to find nothing of that nature in this vessel, and I've been searching since your fleet first arrived in the solar system. But I believe I know what has happened. Will you come with me, please?"

Gloval rose but told the others, "You will all kindly remain here, please."

The jeep was waiting, and the trip through the huge passages and byways of the battle fortress took only a few minutes. Very shortly they were in the engineering section, just forward of the huge reflex engines that were the ship's power plant.

They were in a large compartment that had once held the ship's spacefold apparatus. Now there was some left-over machinery from the pin-point barrier system that had been the ship's main defensive weapon on its precarious trip across the solar system. As there had been for years, there were also the lights.

"When the Zentraedi first attacked Earth, we made our spacefold jump to get to safety," Lang was explaining. "We had no time to experiment, no time to test. A jump that was meant to take us beyond our moon's orbit took us instead to the orbit of Pluto."

"I remember well," Exedore said, scratching his cheek, staring at the giant, almost-empty compartment.

"You made the jump too close to the planetary surface; we were convinced that you were suicidal."

"You gave us no choice," Gloval said in a low voice, thinking back to the appalling devastation and loss of life that day. He did his best to put it from his mind.

"But in the wake of the jump," Lang went on, "the spacefold apparatus just . . . disappeared. Utterly! Simply faded from view and was never seen again. And in its place were *those*."

Lang meant the lights: darting, glowing sparks, fireflies and tiny comets that swarmed and drifted through the space where the spacefold apparatus had once been. Exedore turned to him. "May I borrow some of those instruments you've brought, Doctor?"

It took only a little time to prove his suspicions. "Ah, yes: definite residual Protoculture signature here, but the Matrix is gone. And I detect no other great manufacturing mass, only the lesser animating charges of your weapons and the reflex furnaces."

Exedore lowered the detector numbly. "The secrets of Zor, gone! This long war fought for nothing!"

Lang patted Exedore's shoulder commiseratingly. "Perhaps someday we will find it again; who can say?"

Gloval was shocked to see how quickly the two had become easy in each other's company. "I think we'd better get back to the hearing room," the captain said. "We still have a great deal to talk about."

Deep within the sealed fastness of the mighty reflex engines, something stirred and then was quiet again. It could not be detected by Lang's relatively primitive instruments, was capable of hiding itself even from the Zentraedi's scanners at this range.

As Zor had provided, the last Protoculture Matrix was safe, biding its time, waiting until his great Vision should come to pass.

"It does appear we've made a great mistake," Exedore confessed when they were all back in their places. "But! You cannot possibly deny the power of the female's singing!"

"I wouldn't dream of it," Gloval responded simply, drawing a doubtful look from Colonel Maistroff.

But Bron was on his feet. "He won't deny it because it's true!"

"Minmei's song has incredible power!" Rico added, jumping up too.

Minmei, for her part, gave a shy smile that seemed to have some secret wisdom behind it.

"This is not the first time the Zentraedi have encountered something like this," Exedore told them all. "A very long time ago we were exposed to a culture like yours, and it nearly destroyed us."

"How do you mean that?" Gloval was quick to ask.

Exedore's protruding, pinpoint eyes roamed the room. "To a Zentraedi, fighting is a way of life. Our entire history is made up of nothing but battle after glorious battle. However, exposure to an emotionally open society like yours made our soldiers refuse to fight.

"This, of course, could not be tolerated, and the infection had to be cleansed. Loyal soldiers and the Robotech Masters themselves came in to exterminate all those who had been exposed to the source of the contagion."

The three spies in particular were pale and silent. The rest looked at one another. Exedore went on. "Dolza, our supreme commander, will do everything in his power to avoid making the mistake our ancestors did. When and if he reads my report, he will certainly launch an all-out attack on Earth, especially in light of the fact that the Protoculture Matrix is no longer on the SDF-1."

Gloval's eyes shifted to Rick. "That's the same one mentioned in your report?"

Rick licked his lips. "Yes, sir." *Almost five million warships!*

Exedore nodded. "I know what you're thinking. But you see, these new developments—the defections, the Minmei cult, the mating of our greatest warrior with one of your pilots—change the entire picture."

He looked around at them, the center of their riveted attention. "For, you see," Exedore said, "unless some solution can be found, *we*—Breetai's forces—are in as great a danger from Dolza and the Grand Fleet as you."

* * *

Breetai sat in his chair in the command station overlooking his flagship's bridge.

A projecbeam drew a two-dimensional image of Azonia in the air, the woman who had replaced him in the war against the humans, failed to bring it to a successful conclusion, and been replaced in turn by Breetai.

"Commander!" she began. "How long do you intend to allow this situation to continue?" She was a medium-size, intense Zentraedi female with a quick mind and high aspirations. Her short, frizzy hairstyle puffed within the confinement of her high, rolled collar.

Breetai, arms folded on his great chest, answered in his rumbling, echoing bass, "Any continuation of hostilities would be unwise in light of recent events."

She sneered at him. "Well, I expect a different solution when the Grand Fleet arrives!"

He leapt to his feet. "Grand Fleet? *What have you done?*"

She gave him a smug smile. "I've reported my findings to the supreme commander. And his Excellency Dolza has decided to set the fleet into motion."

"So Dolza has decided the Micronians are a threat, has he?"

"He has," she said triumphantly.

Breetai's anger welled up like a volcano, but suddenly he found himself laughing like a grim god at the end of all worlds. It was the last thing Azonia expected; she watched him, his head thrown back, roaring, light flashing off his metallic skullpiece and the crystal eye, and she felt a sudden sinking sensation in the pit of her stomach.

"You imbecile!" he managed when he could talk again. "You know nothing of history, do you? No, no self-respecting Zentraedi cares! Well, know *this*, my scheming friend: We're doomed along with the humans! We have been infected, and all of us—all—are now considered plague carriers."

"You're certain of this?" Exedore asked quietly, holding the handset tightly in a trembling fist.

The communications patch had been set up hastily,

with no chance for the aliens to encrypt their exchange. Exedore would certainly know that human techs had monitored whatever Breetai had said. Therefore, the captain bent forward, certain that he would hear whatever it was at once.

"You know what this means, then," Exedore said. "I understand." He returned the handset to its cradle and looked at Gloval.

"Captain, you must prepare yourselves to escape this star system. We will help you."

Gloval's face hardened. "And leave the Earth defenseless?"

"Yes."

Gloval squared his shoulders. "Out of the question! We are sworn to defend our planet."

Exedore was nodding wearily. "Yes, I understand. We Zentraedi would not act any differently. What's more, without your help, escape for us would be all but hopeless. The Protoculture Matrix was our great hope for success; the armada's supplies are all but exhausted."

He sighed. "It seems we shall soon be fighting a common enemy."

Maistroff exploded. *What did you say?*

Exedore looked to him. "My Lord Breetai has just informed me that the Grand Fleet is headed for this star system. That means four million eight hundred thousand ships with the destructive force of a supernova."

"All right, then," Gloval said matter-of-factly. "A fight it shall be."

"You're crazy!" Lynn-Kyle was on his feet. "There's no way you can beat a fleet like that! We're finished!"

Max had taken Miriya's hand in his. He told her gently, "I'm so afraid that this might be the end for us. Just when we've found each other."

She squeezed his hand. "I don't care, my love, as long as I'm at your side in battle."

Rick, on the opposite side of the U-shaped table, looked across at them with envy. "Together," he said under his breath.

Exedore had been watching the various reactions carefully and was satisfied. He could tell mighty Breetai that among the military, at least, there were worthy allies.

Now he raised his voice to say, "It's not over yet! There might still be a way!"

"Explain," Gloval bade him, stone-faced.

"Thus far, this vessel has proved itself unbeatable. I will need more information before I can be sure, but I believe there is a way that we can win."

I have therefore concluded that Breetai and his subordinates and all those under their command now entertain such primitive behavioral quirks and abstruse thought processes as to set them completely outside the Zentraedi species and make them a threat to us all.

Every available unit will therefore be mustered in the Grand Fleet to take the action dictated by our ancient lore.

From Dolza's personal log

"REPEATING THIS ANNOUNCEMENT, ALL MILI-tary personnel are to report for duty at once. All leaves are canceled. All reservists are to contact their units for immediate mobilization. Civilians are directed to stand by for further directives; we will be making announcements as soon as further information is available."

Lisa wheeled her jeep into the headquarters cavernous parking lot on two wheels, snapping off the radio. She hadn't been able to get anything on the military freqs, and the civvie bands just kept repeating the same thing.

She dashed into the HQ, flashing her security badge, and, in the situation room, heard the classified announcements.

"Sensors are still picking up extremely high energy levels from lunar and near-Earth regions. This activity is characteristic of enemy spacefold operations. However, they are of a magnitude never before encountered."

She spotted her father and ran toward him. In her mind's eye was the Grand Fleet as she had last seen it, or at least part of it, in and around the moonlet-size hive that was Dolza's headquarters base.

"It doesn't look good," Admiral Hayes was saying to a G3-staff commodore.

"Admiral!"

Her father looked at her, traded salutes with the staffer, and came over to her. He took her by the arm, leading her to a conference room. He sounded brusque as the door slid shut. "Well? What is it?"

She drew a deep breath. "Father, what's going to happen to the SDF-1?"

He didn't reprimand her for the lapse in formality, as he once would have. But there was no sympathy in his voice. "It will be destroyed. We're committing it to drawing the enemy fire away from Earth and the rest of our forces."

"You can't!"

"I'm sorry, Lisa." He didn't sound sorry at all. "There's no other choice."

She accepted that; she'd been around headquarters long enough now to realize that her father was no longer a leader. He was an apologist, an errand boy, for the real rulers of the planet.

She gathered her self-control. "Father, I want to ask you a personal favor. I want you to send me back to the battle fortress."

"No! That's completely out of the question!"

Now it was her turn to flare. "My place is with my crew, my captain!" She waved her hand around to indicate the scurrying futility of the UEDC base. "It's not here, in a hole in the ground, when the people I fought beside need me."

He knew then that he'd lost her. For a moment, he saw the place through her eyes and wondered how he could ever have been so deluded. The Grand Cannon was a sham, and the UEDC were frightened men who had brought the world down around them rather than admit that they were wrong.

He shook it off, his oath to his duty coming to the fore again. But there was real pain in his voice as he told her, "I'm sorry, but—"

"But you won't."

"I can't allow you to throw your life away up there. Lisa, Lisa . . . you're my daughter."

"I'm an officer in the RDF!"

He said it very quietly, "I know that."

"Then reassign me!"

He looked at her angrily now. "Father or no, I promise you this: If you try to leave, I'll have you thrown in the brig."

She was only partly successful at keeping the tears out of her eyes, but her voice was steady. "Yes, sir."

Admiral Hayes despaired of ever winning the battle; he saw that he had lost the last of his family.

Breetai looked up at the projecbeam image. "What now, Azonia?"

She didn't mince words; he had expected no less. "There are no options, great Breetai. Dolza will try to exterminate us now that we have been exposed to the Micronians. I will stay and face the Grand Fleet. It will be an honor to go into battle with you, my lord!"

Some part of him knew what she meant. Wasn't this the battle any Zentraedi dreamed of, a hopeless fight against overwhelming odds in the clash of dreadnoughts as numerous as the stars? Wasn't this the apocalypse to which the Zentraedi looked for their version of immortality?

"Commendable," he said. "May you win every fight."

She drew a breath at the high compliment he had paid her. "And you too, Breetai!"

Her face dissolved as the projecbeam image did, and he turned to another. "Khyron? Your intentions?"

Khyron, languid and condescending, smoothed his beautiful blue hair. "You know my answer. The odds are too great. Why fight if you can't win, Breetai?"

"Why be Zentraedi if you don't know the answer to that, Khyron? But this is as I expected; I wasn't depending on you, anyway."

And so it was all out in the light at this eleventh hour. Khyron had substituted the ruthlessness and savagery that were all he had for courage. The difference came forth only in moments like these, but it was plain.

Now Khyron's facade broke, and he screamed at Breetai, froth leaping from his lips. *"You will be destroyed!"* The projecbeam image vanished.

* * *

On his own flagship, Khyron sat slouched in his command chair like a wounded toad. "All right, let's go." He threw the command over his shoulder to his subordinate, Grel.

"What coordinates?" Grel asked carefully. In such a rage, Khyron was easily capable of lashing out and killing any around him.

"Anyplace else in the universe but here," Khyron brooded, staring off angrily at nothing. There was no response from Grel, and Khyron snarled, "Didn't you hear me?"

Grel calculated his next words carefully. "But sir, we can't run."

Khyron barked a galling laugh. "You think not? Watch, then!" He signaled, and the engines of his flagship came up to power, as did those of all the Botoru ships under his command.

Grel licked his lips, wondering how best to tell Khyron that he hadn't been speaking figuratively. Khyron cherished the practice of beheading the messenger who bore bad tidings.

Breetai paid little attention to the maneuvers of the Botorus. He considered the nearby fabric of space, where the first perturbations of the Cosmic String heralded the Grand Fleet.

Once he had been Dolza's most valued subordinate—had saved Dolza's life from the very Invid attack that had killed Zor. Now he contemplated the stirrings of the universe in advance of the attack and reflected on the incredible way things had turned out there in the Micronian star system.

Hear my thoughts, Lord Dolza! To go down in battle is all we seek, from the highest to the lowest. Mark me well, for this is the final battle of Breetai!

In the hearing chamber, people were exhausted, but the marathon went on. Computers and analysts were hooked in; G-staff members and evaluation teams were ready.

"Dolza will assume you're too weak to fight," Exedore was saying, still animated and prim in the midst of the most tiring activity. "He will divide his fleet and attack from every side, sealing off any avenue of escape. But this maneuvering will give you your only chance."

"Enough background; kindly be specific," Gloval snapped.

Exedore turned to a luminous tactical projection he had constructed with the help of the SDF-1 computers.

"Their flagships will be here, here, here, and here, and Dolza's mobile base will appear here; these are my best projections.

"If you can destroy these vessels, it will throw the entire Grand Fleet into chaos."

"Simple military strategy," someone muttered.

"No; *simple* military strategy—of all-out, straightforward attack and overwhelming numbers—is what has allowed our tactics to remain the same for so long," Exedore countered. "That and the fact that the Zentraedi have never lost a war."

Colonel Maistroff rubbed his face with his hand, as if he were washing. "So, in short, we crush the head of the snake!"

Exedore nodded. He stepped away from the tactical display, pacing toward the place where Gloval sat.

"With their attack forces in disarray, our only chance for survival is to utilize the combined forces of the SDF-1 and our battlefleet. We are already aware of the crude Robotech cannon in your planet's northern hemisphere but consider it a minor element at best."

Gloval came to his feet. "I'm glad that we're now fighting on the same side." He clasped hands with the gnomish little man.

"Yes, so am I." Exedore turned to Minmei, who was watching it all unbelievingly. "And without your singing, this alliance between our peoples would not have been possible."

Kyle had assumed a hard expression, eyes closed, chin sunk on chest, lip curled. But Minmei was in a sort of dream state. "Who, me? *Really*?"

Exedore nodded his head slowly. "While I don't profess to understand Micronians, I now realize the importance of your singing. It touches emotional resources to which we Zentraedi did not have access before—a courage that is beyond mere courage in battle."

He seemed to blush a little; nothing could have surprised them more. Even Kyle was shocked.

"Will . . . will you sing for us?" Exedore got out, face coloring furiously. "So that we may hope for victory? Please, Miss Minmei."

"Of course."

She stood up, in that room where the plans were coming together that would spell the death or life of worlds, the survival or slaughter of billions. She drew a breath and sang in a voice as clear as polished diamond.

She sang "To Be in Love," one of her first compositions, still one of her favorites. It was a simple song, and there was nothing in it of armies or battles. It was about a closeness between two lovers.

Exedore and the three former spies were mesmerized. Kyle, eyes closed, was cold and indifferent. Gloval, Max and Miriya, and the rest watched and listened, immersed. Her voice soared to rebound from the domed ceiling.

Rick was transfixed, too, at first. The fact that he'd lost her didn't make her any less desirable, especially now.

But then a new sound came to him, a sound he recognized even through the intervening decks and bulkheads.

On the hangar decks, the elevators were at work, lifting Veritechs for cat launch. For the final battle.

The finder beams had done their work. Now there was a brutal application of force, and the warp and woof of the universe were ripped apart.

The Zentraedi had refined their targeting. This time, there was no cosmic bow wave of incandescent fire. Instead, a green cloud of some kind seemed to appear—until it became clear that every last mote in the cloud was a warship.

Another cloud appeared nearby, and another. Then two at once, then three. And soon the stars were blotted out. It was as if handfuls of sand had suddenly become ugly battlecraft. More appeared, and more, in dense, well-ordered formations, thicker than any hive swarm.

* * *

"There are too many for sensors to count," Vanessa said, sweating, blinking behind her glasses. "Too many..."

"I have to go," Admiral Hayes told his daughter gruffly. "We'll talk about this later—"

The PA interrupted. "Sensors register immeasurable defold activity. Estimated enemy strength one million, three hundred—correction, *two* million, one hundred thousand—stand by! Stand by! More enemy units arriving!"

Some other, less hysterical voice cut in. "Battle stations. Repeat, battle stations." Alarms and sirens sounded, and nobody had to say that it wasn't a drill this time.

Admiral Hayes swallowed, going pale.

Earth was engulfed in a net of enemy warships. They blotted out the sun's light, appearing in their hundreds of thousands, taking up position for the ultimate confrontation.

Claudia's face appeared in the hearing chamber on a display the size of a movie screen. "Captain Gloval, monitor three shows enemy positions over the western hemisphere."

The view came up. Still the sinister warcraft poured into Earth orbit from nothingness. The drifting clouds of them stretched, established intervals, deployed for total coverage. Great blotches of green, whole clustered space navies, were painted into the picture.

"Well, I'm afraid this is it," Exedore said. It looked like the planet was falling, in time-lapse photography, under a leprous infection of Zentraedi combat green.

Minmei could only stare, her song forgotten. Max and Miriya took each other's hands, and he was grateful that he had been granted the time they had had together.

Even Kyle was aghast. If there was one there who was in the mood for the scene, it was Rick Hunter. He watched the Grand Fleet spread and grow. Nothing left to lose. Okay: A fight it would be.

* * *

Breetai, staring up at the displays that were still functioning on his bridge, watched in awe. It was the greatest single combat fold-jump operation in history, and it came off meticulously. Dolza was doing everything right so far.

Breetai's clifflike jaw set. Opening moves and endgame were two different things.

The night sky over the Alaska Base was lighter, with the reflections of sunlight from the light underbellies of the warships taking up orbit. The stars were obscured, hundreds at a time.

Watching the screens, Lisa heard her father moan. She turned and saw by his expression that he realized, far too late, that the reports of the aliens' strength were accurate and that five million ships were so many more than he had ever envisioned.

CHAPTER

SIXTEEN

And so the Great Mandala spun,
Two halves had learned
They both were one

Mingtao, *Protoculture: Journey Beyond Mecha*

AMONG ALL THE ANNOUNCEMENTS OF THE LOAD-
ing of Decamissiles, the manning of gun turrets, the fran-
tic coordinating of target-acquisition and threat-priority
computers, there came word that Skull Team was to report to its fighters.

"Well. That's us," Max said, looking at the deck and
then up at his wife. He was really at a loss. Some tradi-
tionalism said that he should shield her from harm; but
Miriya was a better flier than anyone else aboard except
Max, and there *was* no safety, anywhere.

More to the point, she would never have allowed him
to leave her behind.

"Yes, Maxmillian," she said, watching him. Rick noticed that in an amazingly short time, they had both
learned to smile *exactly* the same slow smile at each
other at *exactly* the same moment. He did his best to
suppress his envy.

Max put his arm around his wife's slim waist and gave
Rick a wave. "See you out there, boss."

"Count on it." Rick waved at them with phony cheer,
watching them go off to suit up.

Others were finding their way out of the hearing

chamber; Gloval and Exedore and the other heavy-hitters were already gone. The recording techs were wrapping things up quickly, preparing to double in·brass on combat assignments.

Only Kyle and Minmei were left, uncertain, with no place to go. Rick looked up at them and thought about what was happening out there where the void met Earth's atmosphere. Millions of ships were forming up for a greater battle than even the Zentraedi had ever seen before.

Which meant the future looked very dim for one little VT leader who had come late into the business of war. Rick decided in an instant and sprinted off to where Minmei stood.

She was at the top of the steps leading to the table podium; he stopped a few steps below. "Minmei!"

She looked at him oddly. "Yes, Rick?" He couldn't read her, couldn't understand what was going on behind the startling blue eyes. Kyle was at her shoulder, cold and angry, glaring down at him.

Not that Kyle mattered anymore; very little did.

Rick fumbled for words, not coming up with any that would express what he wanted to say, not even managing to get started. At last he got out, "You know I'm not good at this sort of thing."

She did; knew it from the long days and nights they had spent stranded together, knew it from more recent times, when he had been all but inarticulate.

"But I might not see you again," he went ahead. "I want to say that—that I love you."

Her hands flew to her mouth like frightened birds. She mouthed words that made no sound.

"Had to tell you." He smiled bittersweetly. "Take care."

Then he left to suit up, already late in the massive launch schedule of the apocalypse, heels clicking emptily on the deck.

She was frozen by his words; she could move again only when he was out of the hatch, out of sight. Minmei hurried down the steps to catch up.

Kyle was next to her in an instant, catching her arm, bringing her up short. *"Don't try to stop him!"* The doings of the warmakers were their own concern; Kyle had loved Minmei too long to lose her to them now.

She struggled hopelessly to free her arm, the black hair whipping. "Let *go*! I have to *tell* him! Kyle, let me go or I'll hate you *forever*!"

Fingers that could have tightened like a vise released instead. He knew a hundred ways to force her to stay there but not a single one to take away her feelings for Hunter or to keep her from the pilot without making her hate him.

The grip, strong as steel, went limp, letting her go. Minmei wrenched her arm free and raced off after Rick. Kyle stood alone for a long time in the deserted hearing chamber, listening to the emergency directives, the RDF announcements, the preparations for battle.

Battle, death, oblivion—those were so *easy* to face, didn't the military war lovers understand? Living without the one who meant everything in life to you, *that* was the fear that couldn't be overcome, the abyss no courage could see you across.

In the hangars and bays and ready rooms of the combat mecha, thoughts of love and grief had been left behind. Now it was only kill or be killed. Men and women emptied their minds of everything else in a way no outsider would ever understand.

"Arm all reflex warheads," the command came over the PA from Kim Young. The missiles—Hammerheads, Decas, Piledrivers and Stilettos—became alive in their pods and racks.

The attack mecha stood to readiness: lumbering giants heavy with laser-array and x-ray laser cannon, missiles, chain-guns, and rapid-fire tubes loaded with discarding-sabot armor-piercing rounds.

The Destroids stumped out first: waddling two-legged gun turrets the size of houses, running their clustered barrels back and forth in test traverses, ready to bunch up shoulder by shoulder and concentrate fire. Forming up behind them were the Gladiators, Excaliburs, the Spartans and Raidars, all making the reinforced decks resound to their tread, weighted with every weapon Robotechnology could give them.

The March of the Robotech Soldiers.

The SDF-1 gun turret and casemate barrels swung and readied, men and women sweating as they settled into the gunners' and gunners' mates' saddles. Targeting reticles were checked for accuracy; triggers were dry-fired.

The stupendous warrior that was the SDF-1 itself stood ready, covers lifted from its many weapon ports. The two suppercarriers that were the ship's arms, *Daedalus* and *Prometheus*, set for battle and for the harrowing, fiercely dangerous business of combat launches and retrievals.

On the hangar deck, Skull Team warmed up. They would be one of the few teams flying the new armored Veritechs. Max, running things until Rick could get there, threw his wife a quick smile. Miriya blew him a kiss, as she often did when no one else was looking. Kissing was still an amazing thing to her; lovemaking left her at a complete loss for words. But then, it did the same to Max.

She turned back to a final check of her VT. Combat was something she knew intimately, too. Max got the rest of Skull saddled up, resisting the urge to be bitter and preoccupied with regret that he had had so little time with her.

Those were the distractions that got fighter pilots killed.

On the bridge, Gloval arrived with Exedore at his side, and no one thought to say it should be otherwise. The reports of the ship's fighting status came to him from the Terrible Trio and from Claudia.

Gloval led Exedore to the great bubble of the forward viewport, thinking, *Who would have dreamed we'd be fighting side by side?*

But there was an answer to that. It was Gloval, always Gloval—and sometimes *only* Gloval—who had anticipated this day from the moment he had heard of the enemy defections.

* * *

Over the UEDC Alaskan headquarters, fighters looking a lot like VTs but lacking their superlative Robotechnology screamed into the air on alert. It was a brave show that everyone knew to be hollow; Earth's only real hope lay with the dimensional fortress.

Admiral Hayes and several other senior officers stood on a balcony overlooking the vast situation room. They heard echoing updates on the Grand Cannon's firing status, the enemy fleet that was still pouring out of spacefold, the composite picture that made it unlikely that a single member of species *Homo sapiens* would live through the day.

"The projections turned out to be in error," an intel-analysis officer confessed, zombielike. "Against a force that big, we can't hope to win. We couldn't do it even if the Grand Cannon satellites were in place." He was shaking his head slowly. "No way, sir."

Hayes was used to hiding his dismay. He called down to a communication officer, "Lieutenant! Have we been able to establish contact with the aliens?"

Hayes burned at the thought of *why* his superiors were suddenly so eager to talk to the Zentraedi. He avoided any contemplation of how Earth's rulers sounded now that reality had at last been forced upon them. The brave words and the bold posturing had been blown away like smoke in the wind, and UEDC was eager, cringingly eager, to make any deal it could, starting with an offer to make itself an overseer government under alien rule.

Except the Zentraedi weren't making deals today, and Armageddon was apparently the only item on the agenda.

"We're trying, Admiral, but so far it's a no-go," a com officer called up to him.

Hayes himself felt betrayed and a fool. His daughter and Gloval had been correct all along, right down the line. The prestige and honor of his rank had fallen away to nothing, and he saw that he had, very simply, wound up an otherwise honorable career by being the instrument of craven and greedy men.

"Then there's nothing left to do but fight," Hayes said.

Under other circumstances it might have been one of those lines flag-rank officers could hope to have show up in history books. The fact was that Hayes knew he been duped again and again by the politicians. Besides, it was unlikely that there would ever *be* any more history books.

And the only reason to fight was that the enemy offered no alternative—it meant to wipe the human race out of existence.

The Grand Cannon prepared to fire, and the futile squadrons of Earth fighters went out to do their jobs as best they could. Lisa Hayes stared down at her screens and instruments and fought off the urge to weep for the men and women who were doing their jobs in all good faith and were kept, by the omnipresent UEDC propaganda and disinformation, from knowing that they were doomed.

During a few moments' lag time, she paused to regard a close pickup shot of the SDF-1 and to think of Claudia, of Gloval, and of Rick. She found, as her father had told her when she was a little girl, that there were only a few really important questions in life and that combat would make *anybody* ask them.

Why are we here? Where do we come from? What happens to us when we die? And when I do, will I be with Rick, at last, or will I be alone forever?

An update on the cannon's targeting status came in just then, and Lisa had to let those thoughts go.

Rick Hunter sealed up his flightsuit and made sure his gloves were firmly connected to his instrumented cuff rings. They fit smoothly, allowing him maximum dexterity.

The hatch to his quarters signaled, and he thought it was just another messenger with a mission update, all com channels being overloaded. Until the hatch slid back.

"Rick?"

He pivoted and saw her standing in the hatch, outlined against the harsh glare of the passageway lights. She came a step into his quarters demurely but looking him in the eye.

The hatch rolled shut behind Minmei.

They were there in every size and shape, those war-green vessels of the Zentraedi Grand Fleet. Never in their entire history had they been assembled for combat in such a formation.

From his command station, Dolza, supreme commander of the Zentraedi race, considered his target, Earth.

Space was filled with his ships; there had never been a marshaling like this in the infamous annals of the Zentraedi.

And yet he felt misgivings. Dolza knew the ancient lore of his race from Exedore's endless teachings. Against the forces that those records mentioned, the Grand Fleet itself might not be enough.

Perhaps nothing would.

Inside the boulderlike base that was Dolza's headquarters, a thousand miles through its long axis, the supreme commander received word that the fleet was at last all present.

He was enormous, the largest and, but for Exedore, the oldest of his race. Dolza's shaven skull and heavy brow made him look like a granite sculpture.

"My first attack shall be the Micronians' mother planet," he said. "Let all ships stand prepared."

All through the fleet, final preparations for battle were carried out. On the colossal bombardment vessels, the bows opened like giant crocodile jaws, exposing the heavy guns.

Targeting computers accepted their assignments from Dolza's base, ranging their sights across the surface of the world, fixing their aim. The Grand Fleet's engines howled like demons, supercharging the weapons pointed at the helpless Earth.

"I want to apologize to you, Rick," she said. "I mean, about Kyle."

"It's not really your fault," he told her. "I should have

let you know what my feelings were. I should have tried harder, I guess."

"But, I—"

"Oh, Minmei, *it's all right!*" he yelled, frightening her a little. He got control of himself and went to get his flying helmet. *How do I tell her?*

He went to pick up the helmet but saw her reflection in the visor. She was standing silently, watching him.

"I'm a pilot, and you're a superstar now," he said tiredly. "You know it wouldn't have worked for us, anyway. Too much has changed, Minmei."

He went to the viewport, looking down at Earth. "It's strange to think how small our world is," he said, almost distractedly. "It's a pity how much time we wasted, isn't it?"

She flinched as if he had hit her. She could see that he was being cruel on purpose, hurting himself and her, to make the love stop. She opened her mouth to say something that would make him honest again, would clear the air between them.

But at that exact moment the universe lit up. The Zentraedi attack had begun.

CHAPTER
SEVENTEEN

> *Once I wrote here—a younger Minmei did—that I*
> *needed to be my own person, that I had my own shadows to*
> *cast.*
> *But, oh...I didn't realize how terrible that darkness*
> *would be.*

From the diary of Lynn-Minmei

MILLIONS OF BLINDINGLY BRIGHT BEAMS OF PURE
energy rained down on the blue-white world.

First to go were the orbital defenses, the surveillance
satellites and the "armors"—the big conventional-tech-
nology space cruisers. They were obliterated instantly,
vanishing in clouds of expanding gas.

The incredible volley pierced the atmosphere, boiling
away clouds and moisture, striking through to the surface. Buildings and trees and people were vaporized;
everything flammable exploded. The hellish rays set off
tremendous detonations and superheated the air like
thermonuclear weapons.

Everywhere it was the same. Soldiers and civilians,
adults and children, and the unborn as well—the Grand
Fleet favored none and spared none. In the middle of a
humdrum day marked only by some sort of alert the
UEDC wasn't explaining, nearly the entire population of
the planet was put to the sword.

For most, there wasn't even time to scream, only a
hideous moment when light and heat beyond any de-
scription engulfed them, making their bodies as transparent as x-ray images, then consuming them.

Cities toppled, and blowtorch winds scoured the world. Seas were given no mercy, either; Dolza had decreed a carpet-volley pattern to get ships and aquafarming and aquamining installations and the like. Untold cubic miles of water turned into steam.

The beams came like a fusion-hot monsoon all across the defenseless world.

In UEDC headquarters, the ground rumbled but miles of earth and rock saved the occupants from immediate death.

Lisa gaped at an illuminated situation map. The strikes were so numerous that the display computers couldn't discriminate anymore. The face of the world glowed.

"They can't be doing this!" she screamed. "They can't!"

But she knew she was wrong. They were.

"Annihilation."

Gloval stood helplessly, shoulders bowed, looking out the forward viewport. Exedore stood mute at his shoulder. The alien decided that he must, in fact, have fallen victim to the contagious human emotions, because he felt them very strongly at that moment: rage that this should happen, a soul-wrenching sorrow, and an utter, utter shame.

Reading her instruments, a female enlisted-rating tech said in monotone, "They're gone. They're all gone."

In his headquarters base, the immense Dolza looked upon his handiwork and found it good. His guttural laugh echoed in the deep, eerily resonant tones of the Zentraedi.

The Micronian interlude would be expunged from history, he had decided. And any similar race encountered by the Zentraedi would be subject to instant and total termination.

Then, events could be put back on their proper track.

Dolza had to admit that even he, the supreme commander, hadn't had a *true* idea of Zentraedi power until the moment the Grand Fleet opened fire. The irresistible might of it! It filled him with new aspirations, new resolve.

When the humans were finished and the rebellious Breetai and his followers destroyed completely, it would be time to deal with the Robotech Masters.

For too long now, the Masters had treated their warrior servants, the Zentraedi, with the contempt one showed a slave. For too long, that had seared the Zentraedi pride. Moreover, it had come to light that the Masters had told the Zentraedi a colossal lie all along—they had deceived them about the giants' very origins.

The Protoculture secrets hidden in Zor's ship had been an important part of Dolza's master plan to overthrow the Robotech Masters and let the Zentraedi take their rightful place at the pinnacle of the universe.

The accursed Zor had been aware of that and had dispatched his ship to keep it from Masters and Zentraedi alike. The plan had ultimately worked, but in so doing it had brought this day. As Dolza looked out at nearly five million warships, all raining down destruction on Earth, he realized that he didn't need Zor's secrets, didn't need the SDF-1. All he needed was the might of the Zentraedi hordes.

He laughed again, a bass rumble that made the bulkheads ring. Today humanity died. Tomorrow the war against the Robotech Masters would begin.

Rick Hunter clutched the ledge of his viewport. As he watched, the night side of Earth, partly obscured by the enemy fleet, lit up with a myriad of red-hot specks, the work of that first terrible salvo.

"The whole planet," he said numbly.

Minmei came up behind him, walking like a robot, in deep shock. "Are they all . . . are they all dead, Rick?"

He watched the night turn red. "Yes, Minmei."

She tore her eyes away from the sight. "Mother. Father."

"Lisa," he said very softly. His cheeks were suddenly slick with tears.

She started to sing in a lullably voice, crooning a little love song to life and to the planet that was dying. But it didn't last long, and soon her head was buried in her hands.

"So this is how we end," she sobbed. "First the Earth and then the rest of us."

He put a hand on her shoulder. "No, Minmei. This is *not* the end, do you hear me?"

He wished he could sound more convincing. But she wasn't blind; she could see the overwhelming might preparing to turn its guns on the SDF-1 and its Zentraedi allies.

"We still have our lives," he said, shaking her shoulder a bit roughly to make her listen to him.

It was all so unfair, so hopeless. He hadn't felt so angry and powerless since that day in Dolza's base when he and Lisa and Ben were helpless prisoners—

THAT'S IT!!!

He shook her shoulder again with a sudden new conviction. "It's not over yet! Listen, Minmei, I want you to go now and *sing for everyone*!"

She wiped tears from her lashes. "Sing?"

"Yes. I've got an idea."

The smoke clouds were already rising from the Earth, rolling to envelop it and bring on a winter that even the computers couldn't analyze reliably.

In the UEDC base's main control room, Admiral Hayes heard the report.

"There's been no word from any other Council member, sir. Marshal Zukav is still unconscious, and the doctors think they'll probably have to operate. What are your orders?"

In this election year, most of the UEDC members had been caught by surprise by the alien attack, out mending fences and fixing political support. Of them all, only Hayes and Zukav had been present at the base when the attack came, and Zukav had suffered a coronary on the spot.

Now the reins were in Hayes's hands, but they were the reins to a planet that was more cinder than soil.

"Damage estimate to all sectors exceeds any known scale," a voice was saying quietly to one side. "We have indications that a few scattered groups survived the first attack."

The first attack, yes. But now the enemy was no doubt preparing a second and a third—as many volleys as it took to turn Earth into a molten ball.

And so the world would end.

"Did the Grand Cannon survive the attack?" he asked.

An aide was quick to answer. "Yes, sir. It will still function."

Hayes turned to him. "Very good. Then we'll begin the countdown at once, Lieutenant."

The aide hurried off to relay the order. In moments, the vast base thrummed with power.

Gloval looked into the face of his onetime enemy. Breetai stared back, and it would have been a historic moment if everyone had not been in such a hurry.

Breetai gazed down at the mustached, almost disheveled-looking little creature who had outfought and outthought the best warriors in the galaxy; Gloval looked up at a frighteningly massive fellow with a chest as thick as an ancient oak and a metal and crystal cowl covering half his skull.

They spoke with virtually no preamble; they felt they knew each other well.

"Commander Breetai, I want you to please broadcast a simultaneous transmission of Minmei's song on all of your military frequencies."

Breetai's single eye fixed on Gloval intently. "I have no objection, but what is your plan?"

Exedore stepped into the picture to explain. "As yet, the soldiers in Dolza's fleet have had no contact with Micronian culture, m'lord! When exposed to the song, they will be thrown into confusion. And it will also boost the Micronians' morale."

Breetai rubbed his massive jaw. Gloval stared in fascination at the giant mauve hand, the dense black hairs on its back thick as wires. "That *could* provide us with the chance we need to catch them off guard."

Gloval was a bit breathless with this alien's audacity. He himself had been thinking more along the lines of a selective strike. "But—the Grand Fleet is not a force we can attack head-on, Commander!"

Breetai gave him a surprisingly winning smile, coming as it did from a cloned XT soldier whose head was half hidden by a metal and crystal sheath. Breetai plainly savored every word. "Precisely, Captain Gloval. They would never expect us to mount a surprise attack against them."

The main bridge hatchway slid open, and a slender figure stepped in. Minmei looked around nervously at the mysterious landscape of dials, lights, screens, and controls.

"Um, you wanted to see me, Captain?"

He went to her, Exedore trotting alongside. "Yes, Miss Minmei. Lieutenant Hunter has told me his plan. We're going to use it for our counterattack."

Minmei glanced nervously at the communications screen, then quickly averted her eyes from the metal-skulled alien who was staring at her with frank interest.

"You *will* be able to sing a song for us, won't you, Minmei?" Exedore said anxiously.

She forced a smile. How could you go on with life when the world had just died? Simple: You used your acting instincts, keeping introspection and sorrow damped well down.

"Yes, of course. Anything to help out."

Gloval nodded in approval. She had barely exchanged two words with him at the wedding, but there was something about his old-world formality, a kind of lovable stuffiness, that put her at ease somehow.

"I have one special request, Minmei," Exedore put in. "*Could* you do that, er, that is, that *thing* that you do in all your movies? I believe it is referred to as a kiss."

He couldn't have surprised her much more if he had done his Minmei imitation for her. "I—I suppose I could. But why do you need that?"

Exedore dropped into the pedantic, almost effete tones he used when trying to get his point across to stubborn Zentraedi. "I believe it would act as a kind of psychological shock to all the Grand Fleet attack forces, rendering them less able to fight."

She felt like laughing hysterically; there were some

critics who would have agreed with Exedore's evaluation of her acting ability.

But outside the viewport, Earth smoldered. "Well, if it will help."

The clouds were already thick in the night sky over Alaska, lit from below by an infernal glow.

The base throbbed around her, preparing for the monumental cannon shot. Lisa stared at her screens and waited to die.

At the cannon's base, a small city of Robotechnology, subatomic fires whirled; energy crackled and struggled to get free.

Admiral Hayes heard the reports in stony silence. This would probably be the last, possibly the only human shot in the battle, on the last day of the human race; but *somebody* was going to be very sorry they had ever come seeking battle. To go down fighting was much better than simply dying.

The cannon's huge lens, lit with targeting beams, made the undersides of the black clouds closing in on the world red.

Dolza looked around suddenly at an emergency communication tone. "Your Excellency! We've detected a high-energy reaction coming from the third planet!"

But before Dolza could ask for more data or give a single order, hell spewed forth.

It had been apparent from the start that an energy gun buried vertically in a planetary surface would have a very limited field of fire. The planned system of satellite reflectors was supposed to have solved that, but interim measures had been put in place. They showed their worth now.

A beam as hot as the heart of a star sprang up from the devastated Earth. Widened by the lens, it lanced up into the Grand Fleet. A hundred thousand ships disappeared in an instant, burned out of existence like insects in a flamethrower's blast.

Brute servos tilted the lens, angling the beam. No one had been sure whether or not a shot like that would violate all the mathematics of the Grand Cannon and blow the installation to kingdom come, but it turned out that somehow everything held.

Like a flashlight of complete and all-encompassing destruction, the Grand Cannon's volley swiveled through the blockading fleet.

Ships were simply there and then not. Left behind were only component particles and the furious forces of destruction. In that single attack, the human race destroyed more warcraft than the Zentraedi had lost in any war in their entire history.

"The enemy ships are just disappearing, sir," Vanessa said.

Gloval and Exedore stared at the screen, watching the angling and swinging of the Grand Cannon. "Alaska Base survived!" Gloval exulted. The Terrible Trio let out whoops and laughter.

"Lisa," Claudia whispered.

CHAPTER
EIGHTEEN

Well, that was when I decided that ol' Vance needed to ease out of being Minmei's manager and into a new setup. I mean, hey: what does twenty-five percent of Armageddon amount to in real money?

Vance Hasslewood, *Those Were the Days*

MINMEI'S BACKUP BAND AND ROADIES (IF THAT was the proper name for them; they played only one town, but they clocked more miles than any other act in history) were used to taking their time setting up, running sound checks, getting mentally prepared for a concert or recording session. None of that today, though.

RDF techs and other personnel threw the setup together in a few minutes flat, a briefing officer making it clear to the musicians just how important this concert would be. The only one to object, a keyboard man who wasn't happy with the way his stacks had been arranged, was menaced into silence not by the military people but by the other band members. Everyone knew what would happen if the Grand Fleet carried the day.

In her dressing room, Minmei tried to keep her mind off the greater issues and simply concentrate on her performance. Humming, she leaned toward her brightly lit makeup mirror, examining one eyelash critically. It wasn't that she was unaware of the horrifying events taking place all around the SDF-1; it was just that she could do nothing about them except clear her mind and sing her very best.

There was a timid knock at her door, and three visitors entered. "Hi, Minmei," said a rough but friendly voice.

Minmei smiled into her mirror at the reflection of Bron and the other two Zentraedi spies.

"We understand the pressure you're under, Minmei," Rico began.

"Going into battle can be very, um, *taxing*," Konda added helpfully.

"We just wanted you to know we're with you 100 percent and we know you can do it," Bron told her, blushing. The other two nodded energetically.

"Oh!" She turned to them and came to her feet. She had spoken to them only a few times, even including the official hearings and meetings.

But she felt a kinship to them, a bond of empathy. Song had made them leave behind everything they knew, made them risk the unknown and commit themselves to a new life, even though that life held dangers and frightening enigmas. In that, they were very much like Minmei herself.

She put her hands out to them, palm to palm. "Thank you, Konda—Bron, Rico. You're very kind."

Konda cupped his hands around hers, and the other two stacked theirs gently on top. "You three are such wonderful men."

"Minmei," came the stage manager's voice. "Two minutes."

She kissed each of them on the cheek, then she was gone in a swirl of long, raven hair.

Instead of the seats of the Star Bowl amphitheater or a glass wall that looked on a recording studio's engineering booth, Minmei and her band gazed at a great, concave sweep of viewport. The enemy warfleet was deployed before them. Below were the battle fortress's upper works, and beyond the bow, the curve of the blasted Earth.

Combat craft were swarming from the super dimensional fortress; the warships of Breetai's armada were forming up around and behind it, battlewagons and flagships at the lead for a do-or-die first impact.

The cameras and pickups focused on Minmei as she found her mark on the stage. She had decided to wear a simple full skirt and blouse, with a golden ribbon bowed at her throat.

"Wh...what's your opener gonna be?" laughed her manager, Vance Hasslewood, nervously, mopping his brow with his handkerchief.

"How 'bout 'My Boyfriend's a Pilot'?" the bass man joked weakly.

"No," she said firmly. "We'll do the new one."

They had barely rehearsed it; she had completed it only two days before. There was a chorus of objections from just about everyone, but she held up her mike and spoke into it firmly.

"This is the time for it."

Now or never.

Tactical corps and civil defense mecha had been brought out on the decks of the battle fortress and the suppercarriers. With their massed weapons added to the turrets and tubes of the SDF-1, short-range defensive firepower was more than tripled.

Out where the VTs were forming, as the cats slung more and more of them into space, the RDF fliers listened over the command net as Gloval's voice came up.

"Attention, all fighter pilots. Once we enter the zone of engagement, there will be complete radio silence under all circumstances. Miss Minmei's song, and only that, will be broadcast on all frequencies. As you have been briefed, we hope that will distract the enemy and give us the advantage.

"We *must* make maximum use of this element of surprise. Good luck to you all."

Rick heard Gloval out, lowering his helmet visor. Skull Team was flying the few armored VTs the fabrication and tech people had managed to get operational. That meant that Rick, Max, Miriya, and the rest would be out at the very spearhead of the attack. Not something to dwell on.

In his heart, he wished Minmei well, and then he led Skull Team out.

* * *

She looked up to the camera and raised her mike on
cue as the cone of spotlight shone down on her. In the
control room, her image was on all the screens from
many angles.

> Life is only what we choose to make it,
> Let us take it,
> Let us be free

Rick hit his ship's boosters. The blue vortices of its
drives burned and shrieked. The armored VTs left trails
of light, leaping into the dark. Conventional VT teams
came after.

Breetai's tri-thrusters, pods, and other mecha prepared to follow. Gloval and the Zentraedi had wisely
agreed not to mingle their forces; in the heat of battle,
human pilots would have a difficult time reading alien
unit markings and telling friend from foe. Even the hastily added RDF insignia on the tri's and pods might not be
spotted in time.

In the command station of his flagship, Breetai stood
with arms folded across his broad chest, a characteristic
pose, staring up at a projecbeam. As he had admitted so
long ago, hers was a voice to wring emotion from any
heart. Perhaps the course to this moment had been set
when he first heard it.

A tech relayed word. "My lord, this transmission is
being picked up by Dolza's ships."

He nodded, watching and listening to Minmei.

> We can find the glory we all dream of,
> and with our love,
> We can win!

His flagship trembled as its engines came up to full
power. The front ranks of the armada moved forward at
half speed, picking up velocity slowly. The SDF-1, in
Attack mode, was accelerating along in the thick of
them, its back thrusters blazing, a fantastic armored
marionette of war.

Still engulfing Earth, below them, the Grand Fleet lay in orbit, seemingly paralyzed.

The human-Zentraedi alliance swooped down at it.

"What's that on our monitors?" growled one of Dolza's communications officers, his voice harsh and guttural.

His subordinate could barely tear his attention away from the song to answer. Such distraction when a superior was asking questions would have drawn quick, terrible punishment at any other time, but they were both hypnotized by Minmei.

> If we must fight or face defeat,
> We must stand tall and not retreat.

The subordinate shook himself a little and answered. "I don't know, sir, but we're receiving it on all frequencies."

Then they both watched in fascination, ignoring the flashing of indicators and the beeps of comtones.

"We're within firing range," Vanessa said tightly. "No counterattack detected."

"*It's working!*" Exedore cried, watching the battle at Gloval's side.

"This is it," Gloval said calmly. "All ships, open fire."

In that first gargantuan volley, the attacking force's main problem was not to hit its own fightercraft or have its cannon salvos destroy its own missiles in flight. But the Zentraedi were used to that sort of problem, and fire control had been carefully integrated with the SDF-1's systems.

It was an impact almost as damaging as the Grand Cannon's; millions of Zentraedi, gaping at Minmei's performance, died in moments.

Alarms were going off. The few Grand Fleet officers who could force their attention away from the screens could get no response from their troops short of physically attacking them.

As many of the Grand Fleet crews were beginning to

notice the alarms, though, Minmei paused in her song; the band vamped in the background. A tall, dark figure stepped out into the spotlight with her.

Lynn-Kyle wore a look of burning intensity, his long, straight black hair swirling around him, taking her hand. "Minmei—"

"Yes, Kyle; I know," she recited her line. "You've come to say good-bye."

"Yes."

Minmei wasn't exactly sure where the lines had come from; everything was so hurried, so improvised. Weren't they from one of the movies the two had done together? But Kyle was putting more into them than he had ever managed on screen. He had seen her run off after Rick. What was going through his mind?

No matter. He took her into his arms. She turned her face up to his. The camera cut from a two-shot of their bodies pressed against each other to a close-up of a long, passionate kiss, Kyle no longer acting.

In the Grand Fleet, alien warriors groaned and made nauseated sounds.

"How can they *do* that?" "Most disgusting thing I ever—"

And yet there was something about it that kept them from looking away, an appalled captivation. It should be added that among the female units like the Quadronos, there was more absorption and less repulsion than among the males.

But all through the orbiting fleet, moans and growls and other reactions to the kiss turned into shrieks of dismay and pain as the alliance's volley cut through the enemy ships, holing them, blowing them to nothingness.

Rick watched the kiss on a display screen and thought, not unkindly, *Farewell Minmei*.

Then, "Let's get 'em!" he snarled over the tac net.

Someone must have managed to cut off the Minmei transmission from at least *some* of the Grand Fleet's mecha. There were plenty of effective ships, more than plenty.

The Skull Team's armored VTs bore in at the enemy,

releasing barrages of missiles, fighting their way through Grand Fleet pod and tri-thruster defensive screens. Quadrono powered armor came at the VTs, too, less effective now that Miriya no longer led them. Miriya avoided engaging those.

VTs shifted configuration according to the needs of the moment; Battloid and Guardian and Veritech modes were intermingled. Pods and tri-thrusters mixed it up with them and opened fire. Space was one big killing ground.

The armored VTs were faster and more maneuverable than anything else in the battle as well as being more heavily armed. They pierced the enemy formations, ripping a hole for the rest of the attack force to exploit.

Skull Team seemed to be everywhere, unhittable and unavoidable. Many, many Zentraedi saw their Jolly Roger insignia—the skull and crossbones—and died instants later. The heavy autocannon buzz-sawed; the missiles streamed, leaving boiling trails. But for every enemy downed, three more dove in to try to seal the gap.

It's love's battle we must win.
We will win.
We can win!

The range was close now. Around the bowl in which Minmei performed, the ship's mecha opened up. The Destroid cannon in particular put out staggering volumes of fire. Every battery the ship mounted—except for the monster main gun, whose energy demands might have damaged the SDF-1—was working overtime.

The Grand Fleet's losses in the first moments of the battle were awful, but its numbers still gave it a vast edge, and some of the enemy ships were returning fire. The SDF-1 and the armada dreadnoughts forged on, blazing away in all directions. Enemy mecha were starting to get through to the alliance capital vessels now, despite the best efforts of the VTs and the armada's pods, tri-thrusters, and powered armor.

But slowly, seemingly by inches, the allied force drew closer to Dolza's headquarters.

* * *

Max and Miriya were like avenging angels, beyond any mortal power to resist or stop. Faced with the red-trimmed armored VT or the blue, all any enemy pilot could do was resign himself to death.

Rick had part of his commo and guidance equipment tuned for signals of life on Earth, especially from Alaska Base. If there was *any* sign of life . . .

A light cruiser was trying to break past the VTs for a go at the SDF-1. He went in at it, letting go a torrent of mixed ordnance, aiming for the vital spots the defectors had told the RDF about.

The cruiser fired back, and Rick decided this was one head-on he wasn't going to survive. But all at once the cruiser expanded, armor flying off it like rind off a bursting melon, and then the vessel and its crew were scattered atoms and little more.

So violent was the explosion that Rick was distracted, avoiding being damaged by it. When he looked around again, he saw that a trio of Battlepods had loosed multiple spreads of missiles at him, and there was absolutely no hope of dodging them all.

He eluded some, jammed some of the others' guidance systems, shot a few right out of existence—and the special VT's armor protected him from several hits.

But that left still more to go for his vitals. In Battloid mode, he crouched, trying to shield himself. He nevertheless took several, right in the breadbasket. VT armor was good but not that good.

The damaged Battloid, leaving a wake of flame behind it, spun and tumbled for Earth, flopping lifelessly.

CHAPTER
NINETEEN

When you're in the upper-right-hand corner, pushing that envelope, and the "CANCEL" stamp comes your way, you do a lot of thinking.

The Collected Journals of Admiral Rick Hunter

THE CRESCENT MOON HUNG LOW ON THE HORIZON; the landscape of Earth made the two bodies like twins now.

Compared to the barrage that had laid waste to the Earth, the stray beams and rounds from the colossal battle above were barely distant sniper shots. But they were enough to rattle an Alaska Base that was already mortally wounded.

The shattered mouth of what had once been the Grand Cannon was already ringed with bizarre energy phenomena. Crackling discharges, wandering spheres of ball lightning, and fireflylike radiation nexuses had sprung from the tremendous forces loosed by the Grand Cannon and their interaction with both local fields and the fury of the enemy's rain of death.

"Earth Defense Sector four-alpha, come in please," Lisa called into her headset mike as the room tossed. "This is Alaska Base!"

The base heaved again, shaking down dust and debris from the ceiling. The tremors were caused by stray shots from the battle and by the rebellion of the very planet against the obscene things that had been done to it. But they came as well from the interior of the base itself. The installation was dying; but from what Lisa could read from her instruments, it would not be a slow, quiet death.

She had found no one else alive in the base. She had been ordered to see about a glitch in a shielded commo relay substation, had been there just as the cosmic fireworks went off. Being the last survivor in an underground charnel house might be somebody else's idea of a stroke of fortune, but it wasn't Lisa's.

She fought to keep her voice and her nerve from breaking as she tried another call. She kept herself narrowly fixed on the job at hand to shut out the ghastly things she had seen and smelled and been forced to come in contact with in making her way back to her post.

The place was nearly dark, lit only by dim red emergency lights. The weak flow from the fallback power system was barely enough to keep her console functioning. There was plenty of power in the base, power gathering itself for a split-second rampage, but she couldn't tap any of it.

"It's no use. They're all gone," she said numbly. She wondered how long she would last, the only living thing in the city of the dead, perhaps the only human being alive.

Not long, she hoped.

Abruptly, multicolored lines of static zagged across her screen, and her father's face appeared, broken by interference, only to reappear.

"Is that you, Lisa? I'm reading you, but the transmission is very weak."

She let out a long breath. "Thank God you're alive!"

She could see that he was still in the command station. A few figures moved in the gloom behind him, lit by occasional flashes of static or electrical shorts. So others had been spared by the concussion, the explosions and air contamination, the fires and smoke and radiation.

"The Grand Cannon was severely damaged," he admitted. "I don't think it will fire again, but we have to try."

"Oh, Father."

He smiled weakly. "It seems you were right all the

time. The Zentraedi forces are much too powerful for our weapons to handle. I should have listened to you."

Another shock wave shook the base. Admiral Hayes said, "Lisa, you have to get out of here now!"

Get out? What was he talking about? The surface was a radioactive execution chamber carpeted with molten glass for miles all around. She was about to tell him so, to make her way to him, to die with him because it was a better place than the one she was in now, and she knew she would die this day.

Before she could speak, there was some sort of eruption from the Grand Cannon base equipment behind him, and the screen broke up into rainbow distortion, then went dark.

"No!" She threw herself at the console, then sank to the floor, wracked by sobs, as the wailing of the base's power plant built and built for a final, terrible outpouring.

"Father . . . Father . . ."

As the battle draws on, we feel stronger,
How much longer must we go now?

Rick recognized the voice at once, even in the daze he was in from the missiles' pounding. He blinked and saw the Earth whirling before him. His flying sense told him his ship was spinning and sprawling toward the ground, its thrusters only marginally effective in slowing it. He was inside a big, loose-limbed fireball meteor.

Where am I? What happened? Then it came back to him in a rush. As he gained a little control over himself, his VT, taking its impulses from the receptors in his helmet, did the same.

Gotta go to F mode! The bucking and spinning of the dive made it difficult reaching for the one close control. He knew that if the ship hadn't made minimal attempts to control the crash, he would likely never have woken up.

It was the hardest thing he had ever done in his life, but he got his hand to the F lever and yanked it. Damage control systems in his Robotech ship made decisions and blew off the armor and pods with which it had been retrofitted. Somehow, the burning components were jettisoned too.

The Battloid folded, elongated here, shortened there —*mechamorphosed*. And in a moment, a sleek, conventional VT rode the thickening air down toward Earth.

Seems to be handling all right, he thought. *Maybe I wasn't hit as bad as I thought.*

The ship had automatically assumed a belly-flop attitude for atmospheric reentry. The speed of its descent reddened its ablative shielding a bit, torching the air around it.

Oops! Better activate heat shields! In another moment a protective blister of heat-reflective armor, bearing the Skulls' Jolly Roger insignia, slid into place over the canopy. Other vulnerable components were similarly protected.

The heat in the cockpit began dropping at once, and Rick tried to assess his situation. *I'm still alive.* That covered just about all the important stuff as far as most pilots were concerned.

Minmei was still singing. He recalled those last words he had exchanged with her in his quarters as the sirens shrilled for a VT hot scramble.

You can do it, Minmei. Just remember: Today you sing for everyone.

But—I want you to understand, Rick. I'm really singing for you.

And then she had given him a kiss that he had felt to his toes, a kiss that made him feel he didn't need a VT in order to fly.

I love you, he told her; *I love you*, she said.

But it was really good-bye, and they had both known it.

He shook off the recollection; that was the sort of stroll down memory lane that got pilots killed. He was deep in the atmosphere now, his VT trimmed, seeming to respond well. He slowed, bringing the wings out to minimal sweep, rolling back the heat shields, for a look around. Night lay over the wasteland, and clouds closed in above.

He tried to figure out why the VT was descending in the first place, why it seemed to be homing in on something. Then he noticed that the commo system had picked up a signal and remembered that he had given it a certain task.

He swept in lower over the ravaged surface, trying to get a stronger signal. The utter horror of what had been done to his planet made him lock his mind to the job at hand and that alone. His commo equipment had picked up emanations of some kind on the designated frequency.

He turned and banked, climbed through the smoky night. A minute of maneuvering went by, then two, and as if by magic he was rewarded with a signal that came in five by five—perfectly.

"I say again: This is Commander Hayes, Alaska Base. Anyone receiving this transmission, *please* respond."

There was a note of fear in her voice that he had never heard before. Something in it brought home to him forcefully how important she had become to him.

Farewell, Minmei.

He was so eager to reply, to tell her he was there, that he fumbled in opening his transmitter and ignored all proper procedure.

"Lisa! Lisa, it's me!"

"Rick?" She said it low, like a prayer. Then, wildly, "Rick, is it really you?"

"Yes! Are you all right?"

She suddenly sounded downcast. "Yes, but I think I'm the only one."

"Lisa, give me your coordinates. Send me a homing signal."

She waited a beat before answering. "No, Rick; it's far too dangerous here. But thanks."

"Damn your eyes! I've got a fix on your signal, and I'm coming! Now, will you help me or not?" She didn't say no, but she didn't say yes.

"Besides," he said jauntily, "what's a little danger to *us*? I'll get you out of there in no time." He wished he had his long white flying scarf so he could fling it back over his shoulder rakishly.

Suddenly, there was a homing signal. "Rick, I'm so glad it's you," she said in a voice as intimate as a quiet serenade. "Be careful, all right?"

Soon after, the VT dove straight down the shaft of the onetime Grand Cannon. It went from Fighter to Guardian mode, battered by rising heat waves and running a gauntlet of radiation that would have broiled an unprotected human being instantly.

> We shall live the day we dream of winning
> And beginning a new life
> We will win!
> We must win!

She had sung it through, taking longer because of the scene played with Lynn-Kyle, and yet it hadn't been very many minutes since Minmei had begun her song. Nevertheless, Khyron the Backstabber knew, the universe and war in particular turned upon such minutes.

He stood in his flagship, well out of the battle but within striking distance, watching the fight. Lack of sufficient Protoculture to make his escape from the solar system had forced him to come up with a new plan, and the plan seemed more promising every moment.

Grel, his second in command, watched Khyron worriedly. Khyron had shown no aversion to the singing, the kissing. His handsome face shone, his eyes alight with the gleam Grel had seen there when Khyron used the forbidden leaves of the Flower of Life.

"What is your plan now, my lord?" Grel ventured.

Khyron was still watching Minmei. "Mm. Pretty little thing."

Grel couldn't help bursting out, "What?"

Khyron looked at him coldly. "Get me the position of Breetai's flagship." Then he was smiling up dreamily at Minmei's projecbeam image once more.

Grel didn't know what to say and, moreover, knew that saying the wrong thing to the Backstabber had cut short quite a number of otherwise promising careers. He couldn't help blurting, though, "But my lord! Breetai is one of us! You cannot do th—"

Khyron whirled on him in a murderous rage. "How *dare* you? You will follow my orders or else!"

Grel turned very pale and hurried to obey. Khyron turned back to his enjoyment of the song.

But his enjoyment was sinister. He felt a physical, languorous pleasure as he concluded that he was at last coming to a clear understanding of a pure *true* definition of conquest; something more pleasure-giving, if he was right, than all the victories, booty, and worlds the Zentraedi had ever taken.

In seconds, Khyron's flagship was under weigh, followed by the tiny flotilla of those still loyal to him.

People in the control booth and even members of the band had sent the inquiry up the line: Shouldn't Minmei go to another song?

In the midst of the most important battle of his career, Gloval had taken time to give the order personally: no! This song, *this* song was the one!

Now, with Minmei's voice ringing through it everywhere that battle damage hadn't silenced the PA system, the SDF-1 waded deeper and deeper into the massed Grand Fleet. Out on the decks and outerworks, enemy fire was taking a vicious toll of the exposed attack mecha, but the crews of the war machines still kept up intense fire.

Breetai's armada had suffered badly, too, but hadn't slowed.

"Keep all power levels at maximum!" he bellowed as systemry and power conduits blew all about him.

His flagship and its escort, the SDF-1 side by side with them, pressed on, their volume of fire enormous, the rest of the armada striking after in a wedge, probing their way through the disorganized foe.

Many of the smaller fightercraft and mecha on both sides had been snuffed out of existence by the overwhelming volleys being traded; most of the rest had quit the battle's fairway.

"Hell or glory!" cried Azonia, holding her fist aloft, coming in to shore up the alliance's badly crumpling left flank. Her forces threw themselves into the engagement with fanatic zeal.

Dolza's faithful leapt at them with an equal thirst for death and triumph.

* * *

Inside the SDF-1, a direct hit pierced the hold in which Macross City lay. Atmosphere roared out at once like a great river, and more missiles penetrated the hold to score direct hits on the streets of the city. Armored curtains and sealing sections swung into place at once, but still there was grievous damage to the city. Rebuilt a half dozen times, it was fast becoming rubble again. Loss of life was relatively low because most of the inhabitants were on emergency duty elsewhere and practically all the rest were in shelters.

Just before the last curtain rolled into place to seal the compartment and allow it to be repressurized, a last heavy enemy missile somehow sizzled through the gap. By chance, it found a shelter in a direct hit, and the carnage was nothing that belonged in a sane universe.

Repair and rescue crews and medical teams wanted the ship to drop back to give them time to do their work. Gloval bit his lower lip but refused; perhaps all that was left of humanity was aboard the SDF-1, and if Dolza wasn't smashed now, in this moment, none of them would survive.

The request was denied. The battle raged on. It was not the first agonizing time Gloval had felt himself something of a villain.

> *Aside from Gloval, very few of our senior military people seem to be able to grasp the simple truth: The Zentraedi do not truly understand Robotechnology. They use it without comprehending how it works, as many humans use television, laser devices, or aircraft without the slightest idea what makes those technologies function. The Zentraedi were given their weapons and equipment by the enigmatic Robotech Masters. Their control over the Zentraedi is due, in part, to the giants' own ignorance.*
>
> *This means that the Zentraedi are vulnerable in ways of which they are unaware.*

Dr. Emil Lang, Technical Recordings and Notes

MORE DISTURBANCES SHOOK THE UNDERGROUND corridors of Alaska Base as a terrier might shake a rat in its teeth. The titanic supports complained, and the ceilings showered rock dust.

Through it flew the Skull Guardian, maneuvering in very confining space to avoid exploding power ducts and ruptured energy mains. Rick brought the ship to an abrupt halt, hitting the foot thrusters hard so as not to collide with a thick shield door that dead-ended the cyclopean corridor.

But he was in no mood to be stopped. He lowered a phased-array laser turret and aimed with his gunsight reticle. The fearsome power of the quad-mount sent armor flowing in rivulets, but not as quickly as he hoped. He cut back his ambitions and tried for a man-size opening instead of a VT-size one.

In a few moments a circular plug of armor two feet thick fell back from the shield door, leaving a makeshift hatch. Rick gave commands with his controls and with mental images; the Guardian bowed, its nose touching the corridor floor so that he could disembark.

He was barely at the smoking, red-hot opening when he heard her. "Rick!" Lisa was waiting for him patiently at the far end of the short, small connnecting passageway.

He felt like sinking to his knees with relief and— something else. But there was no time for it, and so he tossed his thick, unruly black hair out of his eyes and flickered his eyebrows at her.

"You the lady who called for the cab? I'm your man."

She laughed fondly, nodding. "It's about time." She ran to him, laughing, and he caught her up in his arms, whirling her.

In another few seconds they were in the Guardian's cockpit, Lisa seated across his lap, Rick trying to concentrate on his flying. Strange energy phenomena coruscated and spat all around, a poltergeist zoo of deadly short-term exotica. Purple lightning grasped for them, and green rays ricocheted from surface to surface. Walls blew out into the corridor, sending pieces of shredded armor plate whirling like leaf fragments.

"The reactor's overloading!" she yelled over the din.

Rick somehow ran the dimly lit obstacle course, Lisa's head buried against his chest in case the canopy shattered. After several centuries' time juking and sideslipping through the maze of Alaska Base, the Guardian was back into the vertical shaft of what had been Earth's greatest weapon less than an hour before.

The last layer of defensive ships was riven apart by the irresistible wedge of the allied force. Before them hung Dolza's headquarters like some lumpy, dangling overripe fruit.

But Dolza didn't run; that wasn't the way of the true Zentraedi warrior, and Dolza embodied the Zentraedi warrior code. It was as Breetai had known it would be. Instead, the moonlet-size headquarters came straight at its enemies, surrounded by such escort vessels as it could gather around it.

"Objective now approaching," Vanessa reported.

"All units in position," Kim sang out.

"Target within range. Stand by, all batteries," Sammie said into her mike.

"All escort fighters, break contact and attack objective immediately," Claudia ordered. She paused for a quick glance at the headquarters. Its shape and lines and apparent texture reminded her so much of a mountain in space, falling straight at the SDF-1. Ready to crush them and the Zentraedi who had become humanity's friends; ready to crush everything in its path, as had always been the Zentraedi way.

Claudia's face hardened along grim, angry lines. *Not this time*. She thought of her slain lover, Roy Fokker, and of all the others who had died in the pointless war. *But not this time!*

Exedore, still at Gloval's shoulder, said softly, "Now, Captain."

It was as if someone had run a high current through Gloval. "Open fire!" he barked.

The SDF-1 fired again, in every direction, her carefully hoarded power being used at a fearsome rate now, at a moment that was late in the battle even though only minutes had elapsed.

The armada ships of Breetai fell away to all sides to engage the enemy or lend support as they could. The final mission was the dimensional fortress's alone, and no other vessel in existence could perform it or accompany the ship.

The giant warrior shape's thrusters blared, adjusting attitude, and now the SDF-1 came at Dolza's stronghold headfirst.

"Brace for ramming!" Gloval bellowed, and the orders went forth. The engines shook the great ship and drove it in a death dive.

The two great booms that reared above the ship's head like wings were now aligned directly at the space mountain that was Dolza's headquarters, the nerve center of the Grand Fleet. The booms were separate parts of the main gun, reinforced structures that were, with the exception of the mammoth engines, the strongest parts of the ship. And around their tips glowed the green-white fields of a limited barrier defense, making them all but indestructible.

The SDF-1 plunged at its objective; Dolza's technical operations people, prepared for an exchange of close broadsides, realized only in a last, horrified moment what the dimensional fortress's intention was. By then, it was too late.

The idea of being rammed hadn't occurred to them; no other vessel could have done it. Even Breetai's flagship could have caused Dolza's base little more damage that way than a child could inflict by crashing a kiddie car into Gibraltar.

But this was Zor's final creation, a machine that incorporated most of what he had learned about Protoculture and the secrets of Robotechnology. The booms went through the thick armor of the headquarters moonlet as if it were soft cheese. The SDF-1 was like some enormous stake being driven into the heart of the Grand Fleet.

Once the dimensional fortress was inside the outermost layers of the headquarters' armor plating, Dolza's stupendous ship was even more vulnerable. Bulkheads were smashed out of the way like aluminum foil; structural members snapped like toothpicks. The directed barrier shields glowed brighter but held.

An ocean of air began leaking from the headquarters, and the dying started at once. Power junctions and energy routing, severed or crushed, sent serpents of writhing electrical and Protoculture lightning into the thinning air and serpentining along the bulkheads and decks.

The SDF-1 brought its mighty forearms, the supercarriers *Daedalus* and *Prometheus*, into play. Their bows, too, had been reinforced and mantled with directed barrier shields. Like a giant punching his way through an enemy castle, the ship drove on, destroying all that was in its path, its thrusters making it an irresistible force.

Zentraedi were whirled through the air like dust motes in the tremendous atmospheric currents being sucked toward the opening the SDF-1 had made. They died in explosions and were torn apart, ground up, squashed to jelly, or impaled by the flying, whirling wreckage.

Through it all, Minmei sang. She knew the song was no longer a part of any surprise attack, but she felt now that if she stopped, it might bring about some disastrous halt in the desperate attack. It was as if her song was what was making it all happen; it was a form of magic that she couldn't stop in midspell.

Then the dimensional fortress was opening up with conventional weapons. X-ray lasers and missile tubes, cannon and pulsed beams hammered away at everything before and around them. The ship's path was often obscured by the demon's brew of flame and explosion all around.

Minmei watched, transfixed, at the huge sweep of viewport and sang, wondering if the universe was about to end. Because that was how it looked from where she stood.

But moments later, as suddenly as the drawing aside of a curtain, the SDF-1 broke out into a vast, open place. Behind it was a tunnel with its mouth edged by jagged, bent-out superalloy plate. The Zentraedi gaped as it drifted across the vast space within the headquarters mountain.

Gloval knew the timing had to be split second and perfect, and he had no leisure for preparation.

There were quite a few enemy vessels still inside the gargantuan base, something Gloval had been hoping against. But they were all at rest, unable to maneuver or open fire for seconds more at least, perhaps as much as a half minute. In a battle like this, that was an eternity.

"Prepare to execute final barrage!" he snapped as his bridge crew bent to their work. "Then full power to barrier shield!"

Missile ports opened to let loose the last volley the SDF-1 was capable of firing, the do-or-die knockout punch Gloval had saved for this moment. The fortress's heaviest projectiles—Deca missiles the size of old-fashioned ICBMs, Piledrivers as big as sub-launched nukes —were readied for firing.

The bows of the flatdecks opened like sharks' mouths, revealing racks of smaller Hammerhead and Bighorn missiles.

"Target acquisition on their main reflex furnace," Gloval ordered.

But Claudia was way ahead of him. "Target locked in, all missiles, sir," she said.

In his command post, the looming Dolza tried to believe what he saw before him. "What are they doing? They'll destroy us all!"

If the reflex furnace went, the resulting explosion would certainly destroy the base and everything in it, and quite possibly all ships in both fleets and even the planet nearby. But that didn't seem to be daunting the Micronians.

This isn't war! Dolza screamed within himself. *It's madness!*

So the tiny creatures were willing to die in order to avoid the disgrace of defeat.

They are more like us than I thought! Dolza realized. *They have some source of strength we must learn. What allies they would make in a war against the Robotech Masters!*

"Wait!" he bellowed.

"Fire!" Gloval roared on SDF-1's bridge.

The missiles gushed from the battle fortress, the smaller, faster ones getting a quick lead and leaving corkscrewing white trails. The heavier ones took a bit longer to get up to speed, but they quickly overtook and passed their little siblings. All angled in, on assorted vectors, for the base's reflex furnaces.

But Gloval had dismissed them from his mind as soon as he had given the order to let them fly. There was no time to spare.

"All power to barrier shields!" he snapped, but again his bridge crew had anticipated.

The ship was standing stock still. Every erg of power in it was channeled to the shields, producing first a cloud of scintillating lights around the ship, then a green-white sphere like some exotic Christmas ornament.

"Barrier shield coming to maximum," Kim said calmly. Then, a second later, just as the first missiles began to detonate on target, "Barrier at max, sir."

The enemy ships in the base were opening fire now, but their shots glanced harmlessly off the barrier system.

Gloval barely paid attention to confirmation of that; he had little doubt the Robotech shield created by Dr. Lang could hold out against an enemy bombardment for a few seconds. The real test was coming up.

Dolza watched the awesome barrage hit home on the reflex furnace area of the ship's interior and knew he was going to die.

Even with the protection of its shielding, even with the defenses of desperate, brave Zentraedi captains who purposely threw their ships in the way of the all-out salvo, enough missiles got through to ensure that the base would be destroyed. Many *times* enough.

The reflex furnaces churned, then spewed forth utter destruction. Dolza, watching from his command post, had time only for one thought.

Years and years before, he had watched Zor die. Zor had spoken of some overriding Vision that made the megagenius send the SDF-1 here, to Earth.

Had Zor seen this moment, too? And things beyond it?

Then a terrible light seared him. Dolza howled a fierce Zentraedi war cry as he was rent to particles.

The interior bulkhead of the base began to bulge with secondary explosions, nodes of superhard armor being pushed out like putty by the force of the blasts running through the place. The rift in the reflex furnaces that had destroyed Dolza's command post was expanding, gushing forth blinding-white obliteration.

Ships only beginning to maneuver for the run to safety were caught in it, wiped out of existence like so many soap bubbles in a blast furnace.

The base swelled like an overfilled football, then split apart along irregular seams that hadn't been there moments before. Ruinous light spilled out of it, then it lit the sky over Earth like a star.

CHAPTER
TWENTY-ONE

Francis Bacon said that "In peace the sons bury their fathers and in war the fathers bury their sons." My father warned me when I joined up that this didn't always apply to our family, because we were all military. He might have had some premonition that I would outlive him, but what he didn't foresee was that his daughter would hear taps played for an entire world.

Lisa Hayes, *Recollections*

THE THICK CLOUDS HAD DARKENED THE ALASKAN night to pitch-blackness, but the fighter's night-sight capabilities gave Rick a clear view of what he was doing. The lurching Guardian barely cleared the rim of the Grand Cannon's shaft without snagging a wingtip.

It might be begging for a crash, but he kept going, nursing the fighter along until he was beyond the blighted, red-hot area around what had been Alaska Base.

He was barely clear of the blast radius when Alaska Base went up like a pyromaniac's fantasy of Judgment Day.

He flew in Fighter mode for a long while, casting back and forth across the charred Earth for safe landing, watching his radiation detectors and terrain sensors.

He swooped in over what had been a major UEDC base, according to the maps. But there was only a dry lake bed, its water vaporized by a direct hit, and the remains of what had been a major city. The plane started bucking hard, and he went back to Guardian. The place showed no signs of radioactivity or fallout; he decided to set down.

It was a little before sunrise on a smoky, darkened world that, it seemed, would never see the sun again.

Rick hit the foot thrusters and brought the VT to an erratic, slewing landing. The canopy servos had gotten fried in one of those last blowups, so he yanked the rescue handgrip and blew the canopy off.

Rick and Lisa stood up in the cockpit and looked out at the mutilated landscape of Earth. It was as pockmarked as the moon, with deep cracks and crevasses. Smoke was rolling into the sky from dozens of impact points and from fires that stretched along the horizon. The air was hot, thick with soot and dust. There seemed to be volcanic activity along a chain of mountains to the west. A scorching wind was rising.

The most frightening thing was that there was no water to be seen anywhere.

There was a patch of open sky, but as they watched, the clouds rolled in, blotting out the stars. He wondered how the battle had turned out. From the looks of Earth, it probably didn't matter very much.

Lisa looked at him, pulling the windblown strands of long brown hair away from her face. "Thank you for getting me out of there, Rick." She could bear dying on the surface, in whatever form that death might take. But to endure her last moments among the charred and smoking remains of the base's dead—that would have been more than she could have borne. She extended her hand.

Rick took it with a grin. "Oh, c'mon. It gave me a chance to disobey your orders again, after all." They shook hands, and she let herself laugh just a little.

Lisa sat on the edge of the cockpit. "I'll always be grateful. I admire you a great deal, Rick."

That wasn't what she really wanted to tell him, but it was a start. It was much further along than Rick had gotten in saying what *he* was feeling at the moment. It occurred to him that a world that was a mass grave, very likely smoldering ash from pole to pole, was a strange place to profess love for somebody.

Or maybe not, he saw suddenly. Maybe it was the best epitaph anybody could ever hope to leave behind.

He had already yielded to the hard lesson that life wasn't worth much without it.

He almost said four or five different things, then shrugged, looking at his feet, and managed, "It was . . . it was a pleasure."

A ray of light made them turn. The rising sun had found a slit between clouds, to send long, slanting rays on the two people and their grounded machine. There was no sign of the stupendous battle.

"It looks like the fighting's stopped." She felt so peaceful, so tired of war, that she didn't even want to know the outcome.

"Um, yeah."

"I wonder if there's anyone else around?"

"Huh?"

She looked around to him. "What if we're the last? The only ones left?"

He looked at her for long seconds. "That wouldn't be that bad, would it?" he said softly. "At least neither of us will ever be alone."

"Rick . . ."

He had his mouth open to say something more, but there was a blast of static from the commo equipment as the automatic search gear brought up the sound on a signal it had located. There was a familiar voice singing a lilting, haunting hymn to Earth.

> We shall live the day we dream of winning,
> And beginning a new life!

"Minmei!" Lisa cried. She didn't know whether she could ever change her feelings toward the singer, but right now that voice was as welcome as—well, *almost* as welcome as the company Lisa was keeping.

"Up there!" Rick shouted, pointing. Something was descending on blue thruster flames hundreds of yards long, trailing sparkling particles behind it, weird energy anomalies from the interaction of barrier shield and reflex furnace obliteration.

Rick held Lisa to him. The dimensional fortress settled in toward the lake bed, the two flattops held level, elbows against its own midsection like Jimmy Cagney doing his patented move.

All it needs to do is throw a hitch in its shoulders and sing "Yankee Doodle Dandy"! Rick thought.

The enormous blasts of its engines kicked up dust, but the SDF-1 was landing with the rising sun directly at its back. They watched it sink down, silhouetted against the wavering fireball of the sun, until the land was waist high all around it.

Sunrise was throwing brighter light across the flattened terrain. "What a sight for sore eyes." Rick smiled, flicking switches on his instrument panel.

Lisa laughed outright, surprising herself. Was it right to be happy again so soon after so much carnage? But she couldn't help feeling joy, and she laughed again. "Oh, yes, *yes!*"

"This thing's still got a few miles left in it," Rick decided, studying the instruments. "Let's go."

"Okay!"

She settled back into his lap, and when he put his hand over the throttle, she covered it gently with her own, averting her eyes but leaving her hand there. He moved the throttle forward. Lisa's heart soared, feeling his hand beneath hers.

The Guardian jetted across the devastated landscape, into the sunrise, straight for the SDF-1 and the long shadow it threw. Lisa, her arms around Rick's neck, laid her head on his chest and watched a new future loom up before her.

PART II:

RECONSTRUCTION

BLUES

TWENTY-TWO

> *Why were the higher-ups so surprised that we rebuilt right away, and so quickly? Human feet can wear down a stone, human hands can grind down iron, human perseverance can overcome any adversity.*
>
> Mayor Tommy Luan, *The High Office*

UPON ITS INITIAL ARRIVAL, GLOVAL HAD THOUGHT of the SDF-1 as a kind of malign miracle, since it had kept humanity from destroying itself utterly in the Global Civil War.

There was another miraculous purpose it was to serve, to divert war away from Earth, fight off the Zentraedi, and ultimately break the invaders' power.

But there was a third role in this sequence of events that even Gloval hadn't guessed; indeed, he had unwittingly worked in opposition to it.

The SDF-1 was an ark, as well.

Even after the bombardments, the scorched-Earth attack that had very nearly come to a *no*-Earth situation, the boiling away of much of the planet's water—temporarily at least—into the atmosphere, pockets of humanity had survived. But what chance would they have to resume an advanced culture and technological base?

Very simply, none.

Take mining as an example. Most of the useful minerals that could be mined by primitive means were long since exhausted. The huddled groups of war-shocked people who survived the Zentraedi holocaust were unable to mount even steam-age mining efforts, much less the sophisticated operations it would take to get to the less accessible deposits still remaining in the planet. An unbelievably complex and interdependent world had simply passed away, and there was no means to rebuild it.

Terran technology had used up its one bolt, and there was no such thing as starting over from scratch, because the resources that had let Homo sapiens start from scratch had been consumed long before.

The human race was on its way to becoming a permanent, dead-end race of hunter-gatherers with no hope of ever being more again. History was about to close the books on a vaguely interesting little upstart species; events and the simple facts of life had gone against it.

Except there was the SDF-1, with Macross City inside.

There had been few hard words or unyielding attitudes once the great starship set down in the dry lakebed. Who do you get mad at when the world lies dying?

In their years of wandering and persevering, the residents of Macross City had put most delusions and wishful thinking behind them. They saw what had happened, and it came to them quickly that against any expectation, *they* had been the lucky ones. The castoffs and pariahs were actually the cargo of a new ark.

So in the end that was the fate of Macross City. What was left of it was disembarked, person by person, piece by piece, around the lakebed, and the rebuilding began.

The intellectuals and experts argued about the best ways to reestablish ecological balances and manage moisture reclamation; the people of Macross rebuilt their homes and businesses and lives as best they could, trusting that such things were more important than all the computer projections.

The ship's engines provided power. Its mecha and military people enforced law and order in an ever-growing domain of security. The SDF-1's fabricators and other technical equipment quickly provided a new industrial base, and the population of Macross constituted an urban economic hub.

In the time after that last Armageddon, the SDF-1's name might better have been that of one of its constituent flattops, *Prometheus*. It was humanity's main source of medical care, technical resources, and most importantly, the accumulated knowledge and wisdom of the species *Homo sapiens*.

The nuclear winter scenario was much less severe than the computers had guessed. That was partly because the predictions had been based on faulty models. It was also because the RDF and civilian corps worked around the clock to make it so.

And they had allies. The explosion of Dolza's base had disabled or taken with it his entire Grand Fleet, but a considerable part of Breetai's armada had survived. Many Zentraedi had chosen to go to Earth and take up a life there either in Micronian size or in their own original bodies.

Both races hoped for a new golden age or at least a lasting silver one.

It was a world seared and barren, pockmarked with craters and split with fissures made by war. Everywhere were the rusting mecha of the last great battle. Most of the disabled Zentraedi ships had, for unknown reasons, oriented on the nearest center of gravity—Earth—and driven toward it.

The result was that the planet's surface was an eerie Robotech Boot Hill dotted with crumpled alien warships that had driven themselves partway into the ground like spikes. The reminders of that last day were everywhere, too many to ever dismantle or bury. Only time and the elements would remove the grave markers, and they would not do so in the life span of anyone then living.

But those who were left alive went on a new crusade, the one to heal the planet and put things right again.

Two years passed.

Rick Hunter's VT, in Guardian mode, complained at the strain he put on it in the tight bank. He gritted his teeth but held to it. The old ship, battered as it was, had never failed him yet. With replacement parts and maintenance time in such woefully short supply, the Skull

Leader's craft wasn't in the shape it had been in during the war, but he trusted it.

The Guardian jetted in low over the rust-red, pitted countryside and foot-thrustered to a deft landing. It bowed, nose nearly touching the ground; he jumped from the cockpit eagerly, hardly able to credit what was happening to him.

"I don't believe it! It's impossible!"

He ran across the gritty, fallow soil, back toward what he had spotted. All around were gigantic, jagged shreds and peels of Zentraedi armorplate, twisted and mangled, slowly turning to rust and dust. Off to one side was an overturned Guardian wreck that looked like it had been put through a meat grinder. Its rusting legs stuck straight up into the air like a dead hawk's.

Rick skidded to a halt, the wind moaning around him. He looked down and was astounded.

At his feet, springing from a moist plot of earth somehow enriched enough to sustain it, was a field of dandelions. The irregularly shaped, few-square-yards patch of them was sheltered from the wind by the wreckage and yet, by chance, had good exposure to sunlight.

For a moment he couldn't find words. "Absolutely incredible," he murmured, but that was insufficient. Here, near yet another Zentraedi wreck, the soil had been fortified with something that would support life. He suspected that he knew what that something had been, and it suddenly made him feel very mortal and humble.

"Real flowers!" He knelt, handling them as gently as a lover, inhaling.

Certainly there were flowers in the greenhouses and protected fields of the reclamation projects, but this! It was a thing as wonderful as flight—no, *more* wonderful! Life itself!

He couldn't recall how many times, as a child, he'd raced across a field of these unglamorous flowers, eyes fixed on the blue sky, wishing only to fly. And now things had come full circle; he flew the most advanced aircraft ever known with his eyes trained on the ground, waiting and hoping for just such a sight as . . . dandelions.

I hope this means the Earth is forgiving us, he meditated.

It was a good and precious thing to know that at least one positive sign, however small, had shown itself. There were other omens that were not so good. Rick was privy to a lot of high-level information thanks to his experiences among the Zentraedi and his value as an intelligence source.

There were things he tried not to think about, and three of them had disturbing names: Protoculture. Robotech Masters. Invid.

Three VTs swooped in low over the desolate land, forming up again after completing their aerial recons of assigned sectors. They were newer ships than Rick's, but they looked somehow less sleek and finished. There were those who said the true high-water mark of Robotech workmanship had passed.

"Commander Hunter, come in, please," said Rick's new second in command, Lieutenant Ransom. "This is Skull Four calling Skull Six."

No answer, after five minutes' trying. Ransom thought for a moment. "Bobby?"

Sergeant Bobby Bell, youngest of the remanned Skull Team, appeared on Ransom's display screen. "Yo?"

"I can't raise the boss, kid."

Bobby's round face looked pained. "What d' you think? Renegades?"

That was one of the big reasons for the patrols. Of the many Zentraedi who had gone forth among the humans to try a more peaceful way of life and a chance to open up the more feeling and compassionate side of their nature, some had found that it simply wouldn't work.

The renegades had begun slipping away into the wastelands more than a year before. There was an entire world of salvage for them out there: mecha, weapons, rations, and anything else they might need, provided they could find the right wreck. More importantly, there was the freedom to act as Zentraedi warriors once again, to follow their own brutal, merciless code.

"I think his last transmission came from his search quadrant," Bobby said worriedly.

"I know," Ransom said. "I got a DF fix on it. Let's go."

The VTs formed up, and their engines made the ground tremble. They shot away to the northwest.

The SDF-1 stood like a knight in a bath up to his waist. The two supercarriers floated at anchor, giving the corroding derelict added buoyancy.

Refilling the lake had been a major priority, since not even the fortress's colossal strength could support itself and the two giant warships for long. At the same time that RDF fliers were seeding clouds and Dr. Lang's mysterious machines were working day and night to head off the nuclear winter, combat engineers and anybody else who could be found to lend a hand worked feverishly to make sure the drainage would be ready.

And just over forty-eight hours after the ship's landing, the rains had begun. They gave back some of the moisture boiled away by the Zentraedi attack, but Lang's calculations, supported by subsequent data, showed that much of it was gone forever. Short of importing many cubic miles of water across space from some as yet unknown source, the Earth would never again be the three-quarters-ocean world she had been when she brought forth life.

In time, the rains stopped, and the generations-long job of replanting and refoliating the planet began.

Around the lake the new Macross rose, the stubborn refugees rebuilding their lives yet again. It was the only new population center on the planet so far, the only place where the concrete was uncracked and the buildings tall and straight. There was fresh paint, and there were trees transplanted from the starship. There were lawns and flower beds seeded from plants that had survived the billions of miles of the SDF-1's odyssey.

It was a city where energy and resources were used with utmost efficiency, a town of solar heaters and photovoltaic panels, with a recycling system tied to every phase of life. The Macross residents and SDF-1 personnel had learned the tough lessons of ecological necessity during years in space, and nothing at all was wasted.

That was the sort of world it was going to have to be from now on.

In a neat, quiet suburb of the city served by an overhead rapid-transit system sat a modest little prefab cottage, its solar panels, guided by microprocessors, swinging slowly to follow the sun. As a senior flight officer, Rick Hunter rated off-base housing even though he was single, and liked the idea of getting away from the military when he could, even if his home looked like modular luggage. As Skull Leader, he seldom got a chance to be there.

So Lisa Hayes took it upon herself to tidy up the place when he was away. Her own rather more spacious quarters were nearby.

Neither of them was quite sure what the bond between them meant or where their companionship was going, but she had a key to his place, and he to hers.

Now she hummed happily to herself as she put away the last of the just-washed dishes. *Maybe I ought to bill him for maid services*, she thought wryly.

But she knew better; she enjoyed being in his place, touching the things he touched, seeing reminders of him all around. She hoped that the extended patrol up north didn't last too much longer—that he would be home soon so that they could be together again.

Lisa considered the sunlight streaming through the kitchen window. Polarizing glass was all well and good, but curtains were what that window needed.

Will you listen to me? Curtains! Miss Suzy Homemaker! She smirked at the apron she was wearing. It was doubly funny because she was due back at the base soon for more meetings and briefings on the final construction details of the SDF-2, the new successor to the battle fortress.

And she meant to have a berth on that ship, to be the First Officer if she could, and go to the stars. Ol' Suzy Homemaker herself.

She snorted a laugh as she moved into the bedroom. Seeing it, she sighed. *Why does this place always look like a bear's been wintering here?*

She raised all the blinds, opened all the windows, and

moved around the room slowly, fondly. When she smoothed the sheets to make up the bed, her hands lingered upon them, and she touched the pillows tenderly, remembering his head on them, and her own.

Her wrist chrono toned, reminding her she had to go soon. When she straightened, her eye fell on something she hadn't seen before.

It lay on his desk, next to his spare flight helmet: a photo album bound in creamy imitation leather. Lisa moved toward it unwillingly, knowing she shouldn't do what she was about to do but unable to stop herself.

The album was well worn, had obviously been leafed through many times. The first page made her heart sink. There was a snapshot of Minmei seated on a park swing back in the Macross within the SDF-1, Rick standing behind her. The other picture was a close-up taken of Minmei back at the start of her career, a wide-eyed gamine with flowing black locks framing her face.

Lisa sighed again. *What does he see in her? What's she got except great looks, the singing voice that won the war, and superstardom?*

It was Minmei on every page, glamour poses and home snapshots, portfolio glossies and PR photos. Lisa got angrier and angrier as she thumbed through them.

Why do I have the impulse to strangle this girl?

Along with the anger came a pain so sharp and cold, it took her off guard. Lisa had assumed she and Rick were solidifying something, strengthening the ties between them. But the thought of his keeping this album, taking it out when Lisa wasn't there and fantasizing over it—that was too much to bear.

Having his companionship and friendship without his declared love was something she had accepted, albeit always with a secret hope. But the photo album made her feel she had been taken for granted, a kind of emotional consolation prize. Her self-respect simply wouldn't allow that.

Lisa slammed the album shut, tore off the apron, and strode for the front door. As the door rolled shut to lock, she tossed Rick's spare house key onto the living-room rug, leaving it behind.

We won? When you hear some military moron say that to you, spit on him! Point out the graveyard that is Earth! When he tells you how the military's going to make all that well again too, hold up the ash that used to be your home.

They won, all right, and they'd just love to win again. And every time, it's you and I who lose.

From Lynn-Kyle's tract, *Mark of Cain*

RICK HUNTER SAT IN THE COCKPIT OF THE grounded Guardian and watched white spores take to the wind like miniature parasols. Meanwhile, he wrestled with his thoughts.

The truth was that Earth was a dead end for a pilot. Oh, there was the problem of the rebellious Zentraedi, to be sure, and the various fractious human communities. But the war was over, and there were no flying circuses. Maybe it would be easier to put up with the growing boredom of peacetime life if bigger things weren't brewing out beyond Earth's atmosphere.

Breetai and Exedore seemed to be at the source of it, and Gloval, Dr. Lang, and Dr. Zand. Only everything was so secret that a mere squadron commander couldn't find out a thing. Even Lisa professed not to know anything. But scuttlebutt and the few hints Rick could get from his intel debriefings made him believe that the SDF-2 was slated for a big, big mission.

He was pretty sure that the SDF-2, and such Zentraedi warships as Breetai could get fully functional again, were going to carry the war to the Robotech Masters. Humans and Zentraedi would go out and end the threat forever or die trying.

How could he *not* go? Only . . . that was a voyage and a military operation that might make their previous campaign look like a weekend vacation by comparison. It would probably mean he would never see Earth and Minmei again.

Not that he'd seen much of Minmei in the last two years, but signing on for a trip to far-off star systems would strip away any hope.

But what else was there for him except flying? He wished and prayed that there could be Minmei, but Minmei was so bound up in her glittering career that he rarely saw or heard from her. On the SDF-2 mission, at least he would be with Lisa, and he was becoming more and more convinced that that was where he belonged.

Of course, the odds against surviving would be very high, but that was a combat pilot's lot. And what better cause was there to serve, and die for, if it came to that? He had a sudden vivid recollection of something Roy Fokker had told him.

An American president once said that the price of liberty is eternal vigilance, Rick.

It was on a "day" in SDF-1, out someplace by Pluto's orbit, when Rick joined the RDF. *There's no more flying for fun*, Roy told him, stern and grave. *From now on you fly for the sake of your home and loved ones, Rick.*

"My home and loved ones, huh?" Rick muttered to himself. He flicked a switch, and the canopy descended on whining servos.

"All right; time to go flying, then." He eased the throttle forward. The Guardian's foot thrusters blew soil away and lifted it. Rick was careful to skirt the patch of dandelions as he rose. But the backwash sent hundreds of thousands of spores wafting into the air in hopes of finding some other kind plot of ground.

Rick tucked a single dandelion blossom into a seam of his instrument panel, mechamorphosed his ship to Fighter mode, and went ballistic, climbing toward the sun. He set the commo rig to search for local traffic, part

of the recon mission. The equipment scanned the band
and stopped at a transmission that carried a female
human voice.

> —here by my side,
> Here by my side.

He jolted against his safety harness, reaching to get a
stronger signal. "Minmei!"

There was applause in the background. Another voice
he knew well came up. "You're listening to the beautiful
Lynn-Minmei, broadcasting live and direct from Granite
City! This area is slowly rebuilding through the combined efforts of many wonderful people who are cease-
lessly devoting their time and labor to a project that
many considered hopeless."

Lynn-Kyle. He sounded more like a pitchman than a
costar now, but he still had that same hostility in his
tone.

Granite! Rick realized. *Not far away!* He was already
checking his nav computers.

"People Helping People is the theme of our tour,"
Kyle went on. "And we don't consider the project hopeless at all! How do *you* people feel about it?"

Clapclapclapclap, from the audience, and a few yays.
Those shill questions always worked. Rick's expression
hardened, and he brought his stick over for a bank.

Granite City lay in the shadow of a Zentraedi flagship
rammed like a Jovian bolt into the red dirt. The outskirts
of the place were still haphazard rubble from the war,
but a few square blocks in the center had been made
livable.

There were weakened foundations and angled slabs of
paving and fractured concrete everywhere, but at least
the streets were clear.

This most recent stop in what was to have been the
triumphant Minmei People Helping People tour had attracted something under three hundred people in Granite, plus several Zentraedi who loomed over the crowd
even when sitting and squatting.

The crowd was composed of sad-eyed people doing

their best to believe they had a future. Most were ragged, all were thin, and there were signs of deficiency diseases and other medical problems among them.

But at the urging of Lynn-Kyle and others in the loose-knit network of antigovernmentalists, Granite persisted in refusing to drop its status as an independent city-state or allow military relief teams in.

The Zentraedi were in better shape than the humans; the rations in the spiked ship could sustain them, though for some reason those seemed to have no nutritive value for *Homo sapiens*. There had been a fine cordiality and hopefulness among the people of Granite at first, but now there was growing despair in this dissident model program. Thus, this morale appearance by Minmei.

"Yeah! Let's hear it!" Lynn-Kyle yelled, working the mike at center stage, making beckoning motions with his free hand. The crowd clapped again, a little tiredly.

"And Granite doesn't need any outside interference, either!" he yelled. He had spent fewer than four hours there in his entire life.

"The good people here will take care of themselves and make Granite the great metropolis she once was!"

The applause was even weaker this time around, and the more theatrically knowledgeable in the front rows could detect beads of flop-sweat on Kyle's brow.

"But let's forget, for now, what the military warmongers have brought us to," he said, almost scowling, then catching himself and flashing a bright smile. "As we listen to the song stylings of the marvelous, the incomparable Lynn-Minmei!"

Recorded music came up, and Minmei hit her mark right on cue, mike in hand. She sang her latest hit.

I've made the right move at the right time!
We're on our way to something new!
Just point the way and I will follow!
Love feels so beautiful with you!

Rick followed the song, entranced, until a transmission cut through Minmei's singing. "Commander Hunter, come in, please."

It was Ransom. Rick switched to the tac net. "What is it?"

"You all right, skipper? I've been trying to reach you for some time; thought you might've run into trouble."

Rick let a little impatience slip into his tone. "Is anything wrong?"

Ransom looked at him out of a display screen next to the yellow dandelion, speaking precisely. "Nothing specific, boss. Just wish you'd take your rover radio with you when you leave your ship to look around. I worry, y' know?"

Rick bit back the rebuke he had been putting together. Of course he knew; he would have chewed out a subordinate for doing the same.

He sounded contrite, and it was real. "Sorry, Lieutenant. But I came across something miraculous today."

Ransom stared. "Trouble with renegade Zentraedi? Boss, what is it?"

Rick took the dandelion from its place and held it close to the optical pickup. "Look what I found. An entire field of them."

Ransom considered the flower. "Wait a minute. Your zone wasn't inside the natural recovery planning zone."

Rick was ecstatic. "That's right! But lemme tell ya, there are flowers in the northwest quadrant!"

The usually morbid Ransom cracked a very slight smile. "I suppose we should have known the Earth would be starting her own recovery program. Great news, huh, skipper?"

"Roger that. Look, continue your patrol according to mission plan, Ted."

"I copy, but aren't you coming with us?"

"Not right now," Rick answered. "I'm dropping over to Granite City. If anything serious comes up, give me a yell."

Ransom nodded and hedged. "And, uh, boss . . ."

"Don't sweat it, Lieutenant! When I leave the ship, I'll take my rover! Out!"

Rick did a barrel roll for the hell of it and opened his throttle wide for Granite City.

> If she wonders,
> It's you who's on my mind.
> It's you I cannot
> Leave behind . . .

Rick followed Minmei's voice as someone else might have trod a yellow brick road. From overhead the Zentraedi battlewagon dominated the landscape, but a closer look at the ground showed that the rusting metal peak was a monument to defeat and that the teeming victors were still in turmoil.

Rick left his VT at the edge of town under the care of the local militia CO, who was well disposed toward RDF fliers even if the populace wasn't. Rick got to the concert and missed, by a fraction of a second, getting flattened by the hand of a Zentraedi leviathan who was sitting at the edge of the crowd, shifting his weight.

"I'm so sorry," the alien tried to whisper in his resounding bass. Everybody around them went *Shhhh!* Rick gave the big fellow a nod to let him know it was no offense taken.

> It's me who's lost,
> The me who lost your heart
> The you who tore my heart
> Apart . . .

She's come a long way, but it's the same girl I spent those awful, wonderful two weeks with somewhere in the belly of the SDF-1. My Minmei.

When the song was over, the crowd applauded. Rick applauded loudest of all.

Near a sidewalk café in Monument City, with the SDF-1's shadow coming her way like a sundial, Lisa stared dully at people passing by and ignored her cooling demitasse. The meetings had been delayed, giving her some unexpected free time. Idle hours were more a curse than a blessing.

As she watched, two down-at-the-heels *boulevardiers* ogled a very pert young blonde whose hemline came nearly to her waist. The two did not quite slobber.

"My man, the women were dealt all the aces in this life. They can have anything they want," opined one, a beefy kid who looked as if he stood a fair chance of growing up to be normal. "They can have anybody they wanna have."

Lisa considered that, her chin resting on her interlaced fingers. "That's all you know about it, my fat friend," she murmured, watching the two would-be rakes go on their way. "Here's *one* woman who'd trade every other ace, knave, and king in the deck for one Rick Hunter."

She drew a sudden breath as she looked across Momument City's main thoroughfare. Max Sterling strolled along there, looking as if he didn't have a care in the world, pushing a baby carriage. Miriya held his arm.

They stopped, and Max hurried around the carriage to scoop up his daughter and pat her back, burping her on his shoulder. Miriya looked on serenely with a smile Lisa almost begrudged her.

The very most secret eyes-only reports boiled down to the fact that nobody could quite figure out how Max and Miriya had had Dana, their baby girl. But as proved by exhaustive tests, the child was indisputably theirs.

No Zentraedi male-female reproduction had ever been recorded, making the whole thing that much more extraordinary. The likelier explanations had to do with Miriya's consumption of human-style food as opposed to the antiseptic rations of the Zentraedi and her exposure to emotions that had worked subtle biochemical changes on her. The word "Protoculture" cropped up again and again in the reports, only nobody seemed to understand quite what it was, at least nobody outside the charmed, secretive circle of Lang, Exedore, and a few others.

Like a lot of women and quite a few men, Lisa sometimes thought all that was a crock. Miriya and Max were in love, and so: little Dana.

She looked at the three of them, and for a moment Max wore Rick's face, and Miriya wore Lisa's. The SDF-2 would soon be ready for space trials, but that didn't mean the First Officer couldn't have a family. The starship had been built for a long voyage, for children as well as men and women.

Max and Miriya and their baby resumed their way, and Lisa watched them go. *They look so happy. If only I could make Rick understand!*

Just then, though, two RDF boot trainees wandered up to the café with a street-blaster stereo. The well-remembered voice boomed,

> And the thrill that I feel
> Is really unreal.

"Hew! That little mama sure can sing," the first one said, whistling. "I'd give a month's pay to meet her."

The other blew his breath out sarcastically as the pair sat down a few tables away. "Sure, buddy. Then she takes you away and signs over the deed to her diamond mine to you, right?"

The first one made a very sour face and signaled the waitress. On the eardrum agitator, Minmei sang,

> I can't believe I've come this far.
> This is my chance to be a star!

There doesn't seem to be any way I can avoid you, Minmei!

Lisa collected her purse and left her money on the salver, then rose and headed off down the boulevard.

She was so caught up in her own thoughts, regrets, and preoccupations that she didn't realize—had never realized—how many admiring glances she drew. She was a willowy, athletic young woman with brown hair billowing behind her, a delicate complexion, and a distant look in her eyes. Her insignia and decorations were enough to make any vet, male or female, take notice of her.

If there were an artistic competition for the concept *WINNER*, a simple photo of Lisa at that moment would have won it. Women in particular looked at her, her sure stride and air of confidence, and made various resolutions to be more like this self-confident superwoman, whoever she was.

But that wasn't the way it felt to Lisa. She allowed

herself a rueful half smile. *I guess when the aces were
dealt out, it just wasn't in the cards for me to get the one
I want.*

It was near enough to a joke to make her smile cheer-
lessly. She quickened her pace, off to report to the
SDF-2.

TWENTY-FOUR

I've seen people like Lynn-Kyle before. I'm prepared to believe that he hates war; who among us does not?

But he has the attitude, set in concrete, that virtue is measured by one's disaffection from the power structure under which one lives. Such a person builds a fortress of self-serving piety, resisting authority of any kind at every turn whether for good or ill.

The RDF will continue to defend to the death the freedoms that make this possible.

From the log of Captain Henry Gloval

"**W**HAT A CRUMMY *HOLE!*"

Lynn-Kyle threw his arms wide to take in Granite City, off to one side, and the wastelands all around it.

Minmei sat despondently on a piece of rotting Zentraedi alloy, hugging her knees to her chest, a pink jacket draped over her shoulders against the evening chill, watching him take another slug from the bottle of brandy that seemed to be his constant companion these days.

Things had gone steadily downhill since Vance Hasslewood had moved up in the world to become a booking agent and aspiring theater maven, leaving Minmei's cousin, costar, and lover to take over the duties of manager. Lynn-Kyle's interests went far beyond show business, and he had come to realize that his own fame and popularity were only a pale reflection of hers.

Now he paused. "Lousiest booking so far!" Then he threw back another several ounces, making her wince.

Kyle wiped his mouth on the back of his hand, staining the purple cuff of his suit. "Let's get out of this burg! It's disgusting!"

He was red-eyed and close to the edge, but she said

what was on her mind anyway; she had held it back long enough. "Do you have to drink so much?"

"Listen, don't change the subject!" he slurred. "We didn't even get any money! *This* is our whole paycheck!"

He toed over a wilted cardboard box; out spilled some canned goods, bath soap and so forth, a few vegetables —the same dole everyone else in Granite City was living on. Even though Granite refused to recognize the new Earth government's authority, the government gave what help it could; without it, the city couldn't have kept functioning.

"A stinkin' handout from our military overlords!"

"And what else do we need for survival?" she asked him, watching his eyes. Two years with Kyle had made her older, much older.

"Have you given any thought to taking in a little cash for a change?" he snarled.

She came to her feet, the jacket clutched to her. "No, I haven't!"

If it was going to be another argument, she decided, this time she was going to get a few things off her mind. "This was supposed to be a benefit concert for those poor people who're trying to make their lives work in Granite, not some big-deal career move for Lynn-Minmei!"

She had him, and they both knew it. All at once his ranting sounded like empty talk. He was suddenly contrite. "Aw, c'mon, Minmei. You know I didn't mean anything like that." It was not quite a whine, but somehow it only made her detest him more.

She knelt and began picking up the things he had spilled, brushing dirt from them. "We're getting paid like everyone else is, in the things that keep us alive. I think we should show a little appreciation."

That made him cough on the mouthful of brandy he was chugging. He almost finished the bottle, and his mood swung end for end, as quick as his martial-arts moves used to be.

"Appreciation? I should appreciate the great military mentality that brought us to *this*?" He opened his arms as if to embrace the blighted world.

She straightened and met his stare. "Earth was attacked, and it fought back. I don't want to hear anybody knocking the military. If it hadn't been for them, I wouldn't be alive right now. And for that matter, neither would you."

So, we come to the core of the matter, he thought blearily.

That moment on the SDF-1, with a planet dying at his feet and great fleets slaying one another while he kissed her, was two years behind him. And yet it played over and over in memory, as fresh as if it had happened that afternoon.

The secret that glowed in him like a reflex furnace, the one Kyle would never be able to bring himself to admit to her or even put into words to himself, was that he had exulted in that moment even as he had been repulsed by it.

He had loved it! He had been taken by the drama completely, swept up in the battle. He had cast aside every conviction he ever had and gloried in what was happening. He had hoped with all his soul for human victory.

His father had been a soldier; both family restaurants had catered to the military trade. Lynn-Kyle scorned all of that, scorned military and government and authority in every form. And yet when it had come down to a question of seeing his planet and people die, he had been out there rooting for the home team, as red of fang and claw, as contemptible, as any of them.

He had never lost a fight since his father had pummeled and shamed him into learning the martial arts. Indeed, he'd become a very genius of unarmed combat. But this contest with himself was one he felt fated to lose. As he hated himself, so he had come to make Minmei hate him.

He had seen that the military, with the SDF-1 and Macross as a power base and Breetai and his Zentraedi as allies, was destined to be the force that reunited the planet. Nevertheless, he resisted it every inch of the way, going deeper and deeper into despair as the vast egalitarian movement he had envisioned dwindled away to a few pitiful holdouts.

So if this was going to be the argument that had been

building between Minmei and Kyle for so long, let it be so. He turned his face to an ugly mask with an elaborate sneer. "You're breaking my heart." He swallowed the last of the brandy.

You're breaking my heart.

Twenty yards away, behind a broken piece of cornice at the top of a rise, Rick Hunter squatted with his back against cold stone and listened to Minmei and Kyle.

He sat still as a rock or one of the pieces of dead mecha that now littered the world.

"*Must* you keep drinking?" Minmei said. "It's getting out of hand!"

Kyle upended the bottle and let the last few droplets fall on soil that hadn't tasted moisture in two years. Then he tossed it high, launched himself through the air in a reverse spin kick, a *ki-yi* yell coming from deep within him, turning twice, and popped the little brandy bottle out of existence like a trap shooter.

Pieces of dark glass landed at Minmei's feet. She watched Kyle steadily. "Did that make you feel any better about yourself?"

How can she wound me so easily with just a word or two? he wondered in confusion.

His mood swung again, and there was an endless affection in him for her. She was, after all, the sum of his life. All he had ever really accomplished, Lynn-Kyle saw now, was getting Minmei to love him.

But Minmei's mood was riding a different swing. "Whatever you think of the RDF, there are a lot of fine men and women in it," she said levelly. "Much better people than you are right now."

A moment that might have been a reconciliation and a new start was gone forever. Kyle ran the back of his hand across his mouth again. *All right; we might as well have it all out.*

"What's that crack supposed to mean?"

Minmei was actually shaking a *fist* at him. "It means they're trying to rebuild Earth, while all you can do is drink and feel sorry for yourself!"

"Is that so? Well, I've done a pretty good job of takin' care of your career, little Miss Superstar!"

She had been loud a moment before; her voice was quiet now. "Maybe we'd better split up then, Kyle. So you can look after your own career." She gathered her pink jacket around her.

She had been hurt until her endurance was all gone, and now she only wanted to hurt in retaliation. "I didn't realize I owed it all to *you*, Kyle."

He had his hands out in fending-off gestures. "Wait, wait. I didn't mean—didn't mean I wanted to split up our partnership." "Partnership" was a weak word for what they'd had, but somehow the vocabulary of love was steamrollered by the vocabulary of argument. He felt something slipping away even as he made the choice of words.

She drew a long, deep breath, looking him in the eye. "Maybe not, but it's what *I* meant."

The compass of Lynn-Kyle's emotions swung a last time, and his mouth resolved into a straight, thin line. "Okay, go! Who needs you?" He kicked the empty carton high into the air.

Rick Hunter didn't know exactly what to feel. The fact that Kyle had alienated Minmei might have been enjoyable from a distance, but it was harrowing to see at close range.

And then there was the whole question of going out and intervening. Rick had no illusions about being able to take the tall, cobra-fast martial-arts expert hand to hand, and he had forgotten to bring along the survival pistol from his VT's ejection pack.

Suddenly the rover radio buzzed in its thigh pouch. "Commander Hunter, come in please!" It was Vanessa's voice, sending from the rusting, soggy-footed SDF-1.

He had turned the volume down low when he came out to the edge of the wastelands, following leads to find Minmei. Now he held the rover up to his ear. Minmei and Kyle didn't seem to have heard a thing.

He thumbed the transmit switch. "I'm here."

"Sir, you're directed to lead your flight to New Portland. A residential district is under attack by several Zentraedi malcontents."

"Malcontents." That was what the new world government was calling them so far. But those who had sworn the Zentraedi warrior oath and turned their back on human society were a lot more than malcontents. They had only to walk out into the wasteland and keep going, find the right wrecked ship. If they were lucky, they would find arms, mecha, rations, water, and shelter.

Rick poised for a moment in a pain so precise that it defied any random theory of the universe. Most of what he had come to believe in impelled him to get to New Portland with all possible speed.

Everything else told him to stay there, because this was the moment he could win Minmei back.

But he thumbed the rover's transmit button again. "What weapons?"

"Three battlesuits and four pods, a total of seven," Vanessa's voice came back. That wasn't exactly several, the way Rick saw it, but he had to admit that things probably looked a little different from a worldwide coordinating nerve center like the SDF-1.

These were Zentraedi who had defected to the human side in the Robotech War. They were onetime allies. He held the rover's voice pickup close and said softly, "It'll be taken care of. What's the status on Skull flight? Over."

"They are curtailing their current sweep and will rendezvous with you in New Portland. Out."

He shut off the rover before the sound of static could betray him. He raced off toward his ship. It was a kind of liberation to have some crisis so pressing that he could forget about Minmei for a while. He left the two Lynns to their own devices, and somehow he couldn't help wishing them the worst.

As his VT took off in Guardian mode, Rick saw the tiny, distant figure of Kyle go down on both knees before Minmei. She turned and opened her arms, cradling his head to her breast. Rick hit the throttle, and his VT left a trail of blue fire across the sky.

* * *

Lisa stared up through her window at the rotting hulk of the SDF-1. Beneath it was a thriving, growing city, but its presence put everyone in mind of the war.

"Hmmph! What a view!" As a morale builder, she was wearing a tight blouse with a high, upturned collar. Every once in a while she permitted herself to catch a glimpse of herself in a full-length mirror there in her quarters and admit, *not bad*!

The SDF-1 wasn't bad to look at either, really. The more so because the SDF-2 would be lowered into place, back to back with it, in another day or so. Lang and his disciples had worked out some way to move the sealed enigmatic engines from one to the other. Lisa had heard the briefings, could sort of understand the mathematics Lang scrawled all over every flat surface that came to hand, and had faith in him, but she still thought her new assignment was an unknown quantity.

The comset birred for her attention. She picked up the handset. In seconds she had word of the New Portland raid from Vanessa and was hurrying for the door.

Sunset had come, and a freezing rain, as the Zentraedi ransacked New Portland. They had cut a swath of destruction from the diminished Lake Oswego to the once-great Columbia River.

The pods fired and devastated without mercy. Local militia and police were victims just like the civilians; in the first hours of their rampage, the alien malcontents slew over four hundred men and women of assorted constabularies, police departments, and guard units.

They set buildings afire with a mere brush of their plastron cannon; they trod houses and people flat underneath their pods' huge, hooflike feet.

Now they loomed, three abreast, in the center of New Portland as black smoke roiled around them and the screams of the dying echoed through the rain-washed streets. Blood ran in the gutters.

Down from the night swooped the VTs of Skull Team under Ransom's command. Robotechnology made them all-weather fighters, as dangerous in blackness as they were in light.

"Nobody fires unless they have a confirmed target; there're civilians down there," Ransom said.

Just then New Portland came into view, burning like a skillet of molten metal, smoke funneling up from it to form thickening layers that threw back red light.

Bobby Bell began, "My God! This is horrible—"

"Shut up, Sergeant," Ransom cut him off. "All VTs form up on me. Let's get down there and stop this thing. *And watch your fire!*"

Jeanette LeClair and her best friend, Sonya Poulson, ran through the rain-slick streets of New Portland hand in hand, shivering in the frigid rain, crying for the loved ones who had died, pulses hammering because death was at their heels. Jeanette's birthday a month before had made her eight years old; Sonya's, four days later, had brought them even.

Behind them, a Zentraedi Battlepod stumped around the corner, kicking a traffic light through a brick wall and snapping power lines, then turned its guns on them.

Jeanette fell, and Sonya wanted to keep running but found that she couldn't. She dashed back to her friend, trying to help her up, but she fell instead, and the two of them sprawled on the rain-washed cobblestone street as a huge round metal hoof came down at them. They wept, held each other close, and waited to die.

The pod paused in the act of trampling yet more victims. The armored, lightbulb-shaped torso turned, as if listening to something. Jeanette and Sonya could hardly know that it was receiving an urgent message from one of its fellows.

"Warning! Warning! Enemy fightercraft approaching! Form up to take defensive action!"

The two little girls looked up at the ridges and features of the huge hoof and realized it was pulling away. In moments, the pod had turned and grasshoppered off for some destination they couldn't even guess at, riding its foot thrusters.

Moments later, thunder came down through the sky as Skull Team VTs arrived at full throttle. The two girls helped each other up. Buildings shook and windows

broke to the sonic boom as the RDF fighters swept in
vengefully.

The girls' voices were very small in the middle of all
that, but they cheered nonetheless.

The pods chose straightforward battle, charging out in
a group, firing the primary and secondary cannon
mounted on their armored chest plastrons.

That suited Skull Team just fine; they flew down
through the intense ground fire in Guardian mode, like
eagles for the kill, gripping their chain-guns.

"Let's hit 'em," Ransom said.

"Sure, but we've gotta lead 'em away from the city!"
Bobby Bell yelled.

He was right, and the formation split even while it
exchanged fire with the rampaging pods. The Guardians
turned back, and the pods, firing with every gun, rock-
eted and kangaroo-hopped after.

CHAPTER TWENTY-FIVE

*For the Zentraedi, peaceful life and a disengagement
from their warlike culture was, after all, a profound struggle,
a sort of sublimating battle into which they could hurl themselves. For a time they were content with it, as they were
content with any other conflict.*

*Is it any wonder, though, that with the battle won, so
many of them began to fall prey to a frustrated restlessness?
The fight for peace can be a noble one, but as history and
legend tell us, the warrior-born should beware the disaster of
total victory.*

And so should those about him.

Zeitgeist, *Alien Psychology*

IN THE FOOTHILLS AT THE OUTSKIRTS OF NEW PORT-
land, the VTs stopped running and the mecha clashed in
earnest.

Almost by instinct, the pods came abreast to set up a
firing line. The Guardians dove at them, and the blue-
white lances of energy beams jousted against streams of
high-density slugs lit by tracers.

A concentrated salvo of alien cannon fire took off the
left arm of Ransom's Guardian. "These dudes really
wanna fight," he said grimly. He looped, trying to manage the damage, and unleashed a spread of Stilettos at
them.

*No more tromping on little girls, bozos! Let's see you
pick on somebody your own size!*

"This could be defined as dereliction of duty, Commander," Lisa's voice said in Rick's ear.

"What're you talking about?"

"Where were you?" she said icily.

"Uh, on recon." Guilt made him snappish. "It's within mission guidelines. Why, any objections?"

Back in the command center, she looked down at the latest satnet locater profiles of military aircraft. He had been grounded at the edge of Granite City. No surprise.

"I object when you jeopardize the lives of the men under your command, Hunter."

He couldn't help it; the accumulated experiences of the day just made him lose control as no cool, competent combat flier is supposed to. *"What's your goddamn problem, Lisa?"*

"Your men are in combat, and you're supposed to be leading them, you unutterable moron!" she yelled into the mike, then snapped it off.

Well, there. They had had a grand argument over a command commo net about everything except what was really driving them apart. What satisfaction.

She stalked away from the commo console. "Oh, that man."

"Take cover, take cover," chanted Vanessa in a whisper to the rest of the Terrible Trio.

"I wonder what Commander Hunter did to cause the blowup this time." Sammie blinked.

"Whatever it was, it looks like he'll be on a steady diet of cold shoulder when he gets back," Vanessa replied.

Kim took off her headset and turned to them. "I dunno; d' you think she really loves him?"

"D' you mean to say you haven't heard the latest gossip?" Sammie almost squirmed in her eagerness to tell it. "They say she cleans his quarters. Yeah, yeah, *cleans*! While he's away on patrol. And he doesn't even take her out or anything."

The Terrible Trio thought poisonous thoughts about the male gender.

Kim fanned herself gently with her hand. "It's hard to believe Lisa would get herself roped into something like that. She's too smart!"

Sammie caught her arm. "But wait; that isn't all!"

"*Ixnay*," Kim murmured, turning a sidelong glance. "We're being watched."

"Uh-oh." Sammie hastened to put her earphones back on.

Lisa looked at them resignedly. *Go ahead, girls; I don't blame you. I guess it is funny.*

The pod's cannon hosed concentrated fire into the storm-wracked night sky. The Guardian sideslipped and counterfired with its autocannon.

"Won't these characters ever give up?" Bobby Bell gritted.

But there was a certain fear to it. Zentraedi who had returned to their warrior code, their death-before-defeat belief system, were enemies to be reckoned with.

And then there was a familiar face on an instrument panel display screen. "How you guys doin'?" Rick Hunter asked with elaborate casualness. It was the heritage; he was flying into the middle of a red-hot firefight, and he looked like it was all he could do to stay awake.

"Boss, look sharp," Bobby shot back. "These boys are murder."

Rick's VT dove down through the rain in Guardian configuration like a rocket-powered falcon. "It's okay. I'll take over now. Ransom, Bobby; all of you drop back and stay out of sight."

He went in at them as he had gone in at hundreds of pods—thousands—since the day he first stepped into a VT cockpit. He wove through their fire, rebounded from the ground, and sprang high overhead on Robotech legs.

The energy blasts skewed all around him. "Last chance," he transmitted over the Zentraedi tac frequency. "Cease fire and lay down your arms."

If they had, they would have been the first of the malcontents to do so. But instead, like all the rest, they fired that much more furiously.

He wondered what he would have felt like if their positions had been reversed. The human race was lost and struggling in its own ashes, but how much more so the Zentraedi defectors?

He wondered only for an instant, though; lives were at stake.

Skull Leader came in behind a sustained burst from its autocannon, the tracers lighting the night, blowing one pod leg to metallic splinters. As the pod collapsed, Rick banked and came to ground behind an upcropping of rock, going to Battloid mode.

He reared up from behind the rock, an armored ultra-tech warrior sixty feet tall with a belt-fed autocannon gripped in his fist. "For the last time, I order you to drop your weapons!"

He saw the plastron cannon muzzles swinging at him, and hit the dirt behind the rock. Energy bolts blazed through the air where he had been standing.

When the volley was over, he came up again shooting. The high-density slugs blew another pod leg in half at its rear-articulated knee, toppling it. The third one ran, zigzagging, evading his fire. Suddenly there was only the drumming of the rain on the field of battle.

The Zentraedi malcontents emerged from their disabled mecha slowly. He could see that they carried no personal weapons and knew that the New Portland police and militia would be able to deal with them. The rest of Skull Team went to mop up and make sure the armored Zentraedi on foot were taken prisoner. The malcontents would pay with their lives for the lives they'd taken.

Tonight we won. What about tomorrow?

He was the last one to deplane; Ransom, Bobby, and Greer were already far from the hangars and revetments when Rick dragged himself from his VT, feeling dog-tired. How could peace be so terrible? Peace was all he or Roy or any of the rest had ever wanted. He wondered if there would ever be an end to the fighting.

Then he saw Lisa standing by the fighter ops door. *No peace in my lifetime*, he decided. *Look at* that *warcloud*.

"Why do I feel like I should ask for a blindfold and a last cigarette, Commander?"

"Not very funny, Rick."

"No, I suppose not." He groped for a way to tell her all the things he had thought and been through in the last few days.

But she was saying, "You're ordered to report to Captain Gloval at once."

He considered that, brows knit, turning toward the SDF-1. "Wonder what he wants."

She couldn't hold back what she was thinking. "How was your visit with Minmei?" she called after him.

He stopped. "I enjoyed her broadcast from Granite City yesterday," she said softly.

He drew a breath, let it out, looked down at the hardtop beneath his feet. "Well, I didn't actually visit with Minmei."

He started off again. She caught up, walking right behind. She made it sound as spiteful as she could, hating herself for it the whole time. "Was that because she was so surrounded by adoring fans that you couldn't get close to her, Rick?"

"No."

"Anything happen?" *Why am I putting us both through this?* she wondered, and the answer came back at once: *Because I love him!*

"What *could* happen?" he growled.

"I don't know!" She raced to catch up with him, taking a pale blue envelope from her uniform pocket. She dashed around in front of him, bringing him up short, pressing it into the palm of one flightsuit glove. She turned and walked away from him.

"Lisa, what *is* this?"

"Just something to remember me by," she threw back over her shoulder, not trusting herself to look at his face once more. Her heels clicked away across the hardtop.

The envelope held photographs—Lisa with a niece, on a vacation; Lisa as an adorable teenager with a kitten perched on her head; Lisa on the day of her graduation from the Academy.

"What on Earth?" he mumbled, but he knew. The album, all the rest of it: What had happened came to him in a flash. He had left New Portland feeling like there was some good that he could do in the world, feeling that no matter how bad things looked, there was always hope, and feeling that he was on the side of the angels.

But now, holding the photographs at his side and watching her disappear among the parked combat mecha, he tried to ride out a tide of regret that threatened to wash him away, and he was suddenly sorry he had ever been born.

"Commander Hunter reporting as ordered, sir."

Gloval sat looking out the sweeping forward viewport of the SDF-1, at a blue sky flecked with white clouds. "Please come in, Rick," he said without turning.

"Thank you, sir." Rick came in warily; Gloval did not often use his subordinates' first names.

"I'll get right to the point." Gloval swung around to face him and came to his feet. "The aliens among us are reverting to their former ways."

Rick considered that. He had friends among the Zentraedi—Rico, Bron, and Konda; Karita and others. "The New Portland rebels won't give us any more trouble, sir."

"That incident was only a symptom, Lieutenant Commander." There was something about the way Gloval pronounced your rank that let you know you were a part of a thing greater than yourself.

"We cannot afford to have this occur again," Gloval went on, "or we'll be risking complete social breakdown. I've decided to have some of the aliens reassigned to new locations where we can keep an eye on them."

None of the importance of that was lost on Rick. *We promised them freedom!* It was all coming apart, everything that had seemed so bright two years before.

The rest didn't really have to be said. Gloval was counting on Rick to enforce his directives and letting him know what he would be in for.

Rick Hunter looked at the old man who'd been through so much for Earth, and for the Zentraedi, too, in truth. The younger man snapped off a brisk salute. "Whatever you decide, you have my support; you know that, sir. And you have the support of everyone on the SDF-1."

"Thank you, Lieutenant." Gloval acknowledged the salute precisely but rather tiredly. He didn't look like he had gotten any real sleep in a long time.

They met each other's gaze. "I understand," Rick said.

Minmei shivered under her jacket, leaning against a pylon of Zentraedi wreckage and staring into the sky as night came on Granite City.

So much desolation. And so much bitterness, even between people who should have learned to love one another a long time ago!

She looked to the few lights of the town. Kyle had gone off that way, and she had no idea whether he intended to stop or keep on going, had no idea whether she would ever see him again and no clear conviction as to whether she wanted to or not.

She looked up as the stars appeared. *Oh, Rick. Where are you?*

THE END

The following chapter is a sneak preview of DOOMSDAY —Book VI in the continuing saga of ROBOTECH.

CHAPTER
ONE

Had the Robotech Masters the power to travel as freely through time as they did space, perhaps they would have understood the inevitabilities they were up against: Zor's tampering with the Invid Flower was a crime akin to Adam's acceptance of the apple. Once released, Protoculture had its own destiny to fulfill. Protoculture was a different—and in some ways antithetical—order of life.

Professor Lazlo Zand, as quoted in *History of the Second Robotech War*, Vol. *CXXII*

THE DIMENSION OF MIND...THE RAPTURE TO BE *found at that singular interface between object and essence...the power to reshape and reconfigure:* to transform...

Six hands—the sensor extensions of slender atrophied arms—were pressed reverently to the surface of the mushroomlike Protoculture cap, the Masters' material interface. Long slender fingers with no nails to impede receptivity. Three minds...*joined as one*.

Until the Terminator's entry disturbed their concentration.

Offering a salute to the Masters, it announced:

—Our routine scan of the Fourth Quadrant indicates a large discharge of Protoculture mass in the region where Zor's dimensional fortress defolded.

The three Masters broke off their contact with the Elders and turned to the source of the intrusion, liquid eyes peering out from ancient ax-keen faces. Continual contact with Protoculture had eliminated physical differences, so all three appeared to have the same features: the same hawkish nose, the flaring eyebrows, shoulder-length blue-gray hair, and muttonchop sideburns.

—So!—responded the red-cowled Master, though his lips did not move—Two possibilities present themselves: either the Zentraedi have liberated the hidden Protoculture Matrix from Zor's disciples and commenced a new offensive against the Invid, or these Earthlings have beaten us to the prize and now control the production of the Protoculture.

There was something monkish about them, an image enhanced by their long gray robes, the cowls of which resembled nothing so much as outsize petals of the Invid Flower of Life. Each monkish head seemed to have grown stamenlike from the tripartito flower itself.

—I believe that is highly unlikely—the green-cowled Master countered telepathically—All logic circuits based on available recon reports suggest that the Invid have no knowledge of the whereabouts of Zor's dimensional fortress.

—So! Then we must assume that the Zentraedi have indeed found the Protoculture Matrix, insuring a future for our Robotechnology.

—But only if they were able to capture the ship intact...

The organic systems of the Masters' deep-space fortress began to mirror their sudden concern; energy fluctuations commenced within the Protoculture cap, throwing patterned colors against all the breathing bulkheads and supports. What would have been the bridge of an ordinary ship was here so given over to the unharnessed urgings of Protoculture, so that it approximated a living neural plexus of ganglia, axons, and dendrites.

Unlike the Zentraedi dreadnaughts, these spadelike Robotech fortresses the size of planetoids were designed for a different campaign: the conquest of inner space, which, it was revealed, had its own worlds and star systems, black holes and white light, beauty and terrors. Protoculture had secured an entry, but the Masters' map of that realm was far from complete.

—My only fear is that Zor's disciples may have mastered the inner secrets of Robotech and were then able to defeat Dolza's vast armada.

—One ship against four million? Most unlikely—nearly impossible!

—Unless they managed to invert the Robotech defensive barrier system and penetrate Dolza's command center...

—In order to accomplish that, Zor's disciples would have to know as much about that Robotech ship as he himself knew!

—In any event, a display of such magnitude would certainly have registered on our sensors. We must admit, the destruction of four million Robotech vessels doesn't happen every day.

—Not without our knowing it.

The Terminator, which had waited patiently to deliver the rest of its message, now added:

—That is quite true, Master. Nevertheless, our sensors *do* indicate a disturbance of that magnitude.

The interior of the Protoculture cap, the size of a small bush on its three-legged pedestal base, took on an angry light, summoning back the hands of the Masters.

—System alert: prepare at once for a hyperspace-fold!

—We acknowledge the Elders' request, but our supply of Protoculture is extremely low —we may not be able to use the fold generators!

—The order has been given—obey without question. We will fold immediately...

High in those cathedrals of arcing axon and dendrite-like cables, free-floating amorphous globules of Protoculture mass began to realign themselves along the ship's neural highways, permitting synaptic action where none existed moments before. Energy rippled through the fortress, focusing in the columnar drives of massive reflex engines.

The great Robotech vessel gave a shudder and jumped.

Their homeworld was called Tirol, the primary moon of the giant planet, Fantoma—itself one of seven lifeless wanderers in an otherwise undistinguished yellow-star system of the Fourth Quadrant, some twenty light-years out from the galactic core. Prior to the First Robotech War, Terran astronomers would have located Tirol in that sector of space then referred to as the Southern Cross. But they had learned since that that was merely *their* way of looking at things. By the end of the Second Millennium they had abandoned the last vestiges of geocentric thinking; and by A.D. 2012 had come to understand that their beloved planet was little more than a minor player in constellations entirely unknown to them...

Little was known of the early history of Tirol, save that its inhabitants were a humanoid species—bold, inquisitive, daring—and, in the final analysis, aggressive, acquisitive, and self-destructive. Coincidental with the abolition of warfare among their own kind and the redirecting of their goals toward the exploration of local space, there was born into their midst a being who would alter the destiny of that planet and to some extent affect the fate of the galaxy itself.

His name was Zor.

And the planet that would become the coconspirator in that fateful unfolding of events was known to the techno-voyagers of Tirol as *Optera*. For it was there that Zor would witness the evolutionary rites of the planet's indigenous lifeform—the Invid; there that the visionary scientist would seduce the Invid Regis to learn the secrets of the strange tri-petaled flower they ingested for physical as well as spiritual nourishment; there that the galactic feud between Optera and Tirol would have its roots.

There that Protoculture and Robotechnology were born.

Through experimentation, Zor discovered that a curious form of organic energy could be derived from the flower when its gestating seed was contained in a matrix that prevented maturation. The bio-energy resulting from this *organic fusion* was powerful enough to induce a semblance of bio-will, or *animation*, in essentially inorganic systems. Machines could be made to alter their very shape and structure in response to the prompting of an artificial intelligence or a human operator—to *transform* and reconfigure themselves. Applied to the areas of eugenics and cybernetics the effects were even more astounding: Zor found that the shape-changing properties of Protoculture could act on organic life as well: living tissue and physiological systems could be rendered malleable. *Robotechnology,* as he came to call his science, could be used to fashion a race of humanoid clones, massive enough to withstand Fantoma's enormous gravitational forces and to mine the ores there. When these ores were converted to fuel and used in conjunction with Protoculture-drives (by then called *reflex* drives) Tirol's techno-voyagers would be able to undertake hyperspace jumps to remote areas of the galaxy. *Protoculture effectively reshaped the very fabric of the continuum!*

Zor had begun to envision a new order—not only for his own race, but all those sentient lifeforms centuries of voyaging had revealed. He envisioned a true mating of mind and matter, an era of *clean* energy and unprecedented peace, a *reshaped* universe of limitless possibilities.

But the instincts that govern aggression die a slow death, and those same leaders who had brought peace to Tirol soon embarked on a course which ultimately brought warfare to the stars. Co-opted, Robotechnology and Protoculture fueled the megalomaniacal militaristic dreams of its new masters, whose first act was to decree that *all* of Optera's fertile seed pods be gathered and transported to Tirol.

The order was then issued that Optera be defoliated.

The bio-genetically created giants who had mined Fantoma's wastes were to become the most fearful race of warriors the Quadrant had ever known: the *Zentraedi.*

Engrammed with a false past (replete with artificial racial memories and an equally counterfeit history), programmed to accept Tirol's word as law, and equipped with an armada of gargantuan warships the likes of which only Robotechnology could provide, they were set loose to conquer and destroy, *to fulfill their imperative*: to forge and secure an intergalactic empire ruled by a governing body of barbarians who were calling themselves the Robotech Masters.

Zor, however, had commenced a subtle rebellion; though forced to do the bidding of his misguided Masters, he had been careful to keep the secrets of the Protoculture process to himself. He acted the part of the servile deferential pawn the Masters perceived him to be, all the while manipulating them into allowing him to fashion a starship of his own design—for further galactic exploration, to be sure—a sleek transformable craft, a super dimensional fortress that would embody the science of Robotechnology much as the Zentraedi's organic battlewagons embodied the lusts of war.

Unbeknownst to the Masters, the fortress would also contain the very essence of Robotechnology—a veritable Protoculture factory, concealed among the reflex furnaces that powered its hyperspace drives, the only one of its kind in the known universe, capable of converting the Invid Flower of Life to harnessable bioenergy.

By galactic standards it wasn't long before some of the horrors the Masters' greed had spawned came home to roost. War with the divested Invid was soon a reality, and there were incidents of open rebellion among the ranks of the Zentraedi, that pathetic race of beings deprived by the Masters of the ability to feel, to grow, to experience beauty and love.

Nevertheless Zor ventured forth, in the hopes of redressing some of the injustices his own discoveries had fostered. Under the watchful gaze of Dolza, Commander in Chief of the Zentraedi, the dimensional fortress embarked on a mission to discover new worlds ripe for conquest.

So the Masters were led to believe.

What Zor actually had in mind was the seeding of planets with the Invid Flower. Dolza and his lieutenants, Breetai and the rest, easily duped into believing that he was carrying out orders from the Masters themselves, were along as much to secure Zor's safety as to insure the Masters' investment. The inability to comprehend or effect repairs on any Robotech device, and to stand in awe of those who could was programmed into the Zentraedi as a safety to guard against a possible grand-scale warrior rebellion. The Zentraedi had about as much understanding of the workings of Robotechnology as they did of their humanoid hearts.

So on Spheris, Garuda, Haydon IV, Peryton, and numerous other planets, Zor worked with unprecedented urgency to fulfill *his* imperative. The Invid were always one step behind him, their sensor nebula alert to even minute traces of Protoculture, their Inorganics left behind on those very same worlds to conquer, occupy, and destroy. But no matter: in each instance the seedlings failed to take root.

It was at some point during this voyage that Zor himself began to use the Flowers of Life in a new way, ingesting them as he had seen the Invid do so long ago on Optera. And it was during this time that he began to experience the vision that was to direct him along a new course of action. It seemed inevitable that the Invid would catch up with him long before suitable planets could be sought out and seeded; but his visions had revealed to him a world far removed from that warring sector of the universe where Robotech Masters, Zentraedi, and Invid vied for control. A world of beings intelligent enough to recognize the full potential of his discovery—*a blue-white world, infinitely beautiful, blessed with the treasure that was life . . . at the crux of transcendent events, the crossroads and deciding place of a conflict that would rage across the galaxies.*

A world he was destined to visit.

Well aware of the danger the Invid presented, Zor programmed the continuum coordinates of this planet into the astrogational computers of the dimensional fortress. He likewise programmed some of the ship's Robotech devices to play a part in leading the new trustees of his discovery to a special warning message his own likeness would deliver to them. Further, he enlisted the aid of several Zentraedi (whose heartless conditioning he managed to override by exposing them to music) to carry out the mission.

The Invid caught up with Zor.

But not before the dimensional fortress had been successfully launched and sent on its way.

To Earth.

Subsequent events—notably, the Zentraedi pursuit of the fortress—were as much a part of Earth's history as they were Tirol's; but there were chapters yet to unfold, transformations and reconfigurations, repercussions impossible to predict, events that would have surprised Zor himself . . . had he lived.

"*Farewell, Zor,*" Dolza had said, when the lifeless body of the scientist was sent on its way to Tirol. "*May you serve the Masters better in death than you did in life.*"

And indeed the Robotech Masters had labored to make that so; having their way with Zor's remains, extracting from his still-functioning neural reservoir an image of the blue-white world he had selected to inherit Robotechnology. But beyond that Zor's mind had proved as impenetrable in death as it had been in life. So while Dolza's Zentraedi scoured the Quadrant in search of this *Earth*, the Masters had little to do but hold fast to the mushroom-shaped sensor units that had come to represent their link to the real world. Desperately they tried to knit together the unraveling threads of their once-great empire.

For ten long years by Earth reckoning they waited for some encouraging news from Dolza. It was the blink of an eye to the massive Zentraedi; but for the Robotech Masters who were essentially human in spite of their psychically evolved state, time moved with sometimes agonizing leadenness. Those ten years saw the further decline of their civilization: weakened as it was by internal decadence, the continued attacks by the Protoculture-hungry Invid, a growing rebellion at the fringes of their empire, and heightened disaffection among the ranks of the Zentraedi, who were beginning to recognize the Masters for the fallible beings they were.

Robotechnology's inheritors had been located—*Zor's descendants*, as they were being called—but two more years would pass before Dolza's armada made a decisive move to recapture the dimensional fortress and its much-needed Protoculture Matrix. There was growing concern, especially among the Elder Masters, that Dolza could no longer be trusted. From the start he seemed to harbor some plan of his own; reluctant to return Zor's body twelve years ago and now incommunicado while he moved against the possessors of Zor's fortress. With his armada of more than four million Robotech ships, the Zentraedi Commander in Chief stood to gain the most by securing the Protoculture Matrix for himself.

There was added reason for concern when it was learned that *Zor's descendants* were humanoid like the Masters themselves. The warrior race literally looked down on anything smaller than itself and had come to think of normally proportioned humanoids as "Micronians"—ironic given the fact that the Masters could have sized the Zentraedi to any dimensions they wished. Their present size was in fact an illusion of sorts: beating inside those goliath frames were hearts made from the same genetic stuff as the so-called Micronians they so despised. Because of that basic genetic similarity, the Robotech Masters had been careful to write warnings into the Zentraedi's pseudo-historical records to avoid prolonged contact with any Micronian societies. Rightly so: it was feared that such exposure to emotive life might very well rekindle real memories of the Zentraedi's biogenetic past and the true stuff of their existence.

According to reports received from Commander Reno (who had overseen the return of Zor's body to Tirol and whose fleet still patrolled the central region of the empire), some of the elements under Breetai's command had mutinied. Dolza, if Reno's report was to be believed, had subsequently elected to fold the entire armada to Earthspace, with designs to annihilate the planet before emotive contagion was spread to the remainder of the fleet.

The Zentraedi might learn to emote, but were they capable of learning to utilize the full powers of Robotechnology?

This was the question the Robotech Masters had put to themselves.

It was soon, however, to become a moot point.

Hyperspace sensor probes attached to a Robotech fortress some seventy-five light-years away from Tirol had detected a massive release of Protoculture matrix in the Fourth Quadrant—an amount capable of empowering over four million ships.

ABOUT THE AUTHOR

Jack McKinney has been a psychiatric aide, fusion-rock guitarist and session man, worldwide wilderness guide, and "consultant" to the U.S. Military in Southeast Asia (although they had to draft him for that).

His numerous other works of mainstream and science fiction—novels, radio and television scripts—have been written under various pseudonyms.

He resides in Ubud, on the Indonesian island of Bali.